The Fifteen Streets

Catherine Cookson

Front cover illustration: Fine Art Photographic Library/Thomas Benjamin Kennington

This novel is reproduced under licence from The Catherine Cookson Charitable Trust

This novel forms part of an issue of The Catherine Cookson Collection partwork published by DeAgostini UK Ltd/Planet Three Publishing Network Ltd, 10 Northburgh Street, London EC1V 0AT, and is not for sale separately.

Printed and bound by GGP Media, Poessneck

ISSN 1478-3339

CONTENTS

Chapter One

The Brothers

'Hannah, drop that an' come an' see. The O'Briens are at it again . . . blue murder! Come on. Come upstairs, you can see better from our top window.'

Wiping the soap suds from her arms, Hannah Kelly hastily lifted the lid of the wash-house boiler, scooped off the grey scum with an enamel mug, dabbed the contents of the boiler with a stick, then ran out of the wash-house and across the backyard, thinking as she did so, 'Eeh, I haven't got time for this . . . And our Joe warned me.'

She caught up with her neighbour as she was opening the stair door.

'Who is it this time? The old man?'

'Yes.'

'Who's he at? Dominic!'

'Aye.'

'Are they drunk?'

'Are they ever owt else?'

They scurried across the kitchen to the front room, and automatically took up their stations, one at each side of the window, bodies close to the wall, heads held slightly to the side against the mesh of the Nottingham lace curtains, their arms wound tightly in their aprons.

'My God, what a mess, Bella!'

'He must have thrown them two pictures out since I came down for you.'

'Eeh, God Almighty! It's a shame. Just as Mary Ellen was getting things pulled together again.'

'Look,' – there was glee in Bella's voice – 'there they are at the window throttling each other. Christ!' she exclaimed as something came hurtling through the window into the street, 'which one missed that, I wonder?'

'Eeh! He's thrown the pot through the window. Oh, Bella, that'll bring the pollis. God Almighty, it's awful! It's enough to bring on the bairn . . . she's at the worst time, on eight months.'

'Best thing that could happen. Who wants a bairn at forty-five, I ask you? She should have been more cute. Anyway, she wouldn't listen to me. I told her I could get her a bottle of white mixture from our Harry's Emma who scrubs the wards up at the grubber; the nurses would have given it to her. It would have skited everything out of her.'

'Well, you know she wouldn't do that, she's a Catholic, Bella.'

'Catholic, be damned! They tell 'em to have bairns, but do they bloody well keep them? I'd like to see any priest tell me I must have bairns. Do you know what I'd say?'

Hannah chuckled. 'I've a pretty good idea . . . Look, there she is, there's Mary Ellen. She looks like death.'

They both became silent and watched the woman below picking up the two picture frames from the road. The loose glass splintered about her feet as she shook the frames, and as she shooed some children away from the broken chamber, Hannah remarked, regretfully, 'Pity about that. It was a boody one, too.'

Unblinkingly they watched the woman edge her way indoors, with neither a glance upwards nor to the right or left, although as they knew, she was fully aware of the watchers. Only the children were on the street, staring silently until the door closed, when they drew nearer, and some daring spirits, braving the glass hitched themselves up on the high window sill to get their faces level with the hole. But as they did so the blind was dropped, and Hannah exclaimed, clicking her tongue, 'She shouldn't have done that – dropping the blind right down before dark – it's the sign of a death. It'll be the bairn, likely.'

'Damn good job too. Better if it was her old man though, in case he lands her with another.'

They turned slowly from the window, and Hannah said, 'By, that wouldn't have happened if John had been in; he'd have put a stop to that . . . Funny, isn't it, Bella, that the old man doesn't go for John.'

'Not funny a bit. He's afraid of him, if the truth was known. Old O'Brien and Dominic are both alike, full of wind and water. That's why they fight . . . By God! I wish I was in Mary Ellen's place for five minutes. I'd lay those two sods out with the poker! She's soft, that's what she is, soft as clarts . . . Are you going to stay for a cup of tea?' she added. 'I'll put the kettle on, it won't be a minute.'

'No, lass, I'm not half through, and it's getting on for dark.'

Bella glanced sideways at Hannah. 'Should you come across Mary Ellen – you see her more than I do – and she tells you what it was all about, knock up.'

'Aye, I will. But there's small chance. She's close, is Mary Ellen. You know that.'

'I know she doesn't like me. Thinks I can't mind me own business.'

And she's right there, thought Hannah.

'And anyway, I'm not the same colour as them,' went on Bella nodding her long horse-face. 'Me St Patrick's Day's colour's blue. Wait until next Thursday week when Dominic's wearing his shamrock. There'll be skull and hair flying then. The fifteen streets won't hold him . . . My God, remember last St Patrick's

Day? That was a do, eh?' She laughed at the memory.

'Eeh, Bella, I must be off.' Hannah unwrapped her mottled arms, and banged out the creases in her coarse apron.

'Well don't forget to knock up if you hear owt.'

'I won't.'

Hannah went down the stairs, walking sideways in case she slipped, as the stairs were too narrow for her feet encased in an old pair of men's boots. By the time she reached the bottom she had also reached a decision: she wouldn't tell Bella Bradley what she heard, if she heard owt at all. Too nosy was Bella, by half. She'd rather keep in with Mary Ellen, narrow as she was. At least she minded her own business. And her Joe warned her only last night against Bella Bradley. He said he'd bash her face in if he found her upstairs again – he was nettled after hearing what she said about their Nancy not being all there. He knew Nancy wasn't all there, but it maddened him to hear anyone say it. More so now that Nancy was growing up . . . Hannah sighed. What would become of Nancy? She didn't know. And anyway, there was no time to think now, the washing had to be finished.

Across the road, in number 10 Fadden Street, Mary Ellen O'Brien worked in the semi-darkness behind the drawn blind. She adjusted the block of wood under the chest of drawers – the leg had been kicked off during the last row – and screwed in the knob of the top drawer. She picked up the grey blanket and patchwork quilt from the floor and spread them again over the lumpy bare mattress on the iron bed. She pushed the wicker table back into the centre of the room, and stood leaning on its weak support, breathing heavily. Her eyes, dry with the pricking dryness of sand, looked round the walls. They were quite bare . . . Well, they would remain so. The only two pictures in the house were now gone. Never again would she try to build up. She had told herself, if they went this time it would be the last.

She looked towards the closed door, which led into the kitchen.

She knew that beyond, on either side of the fireplace, they'd be sitting, spent. Their rage and passion flown, they would be like the two halves of one body, accepting each other now that the conflict was over for a time.

She lifted her apron and wiped the sweat from her forehead. If only they weren't so big . . . like giants. She hadn't dared go between them this time because of the bairn . . . She put her hand on the raised globe of her stomach and felt a movement. It brought no sense of feeling to her other than that of apprehension. Why, oh why was she to have this all over again? Hadn't she been through enough in her time? During the twenty-six years of her married life she had given birth to eleven bairns, and only five were alive, for which she thanked God. What she would have done with thirteen in these three rooms only the Almighty knew.

A pain through her breast made her gasp, and she covered it with her hand, lifting up its weight. Last year this time they'd been flat . . . flat for all time she'd thought, for it was ten years since Katie was born. Practically every year since she was married she'd been dropped, but from Katie there'd been nothing. The pain shot through her again, and she remembered such a pain from the past. It was before John was born. She was as strong as a horse then, as small as she was, and she enjoyed the feeling of the pain, anticipating the tugging of the young mouth on the nipples . . . if it lived. It did live, and it was John . . . John, who had never given her any trouble. Oh, if they were all like John, and, at the other end of the scale, Katie. Funny that these two should be alike and the others so different from them. Dominic was different from the day he was born, the year after John. She had always been slightly afraid of Dominic, even when he was a child. It wasn't that he alone suffered from the O'Brien rages, for they all did, except Katie. It was rather that there was something fiendish about Dominic. It showed in everything he did, in his teasing, in his laughter, and especially in his good-looking face. Like John and Mick, he took after his da for his looks. But although they all took after their da Dominic and Mick were better looking than John. When she looked at her eldest son she had the feeling that the features which made the other two good looking made him ugly, and in some strange way this pleased her. To her mind it separated him entirely from them. It was his nose that made the difference, she supposed, with that funny little nob on the side of the nostril. He got that when he climbed the dock wall to get some coal that bad winter. He slipped and his nose was cut on the broken glass set in the top of the wall. The cut did not join properly and gave his face a quaint look from the side. But it wasn't only his nose; John's eyes were different from the others. They were large and brown too, but a different brown . . . dark and kind. That was it, they were kind, like Katie's.

She sighed and rubbed her hand gently round and round her breast. Then, hearing a shout coming through the kitchen from the backyard, she moved her head impatiently – she never thought of Molly unless the girl made herself felt by sight or sound. Molly was . . . well, she couldn't place Molly. She was of a too apparent mixture of them all, and so had no individuality of her own. She was swayed, first one way and then the other; even her rages could be deflected by a stronger will. No, Molly would be no heartache, for she aroused no feeling.

Mary Ellen straightened her shoulders and refastened the top button of her blouse over her straining breasts before walking towards the kitchen door. It was no use standing here thinking; thinking got you nowhere. It was close on five o'clock and John would be in at half past. She'd have to get on with the tea . . . Thank God they fought in here and not in the kitchen. They might have knocked the pan of broth off the hob, and there was nearly fourpennorth of vegetables in besides a twopenny scrag end . . . Well, if you searched hard enough there was always something to be thankful for.

As she expected, her husband and son were sitting one each side of the fireplace, their brows puckered over half-closed eyes. Shane's grey hair was standing up straight in tufts; there was blood on the hair near his temple, and his high cheekbones were showing blue under the tightened skin. At the first glance she saw that his rage wasn't entirely spent, for the muscle was moving in his cheek as he clenched and unclenched his teeth, and his limbs, as always, were jerking with the nerve tick. His knees, in their reddened moleskin trousers, were wide apart, and his feet were crossed below his hands, which were gripping the seat of the wooden armchair. His body looked as if it was still ready to spring . . . No, his rage wasn't spent yet, because he was sober. He'd had only two shifts in this week and had tipped the money up. But Dominic had a full week. For three weeks now he'd worked full weeks. Not that it made much difference to her – she was lucky if she got ten shillings out of him. She often had to meet him at the dock gates to get even that . . . or send Katie. But Dominic's rage was spent because he was drunk and happy.

She took Dominic by the shoulder and shook him. 'Here! Get yourself to bed.'

He lifted his head and smiled crookedly at her, cracking the dried blood on his mouth as he did so. He looked at her out of one merry, brown eye, the other being hidden behind a curling lock of light brown, youthful hair.

'All right, old girl.'

He rose obediently to his feet, and some detached part of her marvelled for the countless time at his docility towards her when he was in drink. Why was it she could manage him when he was drunk? She even found herself liking him in this state. She had no fear of him in drink, when he spoke civilly to her, often with a touch of affection. But it was strange that even in drink she could have any affection for him now, for she remembered the look in his eyes during these past weeks when they lit on her stomach . . . ridicule, scorn, and something else . . . a something for which she could find no word. She pushed him before her into the bedroom, her head coming just to the bottom of his shoulder blades. She always wondered, when close to them, how she gave birth to such great men.

Dominic sat down with a plop on the side of his bed and began to laugh. 'If he wasn't my old man I'd have knocked him stiff. But I'll break his bloody neck the next time he interferes with me. I didn't ask to be set on the ore boat – they want the young 'uns down the holds.'

He fell back on the bed and lifted up his legs, and Mary Ellen immediately swung them down again. She took off his boots and loosened his belt, then unbuttoned his trousers and tugged them off his legs, leaving these looking particularly ludicrous in their tight long pants. Never in all the many times she had pulled trousers off them had she yet been able to conquer the feeling of revulsion. Husband or son, it was the same.

She heaved him up by the shirt front and dragged off his coat. Then she let him fall back on to the bed. She threw the quilt over him and put his coat on top of it, and lifting his trousers quietly from the floor, she put them across her arm and went out, through the kitchen, past her husband, who now sat hunched up over the fire, and into the front room, where she turned out the contents of the trousers pockets on to the table.

There was a half-sovereign, two two-shilling pieces, and four pennies. The half-sovereign he would have to stump up for his board, so she put that back into the pocket again, together with a two-shilling piece. The other two-shilling piece and the coppers went into a little cloth bag that dangled from a pin fastened to the inside of her skirt. It already held tenpence. She had taken to this device of the bag when Shane came back from the Boer War, because he lifted every penny he could get his fingers on for drink.

She went back to the bedroom and quietly placed the trousers over the bed rail, and as she returned to the kitchen the window was darkened by a distorted bulk, and a gentle tap-tap came on the door.

Mary Ellen sighed. As inevitably as the calm which followed the storm would come this tap-tap on the door after any disturbance in the house. She often thanked God for an upstairs neighbour such as Peggy Flaherty. Many a one, placed as she was above the noise and fighting that was almost part of the weekly routine, would have done more than object, she would have brought the pollis; and after a number of such visits they would have been in court and likely turned out of the house. Peggy was a bit queer; still, as God knew, there were worse states than being queer. But today, Mary Ellen felt tired, and even Peggy's well-meant sympathy was an irritant. She opened the door, and would have smiled, if she could, at the quaint tact of this fat, dirty woman.

'I was after warming meself up with a mouthful of stew, Mary Ellen, an' I said to meself, "I'll take a drop below, it'll stick to Mary Ellen's ribs."' She proffered the basin, full of a lead-coloured liquid, with darker pieces of matter floating about on its surface. 'Are you all right, lass?' She peered at Mary Ellen through her short-sighted eyes, looking for a black eye or other evidence of the fight.

'Yes, I'm all right, Peggy. And thanks for the soup.'

'Oh, that's all right, Mary Ellen . . . You'll drink it, now, won't you?'

'Yes, yes,' Mary Ellen hastily assured her, wondering whether Peggy was suspicious of the fate of her proffered balms. She would have to be very hungry, she thought, before she ate anything made by Peggy's hands in that menagerie upstairs. Before he died, Charlie Flaherty earned his living in many ways. At one time, he worked for himself as a tallyman, and when payment was not forthcoming, took the equivalent in kind; so two of the three rooms upstairs were stacked from floor to ceiling with an odd assortment of things, not one of which Peggy would part with, ranging from a stuffed baby crocodile to a collection of books, out of which Peggy was wont to say 'she got the extinsive iducation' she possessed. She spread more false knowledge round the fifteen streets than it was possible to imagine. Many of the inhabitants would have sworn that Henry VIII was Queen Elizabeth's husband, and that England once belonged to the Irish before William the Conqueror came over and took it from them. For the sum of a penny she would write a letter; for a little more, give advice on how to deal with a summons, or a case of defamation of character, or assault. Often this advice, if faithfully carried out, would have got the worried seeker a sojourn in jail. It was strange, that although she was said to be odd and barmy, her advice was still sought. Perhaps it was because it was known that on these pennies she mainly relied for her existence. There was an unspoken feeling in these streets, which, if translated, would have implied . . . you save someone the workhouse and you'll never land there yourself.

'God and His Holy Mother preserve us this day, the trials we have! Is there anything more I can do for you, Mary Ellen?' went on Peggy.

'No, I'm all right, Peggy, thanks.' Mary Ellen looked at the basin in her hands, hoping to convey a hint that she would like to go in and make a start on the soup.

But Peggy did not notice this move; or if she did, she refused to take the hint; for she had something weighty to say. Leaning forward, she whispered, 'Did I ever tell you, Mary Ellen, Mr Flaherty's cure for all this?' She nodded towards the closed scullery door.

Mary Ellen, suppressing another sigh, said, 'No, Peggy.'

'Iducation! No man would fight, he said, once he had iducation. And he knew what he was talking about, for he got about among the gentry, you know, Mary Ellen. It was his theory that once a man got iducation he wouldn't raise a hand to his wife. He might, being a human being, get a bit irritated and say, "Retire to your room before I kick your backside!" or some such thing, but to lift his hand . . . no!'

'There may be something in it.' Mary Ellen again looked at the basin. 'Sure you haven't left yourself short, Peggy?'

'Not at all. Not at all. Anyway you go now inside, and don't talk any more; and get that down you, it'll put a lining on your stomach. And remember, if you want any advice you know where to come.'

She shuffled away, and Mary Ellen closed the door . . . Don't talk any more, and, Retire to your room before I kick your backside! If there was a laugh left in her she would have laughed; but she would remember them, and some night by the fire she would tell them to John, and they would laugh together.

John came in at half-past five. He hung his cap and coat, together with his black neckerchief on the back of the kitchen door, then sat down on a box in the tiny square of scullery and loosened the yorks that bound his trousers below the knee. Before washing his hands in the tin dish that was standing on another box he looked into the lighted kitchen and smiled towards the three children sitting at the table. Only Katie returned his smile, her round, blue eyes sending him a greeting.

Mick called, 'Got anything, John? Any bananas or anything?'

And he answered, 'Not tonight; we're still on the grain boat.'

When John came to the table, his mother set a plate of broth before him, out of which a series of bare ribs stuck up, like the skeleton of a hulk. The smell was appetising, and the eyes of the three children focused on the plate.

Mary Ellen exclaimed harshly, 'Get on with your bread and dripping!' and almost simultaneously each bit into his own inch-thick slice of bread.

She placed another plate on the table and said to her husband, 'Your tea's out.'

Shane turned from the fire and stared at the plate, and from there to his son and the other three. His body started to jerk, first his head, then his arms, and lastly his right leg. His words too, when they came, were spasmodic and heavy with bitterness: 'Served last now, am I? It's a difference when you're not bringing it in. You've got to work or you don't eat . . . not till everybody else is finished.'

John put his spoon down and stared at his father: 'I'll wait until you're done.'

His mother signalled wildly to him from behind her husband, and pointed to the bedroom. John read her signal, but continued to stare at his father, until Shane's eyes dropped away and he growled, 'It's them young 'uns – I was never set down before me father.'

His head jerked to one side as if he were straining at a bit, and Mary Ellen said quietly, 'Don't be a fool! Get your tea.'

'You want to start, you do!' Shane sprang up from his chair, kicking it to one side as he did so. 'It only needs you to start. Belittling me before the bairns! That's a new tack.' He towered like a swaying mountain of rage over the short unwieldy figure of his wife.

Mary Ellen took no notice, but went on cutting bread on the corner of the oilcloth which covered the table, and the children continued to eat, their eyes fixed on their plates. Only John kept his eyes on his father, and Shane lifted his bloodshot gaze from the top of his wife's head to meet John's again. He stared at his son for a moment, his compressed lips moving in and out. Then he swung round, grabbed his cap from the back of the door and went to go out, but as he reached the back door he paused and cast his infuriated glance back into the kitchen again: 'The next bloody thing'll be: There's the door . . . Get out!'

He kicked savagely at the box holding the dish of water. There was a clatter and a splash; the door opened and banged, and only the clink of his heel plates becoming fainter down the yard broke the silence in the kitchen.

When they could be heard no more, Mary Ellen moved. She went into the scullery and, bending down with difficulty, began to sop up the water from the hollowed stones.

Dimly, with a mixture of pity and understanding, her thoughts followed her husband . . . Dominic getting drunk on his earnings . . . John coming in from work. Both of them on full time, and him with only two shifts in. He was getting on and he couldn't work like he used to, and the gaffer picked the young and strong 'uns. His strength was failing – she'd noticed that. Drink and hard work and wet clothes that were often frozen to his skin were at last taking their toll. He seemed to retain his strength for one thing alone . . . if only that would slacken with the rest. It must sometime. Then God, let it be soon.

'I'll help you, Ma.' Katie was on her knees by the side of her mother.

'No! Get up out of that. That's the only clean pinny you've got!'

'Well I haven't got to go to school the morrer.'

'Doesn't matter. Get up out of that.'

'Here!' – John stood above her – 'Let's have it.' He held out his hand for the cloth.

'Oh get out of me road, the both of you!' Her voice pushed them back into the kitchen, and she went on bending and wringing out the cloth. Who did they think did all the other work, the washing, the cooking, the scouring, the humping of the coal, bucket by bucket from the back lane into the coal house because now she couldn't throw the shovelfuls through the hatch?

She partly soothed her irritation by saying to herself: 'You know John's always telling you to leave the coal until he comes in. Yes, but how can I,' – her irritation refused to be soothed – 'with people waiting to get their washing out!' She flung the cloth into the bucket. Oh, she felt so tired. If only she could see a way out of all this . . . if only the bairn was born! Yes, that was the main stumbling block. Once that was over everything would be all right; she would cope, as always.

She went into the kitchen again and said to Mick, 'Go and empty the bucket and wash it out, and bring some clean water . . . See you wash it out, mind!'

Mick's mouth dropped, and he muttered, 'Aw! Why can't she do it?'

He dug Molly in the side, and she cried, 'Look at him, Ma! Stop it, our Mick!'

John took the rib of bones from his mouth: 'Your mother spoke to you.'

'Me ear's bad,' – Mick placed his hand over the side of his head – 'it's been running all day.'

'You going out to play the night?' John asked.

'Yes.' Mick scowled at the table.

'Then empty the bucket.'

John went on picking his bone, and Mick clattered from the table, while Molly sniggered into her pinny.

'You'll laugh the other side of your face in a minute, my girl,' said Mary Ellen. 'Get those dishes washed.'

'Then can I go out to play?'

'Who you going out to play with in the dark, you're not going to run the streets?'

'We're going in Annie Kelly's wash-house; her ma's had the pot on, and it's warm. Annie has some bits of candle, and we're going to put them in bottles and play houses and dress up.'

'Play houses and dress up,' Mary Ellen muttered to herself. Aloud, she said, 'And burn yourselves to death! . . . Well, and only half an hour, mind. And you can take Katie with you.'

'I don't want to go, Ma; I've got to do some homework.'

'What!' the mother and John lifted their heads and stared at Katie.

'You got your sums wrong?' asked John, in surprise.

'No.' Katie shook her head and tried to repress a smile, but her eyes grew rounder and her dimples deeper as she looked at their straight faces.

'Then why have you to do homework?' John asked; 'you never have before.'

'I've got to learn something. Miss Llewellyn asked me to . . . '

'She's Miss Llewellyn's pet, everybody says she is . . . I hated Miss Llewellyn. I was glad when I was moved up.' Molly wet the tip of her finger on her tongue, and in this way she secured a number of crumbs from the table. When she had put them in her mouth, she swung round on Katie, saying, 'You didn't tell me ma Miss Llewellyn gave you a penny the day for learning your poetry first, did you? Nelly Crane told me . . . so!'

The smile vanished from Katie's face, and Mary Ellen looked down on her daughter in surprise, the daughter who was the only one of the family to take after her. She could see this child, as she herself once was, plump and bonny and open-handed. It was unusual for Katie to keep anything.

'Did she give you a penny?' she asked.

Katie neither moved nor spoke, but her eyes, as they looked back into her mother's, became glazed, and she cried out within herself, 'Oh, our Molly! Our Molly!' Now it was all spoilt – the wonderful, wonderful thing she was going to do was spoilt. The Easter egg . . . the real Easter egg in a real box, tied up with a real silk ribbon, was lying in fragments about her! And the picture of herself handing it to Miss Llewellyn was lying with it.

That penny had brought her secret hoard to five-pence. For three weeks she had kept John's Saturday penny and the two halfpennies her mother had given her. Today's surprise penny had meant such a lot, for she had only another month or so during which to get the remainder of the shilling.

Her mother became blotted out by a mist; then she felt John's big hands drawing her to him and pressing her against his knees.

When he bent and whispered in her ear, 'Are you saving up to buy a present?' she experienced the feeling she had felt before that John was in some way connected with God and the priests, because he knew everything.

She nodded her head against the bottom of his waistcoat, and he whispered again, 'Your teacher?'

At this she gasped and pressed her face tightly against him. John exchanged a glance with his mother, and a smile flickered for an instant across her face.

'I think you must be the cleverest lass in the school,' John went on.

Katie brought her head up swiftly and stared at him. 'Why, that's what Miss Llewellyn says! She says . . . she says I'm advanced and I must work at nights and . . . and read a lot.'

'There you are. There you are. Miss Llewellyn knows. She knows when she's on a good thing. What have you got to learn the night?'

'Oh, I already know some of it, the end bit,' she laughed. 'Listen. A man named Shakespeare did it.' She stood back from his knee, threw her long black plaits over her shoulder, joined her hands behind her back, and said:

> 'There take an inventory of all I have,
> To the last penny; 'tis the king's: my role,
> And my integrity to heaven is all
> I dare now call my own. O Cromwell, Cromwell!
> Had I but serv'd my God with half the zeal
> I serv'd my king, he would not in mine age
> Have left me naked to mine enemies.'

John stared down on her face, which was illuminated by the feel of the strange words on her tongue, and Mary Ellen stared at the back of her dark head. Then their eyes met, reflecting the glow of her words, which were unintelligible to both of them . . . But Katie had said them . . . their Katie . . . the only one of them who had ever wanted to learn. With a swoop, John lifted her up and held her on his upstretched hands. Her head was within a few inches of the ceiling, and he laughed up at her: 'Will I push you through to Mrs Flaherty?'

'Eeh! No, John. Eeh, our John, let me down.'

She wriggled on his hands, anxious to get away from the ceiling and the proximity of Mrs Flaherty and her weird house.

As he lowered her to the floor John laughed, 'You'll soon be cleverer than Mrs Flaherty, and then everybody will be coming here and saying, "Please, Katie O'Brien, will you write me a letter?" and you'll say, "Yes, if you give me sixpence." '

'Oh, our John, I wouldn't! I wouldn't ask for sixpence.'

He bent down to her and whispered hoarsely, 'Oh yes you would, if it would get your teacher a present.'

She slapped his knee playfully, then turned her face away to hide the tell-tale glow.

Molly banged the mugs into the cupboard; she banged the door as she went out; then her voice came through the keyhole:

> 'Miss Llewellyn has a swellin',
> An' I'm not tellin'
> Where Miss Llewellyn
> Has a swellin'.'

John turned quickly away from Katie's outraged face, rubbing his hand across his mouth. But he could not rub the laughter from his eyes, and Katie turned on him, her voice full of hurt surprise: 'Oh, our John, you're laughing! Our Molly's awful . . . Miss Llewellyn hasn't got a . . . She's lovely, she's beautiful. She wears a lovely white blouse with a frill at her neck, and her hair's brown and shines all over the place. And Mr Culbert's after her. Cathleen Pearson says he wants to marry her.' Katie's voice broke: 'She's beautiful . . . she's beautiful.'

John sat down by the fire and pulled her on to his knee, cradling her in his arms and soothing her: 'Of course she's beautiful, of course she is. And who's Mr Culbert when he's out?'

'He's . . . he's a teacher at St Jude's.'

'Is he? Is he? Well, he can be the Prime Minister for all I care. But you know what I'm going to do? I'm going to this Mr Culbert, and I'm going to say, "You going to marry Miss Llewellyn and take her away from teaching our Katie? You are . . . like panhacklety!" '

'Oh, our John, you're awful!'

Laughing, she scrambled up and stood on his knees and flung her arms about his neck, endeavouring to strangle him with her small strength.

'Here! Hold on.'

'Eeeh!' – she drew her face back from his – 'You haven't got to say that.'

'What, hold on?'

'Yes. Miss Llewellyn says you've got to say, "Wait a moment," or, "Stop a moment." '

'Do you hear that, Ma?' He winked at his mother, who was now sitting at the other side of the hearth mending a pair of moleskin trousers.

She gave a flicker of a smile and went on adjusting a patch. What was it about these two bairns of hers that brought her such strange joy? To see them playing together like they were now seemed to make up for all the heart scolds of life. She still thought of John as her bairn, although he was twenty-two and six foot one. He would always be her bairn, her first bairn. There were some who said you loved all you gave birth to. Fools! You couldn't love even two alike. Even those two opposite, she loved one more than the other, but she couldn't tell which.

Her mind returned to concrete things, and she said without looking up, 'The front window's out.'

John did not reply, but after a moment put Katie on the floor and, taking a box of matches from his pocket, went to the front room.

Katie was about to follow him, when Mary Ellen said, 'Get on with your homework, hinny.'

It was some time before John returned, and still he said nothing. He sat down on his chair again and took off his boots and put his stockinged feet on the fender, and sat staring at the kettle singing on the side of the hob. Presently he took a loose Woodbine from his pocket and lit it . . . Would it never end? Would life go on like this for her until she died?

He cast a glance at her bent head. The hair was grey, yet coarse and strong, springing from the centre parting and refusing to be drawn flat into the knob behind; but the face beneath was deeply marked with lines. They ran in puckered furrows across her forehead and bit deep from her nose to the corners of her mouth. The mouth in repose, as it was now, looked despondent, without hope. Could you wonder at it! And there was this other thing to happen. And her so little, not much bigger than a bairn herself.

He shifted suddenly in his chair. What could he do? He was helpless. If only he had a decent job, if only he hadn't been pushed into the docks. Well, where else could he have gone? If a lad wanted to make money at fourteen he had to give up all idea of being apprenticed to a trade. It was the same in all the places: Palmer's shipyard, the steel works, the chemical works. Now he'd be a dock labourer for the rest of his life; and he would never earn enough money to make any noticeable difference to her life. Did his father ever feel like this, feel this sense of frustration and helplessness? That's why he drank as he did. And Dominic? Ugh – he made an involuntary gesture with his hand as if wiping his brother away – that swiller!

He lifted his feet up to the side of the pan hob and sank deeper into his chair. Drink was a funny thing once it got you.

He was drunk only once, and could still remember isolated parts of the feeling. It happened the first week he was on capstan work. He had been promoted from hatching at two-and-six a shift and now felt a man. After being paid off, he was walking out of the dock gates with the men when one of them, nodding towards the line of public houses filling the street opposite, said, 'Comin' over?'

He felt flattered, and went with them into The Grapes. He remembered the feeling of his stomach swelling and the continual belching of wind, and his mouth becoming fixed open in a wide grin. It was this grin that was partly the reason why he did not touch the drink again, for he brought the picture of himself over into his sober consciousness, and in it he saw the face of his father when in drink, as he had seen it since he was a child, with the large full-lipped mouth stretched wide, conveying not the impression of geniality but of imbecility. And his cure was completed by knowing, on waking up in bed undressed, that his mother had done for him what she did for his father. It was some time before he could entirely rid himself of the feeling of shame and humiliation when he thought of himself being undressed by her.

There were times when he wanted a drink badly – like today, when his throat felt clogged tight with dust – unloading grain was a dry job. He had gone across to the horse trough outside the gates and filled the iron cup four times. Some of his mates called, 'Cheap that, John.' 'Aye, and no headache the morrow,' he replied. They no longer asked him to join them.

A crescendo of snores came from the bedroom, and he shifted his position again. There was something he wanted more than a drink, and that was a mattress. Could he put it to her now? He looked towards his mother. She'd had enough for one day, he told himself, without anything more to worry about. But when a series of spluttering coughs terminated the snores, he said, 'There's a pitch boat due in shortly; if I get set on her, it'll mean extra. Could you . . . get me a mattress with it?'

'A mattress!' Mary Ellen stopped sewing and looked at him. 'A mattress?'

He turned his head to the fire again. 'I want you to put Mick in the bed; I'll sleep in the cupboard.'

'Oh lad,' – she joined her hands together over the patch – 'you can't sleep on the floor. And anyway, the cupboard isn't big enough, it barely holds Mick.'

'I can leave the door open.'

The sadness seemed to sink from her eyes into her body, shrinking it still further. She turned her gaze to the fire, and her hands lay idle . . . There was no way of getting another bed into the room, even if they could get one. And for John to lie in the cupboard! She shook her head, not knowing she did so.

The cupboard in the bedroom ran under Mrs Flaherty's front stairs; its total length was five feet, and he wanted to sleep in that! If the door was open, it was cold and draughty, even in the summer; if it was closed, it was naturally airless. She often worried about Mick having to lie there . . . but John! And his feet would extend over any mattress – they did through the bed rails, both his and Dominic's. But that wasn't the floor.

She looked at him and saw by the way his face was set that he meant to do it, and if she didn't get him the mattress he'd lie in the cupboard in any case, on Mick's bag of straw. She sighed, and her hands began to work again.

There was no sound in the kitchen except the sound of Katie's pencil and Dominic's muffled snores, until Molly rushed in the back door, crying, 'Ma! Do you know what?'

'Make less noise!' Mary Ellen said.

'But Ma, there's somebody moving in next door the morrer.'

'Wash yourself and get ready for bed . . . Who told you that?' Mary Ellen asked.

'Mrs Bradley told Annie Kelly's ma, and Annie Kelly told me.'

'Then if Mrs Bradley said so, it must be right.' Mary Ellen rose, pulled the table to one side to get at the wooden couch beyond, and began to make up the girls' beds, one at each end.

'Get your things off, hinny,' she said over her shoulder to Katie.

The two girls undressed in the scullery, all except their boots and stockings. These they took off, sitting on crackets before the fire, chatting to each other now quite friendly. Katie sat next to John, her bare feet on the fender sticking out from under her patched, flannelette nightie.

John's fingers moved slowly through her hair. And when the bedroom door opened and Dominic lurched into the kitchen he didn't lift his eyes from the paper he was reading.

Dominic stood near the table, blinking in the gaslight. He yawned, running both his hands over his head; then pulled his belt tighter before coming to the fire. He shivered and sat down in the seat vacated by Mary Ellen, growling to Molly as he did so, 'Move your carcass!' He ran his tongue round his dry lips, shook his head in an endeavour to throw off the muzziness, and stretched out his hands to the fire.

'Any grub?' he asked, without turning his head.

'There's broth,' his mother answered from her bent position over the couch.

Katie looked past Molly to her brother's face. It looked huge and frightening, with the dark stubble around his chin and up the sides of his cheeks, and the darker marks of the dried blood standing out around his mouth. When he hawked in his throat and spat at the bars, she drew her feet sharply beneath her nightie, nearly falling off the cracket as she did so. John's hand, still on her head, steadied her, but he did not take his eyes from the paper.

Dominic saw her frightened glance, and a twisted grin spread slowly over his face. He leaned back in his chair, and after a while Katie's toes came from beneath her nightie again. Her feet were cold, for the steel fender was well below the bottom red bar of the fire. She lifted one foot up above those of Molly, to wriggle her toes in front of the lower bar. There was a hiss, a splatter, and Dominic's yellow saliva was running over her foot.

As she hid her face from the sight and pressed her mouth to stop herself from being sick, she felt John springing away from her. His chair was kicked back, and she flung herself to the floor by the bottom of the fender, lying along its length, pressing close to its brass bars to keep clear of the pounding feet. Molly had sprung to the couch, where she now sat huddled. And before Mary Ellen could reach them John's fist swung out and Dominic reeled backwards and crashed into the cupboard door.

Mary Ellen flung herself on John, crying. 'Lad! Lad!' She beat his chest with her fists in an endeavour to push him back: 'John lad! John lad! For God's sake!'

John did not look at her, but gathered her flaying hands in one of his, and tried to push her aside. But she kept in front of him by pressing her body against his, calling beseechingly up to him, 'Lad! Lad! John, lad!'

His face was bereft of colour; his lips were drawn back from his teeth, and his eyes were like black marble. Through her body she could feel the waves of anger running through his; her breast was pressed against his stomach, which shook with the elemental forces demanding release.

'Holy Mary, Mother of God, Mother of God!' she cried. 'No more the day, lad!' She took no heed of her other son, standing with his fists at the ready behind her; Dominic, she knew, wouldn't fight John unless he had to, for in John he had more than his match. No, it was John she must stop. 'John, lad – John! I can't stand any more this day. Oh, Jesus, Mary and Joseph, you know I can't stand no more the day.'

She felt a great intake of breath coming into his lungs and the rumbling thunder of the words as they were released from his throat: 'I warned you what would happen if you did that again!'

Relief swept through her; he had spoken; she could manage him if he spoke.

He spoke again, and his words now brought a faintness over her; the child in her womb seemed to stop breathing. The words fell into her inner consciousness, to be remembered as would those spoken by a prophet have been, for, like Katie, she felt that John was near the priests and God, for what he said was mostly true. And he said now to his brother, 'One of these days I'll kill you.'

There was no threat in the words, only a quiet certainty.

Chapter Two

A Day of Bonny Lasses

Poverty is comparative. There were those who did not live in the fifteen streets who considered the people living there to be of one stratum, the lowest stratum; but the people inside this stratum knew that there were three different levels, the upper, the middle, and the lower. All lived in 'houses' either upstairs or down; but in the lower end each house had only two small rooms, and upstairs or down the conditions were the same – the plaster on the walls was alive with bugs. These might only appear at night, to drop on the huddled sleepers, but that strange odour, which was peculiarly their own, wafted through the houses all the time, stamping them as buggy. No-one went to live in the lower end unless he was forced. To the middle and upper fifteen streets the bottom end was only one step removed from the workhouse, for its inhabitants were usually those whose furniture had been distrained or who had been ejected from their former houses for non-payment of rent.

There were three nightmares in the lives of the occupants of the middle and upper fifteen streets. And these were linked together: they were the bums, the lower end, and the workhouse.

In the middle houses there were four rooms . . . boxes,

generally, but boxes that were divided, giving privacy of a sort to one or two extra beings. The upper end had only three rooms to each house, and these were either up or down. Here, water was not carried from the central tap in the back lane but from a tap at the bottom of each yard. This stamped the area as selective, automatically making it the best end.

But even into this stratum of the fifteen streets no-one had ever been known to arrive with their furniture in a van. A flat lorry, yes, or a coal cart; at worst, a hand barrow, after dark. These were the three general modes of removal. But a van! A proper one, bearing the words 'Raglan, Furniture Removers, Jarrow-on-Tyne', never.

The street was out to watch with as much interest as if it were a wedding, or a funeral, or, what was more common, a fight. The three O'Brien children had a grandstand view: they stood in a row beneath their front window sill, and behind them, in the room, were the elders, Mary Ellen, Shane, Dominic and John. The sons stood one at each side of their mother and father. They were standing together as a family for once, joined by the common interest, watching in silent wonder as each piece of furniture was carried into the house next door. They had not seen furniture like this before. There was the big, bright, round table, with the thick single leg and bunchy feet like claws; there was the suite of patterned plush, with ball fringe all round the bottom of the couch and chairs; there was the big clock, nearly six feet high; and there was the bed, a wooden one painted white, with pictures on the panels; there were two other beds, but these were of brass. Yet these were outstanding too, for they were neither chipped nor battered. That was not all. There were carpets, two of them, besides a load of rugs one man could hardly shoulder. And the road was strewn with all kinds of things that rent Mary Ellen through with envy; a feeling she thought she was past this many a year. But then, she had never seen owt like this before in the fifteen streets . . . or anywhere else; the mahogany plant stand, with its looped chains, the large china flower pots, the clothes basket full of coloured china, and the little mangle, which looked like a toy but which she knew wasn't. Who were these folks who could own such things, yet had come to live here? It didn't make sense somehow.

She glanced up at John to see what effect all this was having on him, and her eyes left him quickly and travelled down his gaze to the street again. He was looking at a lass who had just come out of the house. Mary Ellen wasn't sure if she was a child, a lass, or a woman.

John, staring at the girl over the brown paper that covered the hole in the window, was being puzzled in much the same way; the girl on the pavement was as shapeless in form as Katie, showing no evidence of either hips or bust. Judged on her figure, she could be a child; and her face too had something of the immaturity of the child in it. Yet it was old. No, not old – he rejected the word – wise, that was it . . . and bonny too. Yes, she was bonny, that pale skin against the dark hair. The hair was unusual in that it hung loose about her head. Cut short, boyish fashion, it was like a dark halo. He was curious to see more of her, and, as she turned to speak to the old man with the white hair, who was directing the unloading, he unconsciously bent forward.

Whatever she said brought a smile from the long, serious face of the man, and she smiled in return: and John knew them to be related; it was as if the same light shone from them. It illuminated their faces, and seemed to convey a ray of light even to himself, for he found his face relaxing into a smile as he watched them. He wondered who they could be. Was the man her da, or her grandda? And the little lad running to and fro was evidently one of them, for he had the same pale skin and dark hair.

As John considered the fine furniture and their fine clothes, his smile faded. The old man was wearing a suit and a collar and tie, as though got up for a do, and the girl, a blue woollen dress with a little woollen coat of the same colour. It looked neat and trim and was as unlike anything the lasses of the fifteen streets wore as John could possibly imagine.

The two removal men were struggling to get a chest of drawers through the front door. It was the biggest chest John had seen in his life; it was taller than himself. He could see only one of the men, who was bearing the weight of the bottom end and was stepping backwards and forwards under the other's directions. John knew what had happened. The front door did not lead directly into the front room, but into a tiny square of passage. The other man had got his end stuck in this passage.

The old man's assistance was to no avail; and John watched the girl glance about her at the dark, huddled figures blocking the doorways. Then her eyes came to the window and met his. For a second they looked at each other, and he noted the surprise and curiosity in her glance, and realised in a flash that to her he must appear as if he was standing on something to look over the brown paper. Humorously he thought: I'd better show her it's me all the way. I'll give them a hand with those drawers . . . and damn the tongues! He turned, to find Dominic, who was nearer the front door, looking at him with eyes full of mirthless laughter. Dominic slowly hitched up his trousers, buttoned his coat, then went out into the street.

With a feeling of frustration mixed with anger, John watched Dominic speak to the girl, and saw her look sharply from Dominic's face to the window as if to reassure herself there were two of them. Then she smiled on Dominic, and he bent his broad back under the chest, taking the weight off the men, and in a few minutes they all moved into the house.

John and Mary Ellen turned from the window and went to the kitchen. Nothing had escaped Mary Ellen; she had followed the desire of her son and felt Dominic interpret John's thought and use it against him. She said, 'Come and finish your dinner, lad, it'll be kissened up to cork.'

Taking three plates out of the oven, she called to her husband. Shane, looking mystified and his head jerking, came to the table. 'Must be bloody millionaires,' he said. 'Know who they are?'

'No,' she answered. 'I know nowt about them.'

The meal was eaten in silence. Once or twice Mary Ellen glanced at John, but his face was closed, telling her nothing. She got up to clear the table, and muttered impatiently when a face was pressed against the window and a voice called, 'Can I come in, Mrs O'Brien?'

Mary Ellen's brows knit together, but she answered pleasantly, 'Oh, it's you, Nancy. Yes, come in.'

A girl of sixteen sidled into the room. Her face was flat, almost concave, and her nose and eyes seemed to be lost in its centre, as though a force were sucking them in. The expression was serious and earnest, like that of a child struggling to be impressive. She began with quaint ceremony, 'Hallo, Mrs O'Brien.'

And Mary Ellen answered kindly, 'Hallo, Nancy.'

'Hallo, John.'

John turned from the table and said, 'Hallo, there, Nancy.'

'Hallo, Mr O'Brien.'

Shane growled something, keeping his eyes directed towards his plate. And Mary Ellen, thanking God that the rest of the family weren't in to lengthen Nancy's usual formal greeting, said, 'Sit yourself down, Nancy.'

Nancy sat down, and John said to her, 'Still like your place, Nancy?'

'Yes, John,' she answered; 'I've nearly been there a month now.' It was a curious defect of her speech that her mouth never closed; her lips refused to meet, so her voice sounded nasal, like that of someone with a harelip.

John answered tolerantly, 'Yes, you have, Nancy,' knowing that the time she had scrubbed and cleaned in the Fitzsimmons outdoor beer shop was nearer to four years than four weeks – time had no place in Nancy's mind. Her body gave the impression of uncontrolled strength; her long arms hung out from the short sleeves of her coat, a brown, faded thing, and her boots looked too small for her big feet.

John said kindly, 'You look very nice the day, Nancy.'

She smiled at him, stretching her face; then, preening herself and dusting down the front of her coat with her red hands, she said, 'This is a new coat. Me ma bought it. And these boots too. And I've got a silk dress, with a sash. And I'm going to get a hat with a feather in.'

Shane's chair scraped back and he went to the front room. Mary Ellen looked after him for a moment – he never could stand the senseless prattle of Nancy. She went into the scullery to wash the dishes, glad that John was in to cope with Nancy should she start laughing . . . Oh, Nancy's laughter! Mary Ellen shuddered. She thought she was afraid of nothing on earth as she was of Nancy Kelly's laughter – it put the fear of God in her. But John could manage her – he always had; he made her think she was like other lasses. She could sense John's pity for Nancy; it was like her own, but without the strain of fear that ran through hers.

She heard Dominic coming up the backyard, whistling. He was pleased with himself for outwitting John, she supposed. She hoped to God he did nothing more to aggravate John's feelings; the sick premonition of last night was still partly with her. She was more afraid of John's rages than of either Shane's or Dominic's, for his were stronger, being made more fierce through sober justification.

Dominic came in and surprised her by closing the scullery door and so shutting them off from the kitchen. He stood near her as she bent over the dish, and said softly, 'Any chance of you lending me the money to get me clothes out?'

She looked up at him, her hands still in the water. 'I've only got the rent. You put your suit in, you'll have to get it out.'

'I'll give it to you back next week.'

'I haven't got it; I only have a few coppers left for the gas over the weekend.'

Dominic's suit had been in pawn for more than a month, and he had made no effort to get it out, even on his full shifts. Without it he was tied to the house and spent his Sundays in bed, for by some unwritten law no-one went out of doors on a Sunday dressed in their working clothes. Even if a man possessed a shilling to 'get a set in', he never showed his face inside a public house unless he was 'tidy'.

Strangely enough, Mary Ellen realised it wasn't tomorrow Dominic was thinking of, but tonight, and that new lass next door; although how he'd had the nerve to ask such as her out, she didn't know . . . But then she did. Dominic had the nerve for anything if he wanted it badly enough. She said cuttingly. 'Why don't you ask one of your cronies for it?'

He cast her a sidelong glance, in which she saw the sharp, questioning look – he wondered how much she knew. She knew more than he thought she did, to her sorrow. There was a certain woman of the docks, Lady Pansy, so-called because of her style in her heyday when she entertained nothing less than a chief engineer. But times had changed, and with them Lady Pansy's figure and face. Although she couldn't claim big money now she still liked her men young and strong, and Mary Ellen knew that all the money from Dominic's full shifts was not spent on drink – the thought made her sick – and the woman was as old as she was, if not older!

If Mary Ellen's refusal dampened Dominic's spirits, he hid it successfully, for in the kitchen he was extra hearty, forestalling Nancy's greeting by giving an imitation of herself.

'Hal-lo, Nan-cy!'

'Hallo, Dominic.' Nancy wriggled on her chair.

Dominic went and stood over her: 'What's this I'm hearing about you, Nancy? They tell me you're courtin'.'

'Eeh! Who told you that?' The girl wriggled in agitation. 'Eeh! I'm not . . . am I, John?'

John said nothing, but left the table and took a seat by the fire. He knew where Dominic's teasing would lead.

'Well, that's what I heard,' Dominic went on; 'I thought you were goin' to wait for me. Nice one, you are.' He pulled his belt tighter in feigned annoyance.

'Eeh, Dominic! I haven't got a lad, I haven't. I don't let them come near me. If they touch me, I yells I do.' Her face gathered itself into a troubled pucker.

John thrust the poker between the bars and raked savagely – he knew that Dominic's tactics were more to madden him than to tease Nancy.

Dominic laughed, and went on, with mock seriousness, 'Let's get this settled. When are me and you goin' out for a walk, eh?'

Mary Ellen came hurriedly into the kitchen: 'I think you'd better be going home now, Nancy, your ma will be wondering where you are.

As Nancy stood up, Dominic said softly, 'I'll get another lass, mind.'

And Mary Ellen cried, 'That's enough of that! Get away home now, Nancy.' She turned to the girl and led her, trembling, to the door; but before they reached it, it opened, and Hannah Kelly herself stood there.

'Oh, this is where you are,' – she looked unsmilingly at her daughter – 'I guessed as much. Go on, get yourself over home.'

Nancy slid by her mother, and Hannah came in and closed the door. Her manner was conspiratorial. 'Well, what d'yer think, eh? D'ye know who ye've got next door, Mary Ellen?'

Mary Ellen shook her head.

'My God! Ye'd never believe. They call this the Irish quarter, but what with the Jews and the ranters . . . and now this! Well, my God, I ask ye!'

'What are they?' asked Mary Ellen bluntly.

'Spooks!' Hannah's head came forward, impressing the word.

'What!'

'Spooks. He's called The Spook in Jarrow and Howden and round there. Remember a bit back when the Irish navvies burnt a hut down and the pollis had to get the man away? Well, that was him. He was givin' a service or somethin'.'

Mary Ellen turned and looked from one to the other of her sons, who were now both listening to Hannah Kelly with interest.

'Dorrie Clark knew who he was the minute she set eyes on him, and she was tellin' Bella Bradley that when she was delivering once in Jarrow, he came in and wanted to lay his hands on the woman. That's what she said . . . lay his hands on her! Did ye ever hear owt like it? To ease her labour, he said, because she'd been in it four days.'

Mary Ellen looked distinctly shocked. 'Did she let him?'

'Did she hell! Ye know old Dorrie. She said she kicked his arse out of the door. And she would an' all, full of gin or not. But my God, there'll be the divil's fagarties around these doors before long! Mark my words; ye'll see.'

Mary Ellen was evidently disturbed. She looked from one to other; then she addressed John, 'What d'you make of it?'

John turned away, and went to the bedroom, saying, 'I don't know; they looked all right to me.'

Hannah laughed and called after John, 'Mind yerself, John lad, that she don't lay hands on you. They say the lass is as bad as the old man.' Then turning to Dominic, she said, 'And you there, ye've soon got yer leg in.'

Ignoring her jibe, Dominic asked: 'D'you know what the old man works at?'

'Now that's another funny thing,' – Hannah pointed her finger at him – 'he's the Mr Bracken that has the boot shop in Jarrow.'

The three of them looked from one to the other, and the same question was running through their minds: 'Why did a man who owned a boot shop come to live in the fifteen streets?'

In the bedroom, John pulled the wooden box from beneath the bed and took out his suit. It was too creased to wear, so he knew it hadn't been in the pawn; had it been in his mother would have pressed it ready for him. Taking a dirty raincoat from the back of the door, he stood pondering a moment whether he should change his black neckerchief for a white muffler, but decided against doing so. He would keep it for tonight, when he would be going to the Shields to have a look round the market and perhaps go to the second-house somewhere. Now, he was just going for a walk.

He did not bother to change his working boots, but went into the kitchen and finding his mother alone, asked, 'Will you put an iron over my suit?'

'Yes, lad,' she replied. 'Are you off for a walk?'

He nodded. 'Where's Katie?'

'Here she is, coming up the yard,' said Mary Ellen.

'Want to come?' he asked her.

'Oh yes, John. Yes!' In her excitement, Katie hopped from one foot to the other.

'Not with hands and face like that,' he said. 'What have you been up to?'

'Playing shops . . . I won't be a tick; wait for me. '

Mary Ellen was already pouring the water into the dish; and after a few minutes Katie, her face shining and a round straw hat lying straight on the top of her head, was walking down the yard with John.

He took her hand, and they went along the cobbled back lane to the main road.

'Where shall we go?' he asked her.

'Oh, the country, John. Up the country!'

'Simonside?'

'Yes. Oh yes, Simonside!'

The day was cold and clear, with the wind blowing straight in from the sea. The sky was high above the housetops and above the towering cranes, which reared up inside the stone wall edging the road opposite the fifteen streets.

John looked up at the white tufted clouds moving swiftly across the sky, and said, 'Look up there. They look like a fleet of white brakes off for a day's outing, don't they? I bet they're off to the country, too – Morpeth or some place.'

Katie chuckled. This was one of the many reasons why she loved going for walks with John – he made up stories about everything. She glanced up at him, her eyes twinkling: 'I bet when they come back they'll be singing, like the people do on the brake trips:

"Aa'm back to canny auld Jarrer,
A hip, a hip hooray." '

She giggled, and John tilted her hat over her eyes, saying 'Saucy piece!'

They walked by the side of the wall for some way, until they came to the chemical works and the tram sheds. Then, further on, as they passed a narrow cut, bordered on one side by the end of the chemical works and on the other by the railings which fence in part of the Jarrow slacks, John asked her, 'Do you want to go down the slipway?'

Katie shook her head quickly and shuddered.

'What are you frightened of?'

'It's that black mud – it's deep, and if you fell in you'd never get out.'

'But the tide's up now, and there might be a little boat moored there . . . All right, all right,' he laughed when Katie shuddered again; 'but you never used to be afraid of the slipway.'

She didn't say that Mick had dragged her down there and pretended he was going to push her in. He had held her over the stone coping, and she had gazed, petrified, at the silvery black, slimy mud sloping away from just below her face to the narrow stream of water at the bottom, running slowly beneath its shot-coloured oily surface. She didn't dare tell her mother in case John got to know, for then he would have gone for Mick.

They came to the Jarrow slacks at the point where they were open to the road. The water was lapping just below the bank, a few feet from the edge of the pavement. The large, square stretch of water was covered with timbers, roped together in batches, right up to the gut.

There was a permanent way, starting below the pavement and reaching to the gut, running through the middle of them. It consisted of logs, a foot wide, lashed end to end and to each side of posts driven in at intervals over the stretch. In parts, the logs were black and rotten and looked as safe for foothold as a loose rock on the edge of a precipice. But children were playing on them with happy unconcern, jumping from them to the roped timbers. Some children were far away over the timbers, lying flat along the edges, trying to rake in pieces of wood that were floating by. And the sight of them brought back the past vividly to John. How many times had he perilously stood on the end timbers, near the edge of the gut, and waited for the tide to come in, bringing with it its driftwood. Often, for weeks on end, this wood was their only source of warmth, but often again, they had to do without the warmth whilst he hawked the sack of wood around, trying to sell it for twopence. He seldom succeeded; coke was the best sell. If he followed the coke carts from Jarrow right into Shields he could pick up as much as two bucketfuls each trip. Pieces would roll off the cart as it jogged along, especially when it crossed the tram lines. He'd get twopence for the coke, and if he could follow the cart three times, that meant sixpence. But he rarely completed the third journey, for his legs became so tired. He remembered the melancholy feeling that would settle on him as he followed the carts. It seemed to be worse when the sun was shining . . . That was an odd thing he hadn't entirely grown out of – he didn't like the sunshine. For years this feeling vaguely puzzled him. Then one day the reason was made known to him. The sunshine, he discovered, showed up his surroundings. It brought a queer kind of pain to him. On a dull day, the docks, the coal dust, the houses, the rattling trams, and the people all seemed to merge into one background; but when the sun shone, there they all were, standing out in relief, dirty, stark, tired; and in some odd way it hurt him . . . The feeling was coming on him now, and he tried to ignore it, for it always made him start thinking; and when he thought, he got mad at things. As his mother said, thinking got you nowhere.

Katie plunged him further into the trough by exclaiming, 'You know, when I grow up, John, I'm going to be a teacher.'

He squeezed her hand and said, 'I bet you will too . . . headmistress!'

A teacher! Would Katie's dreams ever be fulfilled? He couldn't see it happening. She would go into a place at fourteen like the other lasses, and the bright eagerness would die. Her dreams, like his own when a lad, would be lost in the fight for food . . . It was funny, but that was all life amounted to . . . working life out to keep it in – working for food and warmth; and when the futility of this was made evident, blotting it out with drink. What did it all mean, anyway? What was living for?

When in this state of mind he always asked this question. The priests had one answer; but that had long ago ceased to satisfy him. Now he was asking himself another question: Had he to stay round these quarters until he died? He wasn't happy around here, yet when he moved out of this quarter, as he was doing now, up into Simonside, the lonely feeling became intensified and he felt lost, and some part of him wanted to get back again into the fifteen streets, into the docks, anywhere but near these grand houses that stood back from the Simonside bank, with their drives and large gardens. He couldn't understand why his sense of loneliness should be greater away from the life that was irking him.

He was being daft, he told himself – just daft. He should get himself a lass. That's what he needed. He was twenty-two and he'd never had a lass. He had never kissed a lass, not even in a bit of fun. Katie was the only one he kissed. He knew there were one or two in the fifteen streets who would come at his nod, but he hadn't nodded. His flingings and tossings in bed at night had equalled Dominic's, and many a time he promised himself to ask Jenny Carey or Lily McDonald to go out on a Saturday night; but with the light of day he forgot about them.

Lately, Dominic hadn't tossed so much. And once or twice John had been tempted to seek his cure; but then again, the temptation vanished with the light.

'Look, John,' said Katie; 'there's Father Bailey.'

The priest was coming down the drive of one of the big houses, and he waved to them, calling, 'Hallo, there.'

John stopped and said, 'Hallo, Father.'

He wouldn't have stopped had it been Father O'Malley; but then, Father O'Malley wouldn't have called 'Hallo, there.' At best, he would have inclined his head slightly. Not even if he knew you hadn't been to mass would he speak to you on the street; he would wait till he had you indoors, then raise the roof on you. But Father Bailey was different. Even when he was chastising you for not going to mass he was nice about it.

'Are you going for a walk, the pair of you?' The priest smiled, first up at John then down on Katie; and not waiting for an answer, went on, 'It's just the day for it. You know, John,' – he took a step backwards – 'I believe you get taller.'

'It's the clothes, Father; they've shrunk.'

'Well, there may be something in that, but I've always had the idea I came up to your shoulder. It must have been just an idea.'

He turned to Katie. 'And now, Katie O'Brien, what honours have you been gathering on your head this week? Do you know we have a clever girl here, John? Every week I hear something about Katie O'Brien. She's the top of her class for this, that, and the other. It'll be teaching the teachers she'll be in the end.'

'Oh, Father!' Katie O'Brien lowered her head and blinked at her boots.

The priest patted her straw hat. 'I'm just on my way up to the fifteen streets; I'll look in on your mother. How is she, John?'

'Oh, just middling, Father.'

'And your da, and Dominic?' There was a question in the priest's eyes.

They held John's, and he replied gruffly, 'Things don't change.'

'Oh, you're wrong there, John; every minute of the day they're changing.'

'Yes? Well I haven't noticed it.'

Father Bailey patted Katie's hat again, but still addressing John said, 'We never do. But look ahead, John . . . Shall I be seeing you at mass tomorrow?'

'I don't think so, Father.'

'Oh! This'll never do. Not at all, at all! I'll have to come and have a crack with you soon. But I must be off now. Enjoy your walk, both of you. Goodbye. Goodbye.'

'Goodbye, Father.' 'Goodbye, Father,' they said, and continued their way up the Simonside bank, past the little school and into what was termed the country, a few fields with hedged lanes between. If you didn't turn round and look back you could imagine there were no docks, no pits, no drab grey streets; and if you could stretch your imagination you could visualise these fields with their straight rows of tender green going on for ever.

'Shall we walk to the Robin Hood?' Katie asked.

'It'll be too far for you,' said John.

'No, it won't. I could walk miles and miles.'

She skipped on ahead of him, leaving him with his thoughts – thoughts of the priest; of this lonely feeling; and of the lass next door. His mind dwelt on the lass: Would he like to take her out? Good God! He'd never have the nerve to ask the likes of her, even if she were free – she was different somehow . . . Then why was she living next door? . . . There was no answer to this. And Dominic, he wouldn't be backward in asking her. But no! Surely he wouldn't have the cheek, the state he was in with drink, and that woman. Yet why did he go out and give them a hand? It wasn't with any idea of helping, but to speak to the lass . . . Anyway, why was he thinking about all these things that didn't matter a damn! Hadn't he other things to think about? His mother in her trouble; and the house with hardly a whole stick standing.

But the sun and the wind were changing his mood – he didn't want to think, he only wanted to wander here in this quiet road.

He took off his cap and let the wind play through his hair. He ran his hand through it, and felt the freedom of being uncovered out of doors. It was such a relief to walk with his cap off, and no-one would see him here so it didn't matter, for it was another unwritten law that a woman did not go out without a hat or a shawl covering her head, nor a man a cap.

Katie came running back to him, exclaiming, 'Oh, John, your hair looks just like Miss Llewellyn's with the sun shining on it! It's all brown and shiny.'

'What!' he exclaimed. 'Miss— Don't be silly.' He ruffled it more.

'It is though.'

'Go on with you!' He took her hand and pulled her to his side, and they walked on until they came within sight of the Robin Hood, then turned towards Simonside again. Katie sang hymns, school songs, and rhymes, one following on the other without pause, while John walked along in strange contentment, listening to her.

They were nearing the top of the bank, where it dipped to the docks, when her singing ended abruptly and he felt her hand tugging on his. He looked down on her upturned face. It was alight with pleased surprise – her eyes were wide, sending him a mute message. Wondering, he followed her gaze, and saw a woman coming towards them, a young woman. She was taller than average, and wore a brown cloth coat with a full skirt. It was nipped in at the waist and gave emphasis to her bust. She carried her head high, and her hat, which was green and had a brown feather curling round its brim, appeared like a crown set on the top of her head.

As she came nearer, John became aware of her hair. It fell over her ears in soft folds, and when he noticed the colour, he connected it with Katie's excitement and thrust his cap on his head. Good God! Miss Llewellyn – and she not much more than a lass. And he'd thought she was getting on . . . well, in her thirties. She was looking directly at Katie and smiling.

He looked beyond her, but to his horror she stopped as she came abreast of them and said, 'Hallo, Katie.'

'Hallo, Miss Llewellyn.'

John felt Katie's fingers opening and shutting within his palm.

'You are a long way from home.'

'Yes, Miss Llewellyn.' Katie was breathless.

John gave a sidelong glance at the bent head – he could dare this because she wasn't looking at him. He had never before been so close to such a face. Katie said she was lovely. Katie wasn't far wrong. The skin of her cheeks was a soft, creamy pink, the nose was short, and in striking contrast the mouth was wide and laughing.

When she turned her eyes on him, he switched his away; and he fumbled in the pocket of his coat for his red handkerchief as she said, 'You're John, aren't you?'

He felt his eyes forced back to her, to look her full in the face, and for no reason he could understand he began to tremble inside – almost, he felt, like the jerking of his father's limbs, only invisible. He was painfully conscious of the cap on his tousled hair, of his dirty raincoat, of his neckerchief, and of his big boots, with their leather laces showing numerous knots. His Adam's apple moved swiftly, and he swallowed, but no words came.

And she went on, 'I've heard such a lot about you.'

Her voice, too, was like none he had heard before. Like her face, there was laughter playing around it. Was she laughing at him? Very likely.

He knew she was, and though he felt it was kindly laughter the hot colour flooded his face when she said, 'I don't suppose you know, but you are a combination of Prince Charming and God to a certain young lady.'

He thought quickly, as he found himself doing at times, and spoke before he could stop himself: 'Neither of them would be flattered. And if the last one hears of it there's not much chance of me getting up there.'

Her laugh rang out, joyous and infectious, and to his utter surprise he found himself laughing with her.

Katie stood looking up from one to the other. She did not join in with their laughter, her happiness was too profound - Miss Llewellyn laughing with their John!

When he thought of it later, he was surprised at her next remark - and her a Catholic and a teacher too - for she said, 'I don't suppose that will worry you very much. I should take the heaven you're sure of.' Her words seemed to confuse her slightly and the tinge of pink grew deeper in her cheeks.

He made no answer, thinking that if this life was her idea of heaven he'd bet on the one up there. The wind swirled about them, and she turned her back to it, leaning slightly back and holding her hat on with both hands. Then she terminated the meeting by saying, 'Well, I'll see you on Monday morning, Katie,' and to John, 'I'm glad I've met you in the flesh, for now when I listen to your sayings being recorded I'll be able to place them. Goodbye. Goodbye, Katie.'

'Goodbye, Miss Llewellyn.'

'Goodbye.' John did not turn immediately away, but watched her bending against the wind, the coat pressed against her legs. And he saw that she wore shoes and that her ankles were thin.

He turned away, and Katie, walking close by his side, sighed. They looked at each other and smiled secretly, then walked on in silence, until John asked, 'You don't tell her all I say, do you?'

'No. Oh, no!' Katie lied firmly. And in the next breath she exclaimed, 'Isn't she lovely!'

He stopped and looked towards the docks, and Katie went on, 'And isn't it a lovely day!'

'Grand.' The word seemed to answer both her questions.

Far away in the distance he could see the masts of the ships, disembodied things, seemingly borne on air. He looked up at the sun, and for the first time in his life felt glad to be out and under it. He thought of the lass next door and of the lovely lass just gone, and he said, more to himself than to Katie, 'Yes, it's a lovely day; a day of clean wind and far mastheads, and bonny lasses.'

Katie stared up at him. Oh, their John was wonderful, the things he said! A day of clean wind and far mastheads, and bonny lasses! It was like . . . well, not like the poetry she learnt at school . . . and yet it was. Oh, and Miss Llewellyn had seen him! She had seen how wonderful he was.

Mary Llewellyn, walking briskly away in the opposite direction, was smiling no longer. Her face was thoughtful, and her eyes sad. So that was John. Poor soul! Poor soul!

Chapter Three

St Patrick's Day

Mick led the Catholics, not because he was the eldest but because he was the biggest. At the top corner of Fadden and Blacket Streets he marshalled his gang, twenty-five in all, and saw that they were supplied with weapons. He made sure that the innocent-looking paper balls dangling from lengths of rope or string each had a good-sized stone in its centre. About twenty yards away, at the corner of Whitley Street, the Protestants were gathering, and their leaders were doing much the same as Mick. This was to be the climax to the day's badgering and cornering of individuals and isolated groups, of swinging the paper balls round the heads of victims, whether Catholic or Protestant, and asking the terrifying question, 'Are you blue or green?' Pity help the individual who had the courage to defend his colour to the opposite clan, for he was often hit until he was sick or rescued by some indignant passer-by.

Mick's gang were protesting loudly that it wasn't fair, for the ranters had three separate gangs – the churchies, the chapelies, and the odds, the latter group consisting of Jews, Salvationists, and a Quaker.

Mick exclaimed loudly that three lots were nowt, for they'd bash all their bleeding heads in. Adroitly he spread out his men in the form of an arrow, placing the bigger boys at the head.

He took a long time over this, for he was enjoying his momentary power and the admiration of the younger children swarming on the top of the stack-yard wall that hemmed in the ends of the fifteen streets.

Someone began to sing the hymn:

> 'Oh glorious St Patrick, dear Saint of our Isle,'

and all the children on the wall took it up:

> 'On us, thy dear children, bestow a sweet smile;
> And now thou art high in the mansions above,
> Oh glorious St Patrick look down in thy love.'

The ending was the signal for the advance, both sides moving slowly towards each other. Then, with a rush, there was a swirling of balls, and there were screams and cries of 'Long live Ireland!' 'Up the shamrock!' in which were mingled 'England forever!' and 'God save the King!'

Hard blows were struck by the arrowheads. But they had learned no lesson from last year; so their balls became entwined, and many combatants had to stop and free them, and whilst doing so a number of them laughed, especially if their enemy happened to be a pal on the other three hundred and sixty-four days of the year. And so the fight became spasmodic, lacking the ferocity of the earlier battles; it became a mêlée of half-hearted punches and pushes. And the jeering from the mixed supporters on the wall became derisive.

Mick realised there was something lacking. He fell back with his side and engaged in a battle of vituperation!

'Protestant, Protestant, you dirty lot,
Yer backside's blue and yer nose all snot!'

to which the Protestants replied:

'Catholic, Catholic, ring the bell,
When you die you'll go to hell.'

It was all very half-hearted – the excitement seemed to have died in the completion of the preparations.

Mick felt a definite sense of disappointment and feared the flatness of the fight might be put down to his leadership, and that Big Geordie Flannagan might be picked to take his place. He looked round for some sign that would be the means of leading him to fresh applause. And like manna from heaven he found it. Standing solitary at the top end of his own back lane was the boy from next door . . . the spook's lad.

The boy was looking from one group to the other with evident curiosity. His face looked all eyes, and Mick was quick to detect a gleam of fear in them. With the true instinct of a leader, he first of all planned to cut off the enemy's retreat. So he called three of his best men to him, and in a few words told them what he intended doing, and dispatched them down Fadden Street with orders to come up the back lane. A few more whispered words to other members of his gang, and they stopped yelling and stood looking towards the boy.

As soon as Mick saw the three outriders coming up the back lane he called out loudly, 'Look! There's the spook!'

After a moment's hesitation the word was taken up, 'The spook! The spook!' Those on the other side stopped their abuse and they too turned towards the boy, whose face had blanched. He did not turn and try to escape down the back lane, for he knew, from the laughs behind him, that that escape was cut off. Instead he tried to think of what his grandfather had told him to do when confronted with hostile thought, but terror swamped any thinking.

Fascinated, he watched the two opposing sides converging on each other and the children swarming down from the wall. They began to form a solid mass before him, and he listened to shouts that weren't new to his ears:

'His da's a spook!'

'Me ma says he's a divil.'

'Me ma says if you bless yersel' when you pass him he can't do you any harm.'

'Me da says the priest put a curse on him an' he was kicked out of Jarrer, an' he'll wither away.'

'Mr Roberts, our minister, says they're evil and we mustn't have any truck with 'em.'

On and on it went, not loudly or angrily, but steadily and defiantly, and in some faint way the boy detected fear of himself in their voices. Yet he knew what that fear would make them do. It wasn't the first time he had been in a similar situation, but he found that repetition did not make him more brave.

Mick too was aware of the fear. The crowd of them would do nothing, he thought, just call the spook names and perhaps throw a stone or two, until some woman came out from her backyard and scattered the lot of them. He wanted a chase, some life in the proceedings.

Again he gave instructions to others of his gang, who sped away to block the ends of the streets, all but the last one. Then he yelled out to the crowd, proclaiming himself leader and a man of fair play, 'Give him a chance . . . Let him away! Give him a start!'

Molly, who was standing near him, whispered, 'Where you goner chase him?'

'The gut,' he whispered back without looking at her, for his eyes were now fixed on those of the boy.

The boy was shivering in stark terror; he knew what this

chance meant; it meant running, running, running until his whole body sobbed and his trousers became wet. And he knew that long after the fear would have passed the feeling of his wet trousers would remain. But it was either running or being stoned here.

A gap appeared in the crowd and Mick's voice yelled, 'Come on, spooky! We'll give you a start.' He was leading them all now, the Catholics, the Protestants, the Chapelies and the others. He kept yelling, 'Let him through! . . . Come on, spook. We'll give you ten for a start when you're through.'

There was a whirling in Mick's blood when he saw the boy begin to move, and a stream of saliva trickled from the corner of his mouth. The boy, his face the colour of dirty dough and his eyes stretching the skin, came abreast of Mick. He would never reach the gut, Mick thought – he was too small. They would drag him there.

Suddenly he threw his arms out wide, a signal that no-one must move and shouted, 'One!'

At the sound the boy became galvanised. He shot away, and Mick, when he noted the speed with which the boy ran, quickened his counting, almost choking with suppressed glee when he saw the boy's maddened terror on realising the exits of the streets and back lanes were blocked.

'Ten!' was a scream in Mick's throat. He was off, ahead of the milling, screeching children. They stumbled into each other, kicking and pushing to get a clear road. Some left the main chase and ran down the streets, knowing that this would be the quickest way and that they would pick up the chase again on the main road, the word had been passed, 'To the gut! To the gut!'

Among those who diverted was Molly. She sped down her own street her hair and legs flying. And she almost cried with vexation when she saw her mother step from their front door.

'Here!' Mary Ellen caught at Molly's arm, almost unbalancing herself. 'Have you gone mad? What's all the screeching for?'

'Aw! Ma, let go.'

'Get inside!' said Mary Ellen.

'Aw! Ma, I'm goin' with our Mick.'

'With Mick? What's he doin'?'

'He's . . . he's . . . They're chasin' the lad next door to the gut.'

Mary Ellen brought her hand across her daughter's ear with a crack. 'Get yersel' inside – I'll gut you! A big lass like you running mad with a lot of lads!' She pushed Molly before her through the front room, calling, 'John!'

John came out of the bedroom asking, 'What is it?'

'It's our Mick . . . he's chasing the lad next door to the gut. There's dozens of them running mad!'

'Are you sure it's Mick?'

'Ask her.' Mary Ellen pointed to the snivelling Molly.

When John looked at Molly she hung her head, and Mary Ellen said, 'Go and see what he's up to, lad; for if the pollis catches him at anything down there they won't give him another chance, after catching him loosening the timbers that time.'

'Why are they chasing the lad next door, are they playing at something?' John asked Molly.

'No,' Molly muttered into her chest. 'It's because he's a spook.'

John hastily put on his coat and left the house; and as he went out into the back lane he bumped into the girl from next door. She was running, and gasped, 'I'm sorry.' She smiled faintly at him and ran on again.

He did not speak, but hurried after her. He guessed where she was going . . . someone must have told her. Children were straggled along the road; most of them, frightened by the thought of the gut, especially as it was getting dark, had given up the chase.

One bold spirit addressed John: 'Your Mick's goin' to push the spook into the gut, Mr O'Brien.'

John knew that between Mick and Dominic there was only the difference in years; the cruelty was already fully matured in

Mick, and he was quite capable of doing what this boy said. He set off at a run and caught up with the girl before she reached the short cut leading to the gut. Shortening his step to suit hers, he said, 'Are you looking for your brother?'

She nodded, but did not speak; and John again had the impression of age. There was a similarity, he noticed, between her expression and that which was more often than not on his mother's face . . . This wasn't the first time she'd gone to her brother's aid – by God, he'd break that young rat's neck!

'You go back, and I'll see to them,' he said to her. But she shook her head.

As they turned down the cut, the shouting came to them, and John sprang away from the girl and ran on ahead.

With the intuition of the young, his coming was noted and the boys crowding round the disused boathouse on the edge of the gut gave the cry, 'Look out! Scatter!'

The size of John looming out of the gathering dusk and the fear of being caught and held responsible gave aid to their legs. They made for the opening near the boathouse, and like dots of vapour they disappeared across the disused ground adjoining the slacks.

John pulled up at the slipway. There was no sign of the boy. Likely, he had taken refuge on the wall round the corner. The wall supporting the slipway turned sharply at right angles, bordering the gut for a considerable distance, and ended abruptly where the gut was deepest, for the swirling tides had by slow degrees loosened its large granite stones, and many of these now made only a row of pinpoints in the mud. The wall was just above ground level and was eighteen inches wide on the top, but from its back edge arose a six-foot fence of stout sleepers.

John walked sideways along the wall, pressing his back against the sleepers, and as he turned the corner he saw the boy and Mick.

The boy was standing up against the last sleeper of the fence, Mick was lying flat along the wall; and there was no sound from either of them, except the whack of the stick as Mick hit at the boy's legs, trying to dislodge him into the black, oozing mud. So lost was Mick in the relish of the moment that he did not hear John's approach. The first he knew was the sound of harsh breathing over him; then he was whipped to his feet and for one sickening second he was hanging in mid-air over the mud. John brought him to his feet and shook him until his head rolled on his shoulders.

'Get home and stay there! If you're not in when I get back it'll mean twice as much when I find you.'

Mick clutched at the sleepers to steady himself, and growled, 'You hit me and I'll tell me da.' Then he retreated hastily along the wall, and John went on to the boy.

In the dim light the white face shone at him, and he said soothingly, 'It's all right, sonny, it's all right.'

The boy did not answer, and John said, 'Come on, give me your hand.'

But the boy still did not move; he seemed petrified into dumbness, and his fingers held on to the sleeper as if glued to it. The wall ended directly below this sleeper, and the rising tide was already creeping towards its fallen stones.

As John unbent the boy's fingers he saw that they were bleeding, and he wished for the moment he would have Mick under his hands. When he picked him up the boy lay stiff across his arms like something frozen hard. The girl was standing at the corner, her face as white as her brother's, and she clutched at them both, saying, 'Is he all right? Oh, David, are you all right?'

'Steady!' John said. 'Let's get off here.' And she went before them along the wall to where it met the ground.

As John put the boy down she drew David into her arms, crying, 'Oh, my dear, what have they done?'

The boy shuddered, and his body fell against hers, and she

soothed him, saying, 'There! There! . . . We'll go home – Grandfather will soon be in and everything will be all right.'

But when she took his hand to walk him up the bank his legs gave way beneath him, and he fell forward. John picked him up again, saying, 'You'd better get him to bed.'

As he strode up the road with the girl trotting by his side and holding on to her brother's ankle, he thanked God that most of the people were indoors having their tea and that the corners of the streets were deserted by their usual batches of men, for he felt self-conscious in doing this rescue act.

The door was open and the house lighted just as she had left it; and as John passed through the front room and into the kitchen he had the impression that his home next door was a hundred miles away. He became conscious of his big, dirty boots on the carpet, and when he laid the boy in a chair, drawn up to the fire, the comfort of it was conveyed to him by his hands sinking beneath the boy into the upholstery.

The girl ran into the bedroom, and returned with something in a glass. David drank it, then asked, in a thin, small voice, 'How long will Grandfather be?'

'Not long, darling.'

The girl was kneeling by the chair, and John, looking down on her, repeated to himself, 'Not long, darling.' Never before had he heard the word spoken, except in derision. How strange these people were.

He was turning to go, saying, 'I hope he'll be all right. My brother will be dealt with,' when the girl sprang to her feet.

'What are you going to do to your brother?' she asked. 'Thrash him?'

'What else?'

'Oh please!' her words tumbled over one another – 'Please don't do that! It won't do a bit of good . . . not the slightest, just the opposite.'

John frowned down on her in perplexity: 'What do you expect

me to do? Let him off? He might have killed the lad there—' He nodded towards the chair.

Her eyes, set deep in her white face, looked black and enormous, and she began to plead with him as if her life depended on it: 'But he didn't! You must talk to him, point out where he was wrong . . . Will you? . . . Please. But don't thrash him; you'll only thrash it into him.'

'Thrash what into him?' John's brows drew closer together.

'The fears, the inhibitions . . . all the things that drove him to do what he did.'

John stared at her. What was she getting at? Was this part of the spook religion? She was strange, not in sayings alone, but in her looks; her curveless body, like a lad's, was as attractive as any bulging bust and wobbling hips.

He turned away from her and went towards the kitchen door, but she hastily blocked his exit: 'Please! . . . Oh!' – she closed her eyes and moved her head from side to side – 'if only Grandfather was in he'd explain so much better than me . . . But you mustn't thrash him.'

Looking down into her strained face, John saw that for the moment, the thought of Mick being thrashed had entirely eliminated the worry for her brother – she was like no-one he had met before . . . she was really in earnest that Mick should be let off. But he knew Mick, and she didn't, so he said, 'Do you think he would understand a talking-to? No. The only thing Mick and his like understand is the thick end of the belt across their . . .' Somehow he couldn't say 'arses' in front of her, so he ended lamely, 'You see. You don't know them.'

'Oh, but I do,' she said, smiling faintly, trying to override his last remark; 'I've known dozens of Micks. Look—' She put out her hands and caught hold of the lapels of his coat. The gesture was almost childish in its naturalness, and he looked down at her hands, then at her face close beneath his own; and an odd sensation passed over him . . . Hannah Kelly said, 'Mind she doesn't lay hands on you, lad.' But this wasn't the kind of laying on she was referring to. If a lass of the fifteen streets laid hold of him, there would be a particular meaning to it; they would lark about a lot before she did this though, and afterwards his arms would go round her. He had seen the process enacted at the corner ends and in dark places in the back lanes. Often, when a lad, he watched the climax with an envy that dissolved into loneliness. And now here was this lass with her hands on him, and the sensation he was experiencing was almost one of reverence, similar to that which he at one time felt for the Virgin . . . But he didn't want to feel reverence for her, or any other lass. She was fetching and he wanted . . . He lifted his hand and covered one of hers – it wasn't much bigger than Katie's, but it was different. His blood began to warm with the feel of her, and he smiled slowly. Her soft, curving mouth was just below his, and as he watched it move, it fascinated him. He wasn't fully aware of the words it was forming until she stepped away from him, taking her hand from his and saying, 'If you had to treat a dirty wound, you wouldn't rub more dirt into it, would you?'

Still on about Mick . . . He came to himself, and said thickly, 'I'm sorry; I'll have to deal with him as I think fit.' A feeling of bewilderment and frustration, mixed with annoyance was filling him; and he passed her, saying gruffly, 'He'll have to take what's coming to him.'

It was with relief he entered his own kitchen. Here were people and things he could understand . . . and manage. Going straight to the wall by the side of the fireplace he unhooked the razor strop.

'Is the lad all right?' Mary Ellen asked.

'Just,' John answered briefly. 'Come on,' – he motioned with his head to Mick.

'I'm not comin'. I'll tell me da!'

'Go canny, lad,' Mary Ellen said to John.

Go canny. Here was another one. 'Go canny!' he rapped out at her with unusual irritation. 'Do you know he nearly killed the lad! As it is he's practically sent him out of his mind. It's as well for you you got hold of Molly when you did, or you'd have something more than a thrashing on your plate the night. Go canny!' He flung round from her and pointed to the door.

Mick began to snivel and cried, 'Ma! Ma, don't let him!'

Mary Ellen turned from Mick to the fire, and John seized him by the collar and pulled him to the door, there to meet Dominic coming in.

Dominic looked from one to the other before eyeing John through narrowed lids: 'What you at? Playin' boss of the house again?'

'You mind your own damn business. If you'd had a little more of it there might have been an improvement in you!'

Mary Ellen hastily broke in, addressing herself to Dominic, 'He's nearly killed the little lad next door.'

After a moment, during which he glanced from one to the other, Dominic stepped aside, and John pushed Mick before him down the yard and into the wash-house.

Mary Ellen found herself staring at Dominic; she couldn't quite take it in; he was sober, solid and sober; and it St Patrick's Day! And added to this surprise was another; for when he took his cap off she saw that he'd had a haircut . . . a proper one; his thick, brown, curling hair was neatly trimmed up the sides, making him, even with the dust of the ore on him, look more attractive. He hadn't come in to tea and she imagined him to be in the bars; but he must have been having a haircut!

She went to the oven to take out his tea, a plate of finnan haddock, but he said, 'I don't want that yet.'

With further amazement she saw him wash himself quickly, take off his yorks and change his coat. He was banging the dust from his trousers as he hurried past her to the front room.

'Where you off to?' she asked.

Dominic paused a moment, and the expression she hated, a mixture of scorn, cocksuredness and craft, came over his face. His eyes flicked over her; and her throat contracted with dislike of him. He said heavily, 'Where d'yer think?'

She stood still, listening to him going out of the front door, and between Mick's howls out in the backyard, she heard the knocker of the next door banging. Her fingers moved nervously back and forth across her lips . . . How would it work out? Candidly she wouldn't care if Dominic left home tomorrow and she never set eyes on him again, but there was no such luck as that happening; he was here and he was going after that lass. It would have been bad enough had she been a Protestant – that was something you could lay your finger on – but what these people next door were was something beyond her ken, something dark and mysterious, something not far removed from the devil; for whoever heard anyone connected with God daring to say they could cure people! Even the priests wouldn't dare. And then another strong point proving their ungodliness was all their fine things. God didn't shower gifts on those He loved – He pointed out the road of poverty to them. Father O'Malley could be hard, but he was right in some things; if you got your reward here, then you could make sure it wasn't from God.

From last Saturday, when they moved in, she had made up her mind to have no truck with them. At odd times she had stopped working and found herself listening to the girl singing. The first time she had heard her she was shocked; she felt it was indecent somehow, almost as bad as if she had seen her walking naked, for it wasn't like a woman singing to a bairn, nor yet over her poss tub, but was high and clear and without restraint. And the morning she heard the singing before breakfast she was bewildered; for even if you had something to sing about you wouldn't do it before breakfast, unless you were prepared to cry your eyes out before supper . . . No, she wanted no truck with them. Yet here was John saving the lad and braying their Mick, and Dominic in next door pouring sympathy over the lass in his best manner. And he had a best manner, Mary Ellen knew; but she also knew it was an impossibility for him to keep it up. Well – she again fastened the errant button of her blouse and momentarily lifted the weight of her body – that was as far as things were going, if she could help it . . . not one of them would darken this door!

She crossed herself swiftly and murmured, 'May the Lord bless us and preserve us from all evil, and bring us to life everlasting. Amen.'

Chapter Four

The Conflict

Mary Ellen's temper was fraying thin. The weather was bad enough with the rain pelting down and the wind howling as if it was December, but to have them all in the house except Mick and Molly, who were at school, was too much. Neither John nor Dominic had been set on this morning; a mailboat had come in with a cargo of fruit, but the gaffer had given the work to the men who had not been set on the recent boats. It was bad enough that they were off work, but to have them all stuck round her like this was too much of a good thing. And what was more, she was feeling a little sick with the heat of the oven and the smell of the dirty working clothes put to dry all round the kitchen . . . If only this other business were over. She was tired of it all – her body was so bairn-weary. She was feeling now that things were getting beyond her.

Even Katie could draw no kind word from her, and she pushed her to one side to get to the oven, saying. 'Get out of me way, bairn.'

Katie was home from school because her boots leaked; and her eyes were streaming, not only as the result of a cold but with crying. She hated to be off school, more so now than ever, for Miss Llewellyn had said that if she worked hard she could sit for an examination, which might be the first step on the road to her becoming a teacher. She had tried to tell her mother, but Mary Ellen snapped at her, and even John did not seem interested.

She looked towards him now. He was sitting in the corner on the far side of the fireplace mending her boots. He had put odd pieces of leather on the soles and was now cutting up an old boot to get enough leather to sew across the slits. She returned to her book, the only one she possessed, a Grimm's Fairy Tale, and she knew each word by heart.

The front-door knocker was suddenly banged, and without waiting she went to answer it. It had been knocked twice already this afternoon, once by a tallyman and once by a man begging. The beggar wasn't pleased when she brought him a slice of bread. He bent it up and put it in his pocket, and her mouth watered, for it was new bread from a flat cake just out of the oven; it was a long time till teatime, and she had got out of the habit of asking for bread between meals for she remembered times when they all had bread at teatime except her mother, and she was frightened that this would happen again.

It was Mrs Bradley at the door, and she asked, 'Is yer ma in?'

Katie said, 'Yes.'

'Then tell her we're gathering for poor Mrs Patton's wreath . . . Here, take her the paper.'

Katie took the paper and went into the scullery to her mother. 'It's Mrs Bradley – she's gathering for flowers, ma.'

Mary Ellen's lips set in a tight line as she read down one side of the list and halfway down the other . . . shillings, sixpences . . . only two or three threepences. She gave a sigh, and lifting up her skirt took fourpence from the little bag and handed it to Katie, together with the list.

As Katie passed John he asked, 'What's that for?' But before she could reply, Mary Ellen called, 'Go on, you, Katie,' and Katie went on to the front door. Mary Ellen knew that John didn't hold with gathering for wreaths, but what could she do . . .

and that Bella Bradley collecting!

John knew what he would have done . . . the gathering for wreaths had always irked him. They would collect as much as two pounds and spend the whole lot on flowers, when the widow, if it was a man who had died, was more often than not destitute, and within a week the bairns would be crying for bread. They knew this only too well, the women who took it on themselves to gather, yet they still bought flowers to show respect for the dead. He snorted and banged the hammer on the last, sending a pain through his knee. It made him mad! He knew that, even if there was no insurance money, besides collecting for the flowers they would collect for cabs, to make the dead look decent. They didn't collect for the hearse. No, that could be ticked, to be paid off at so much a week. But the undertakers weren't so ready to tick cabs. And if it was for one of the Irish, the relatives would pawn, beg, borrow or steal, but they would have a bit of a wake. It was all crazy! And yet he understood from his mother that the funerals were nothing like they used to be, for in her young days, she told him, she longed for the Irish to die so she could go to the wake with her mother and have a good feed.

What had she put on the list, he wondered. Whatever it was, by this time next week they would be glad of it; for if they were not set on there wouldn't be a penny in the house.

Many things were beginning to make him wild. And on a day like this, tied to the house, he had nothing else to do but think. Lately he had been feeling the desire for someone to talk to, someone who could answer questions. Once or twice he tried to talk to Father Bailey, and endeavoured to have the material in his mind formed into concrete questions; but when he was with the priest he found it was no use – he knew what he wanted to say but couldn't get it out.

His mother was always saying thinking got you nowhere; you must have faith and rely on that. Faith! He looked at her now, pounding a great piece of dough, the second batch of bread she had baked today. What had faith done for her? She could hardly get her arms into the bowl for the roundness of her stomach. He took his eyes from her. Where would they put the bairn when it came? He'd have to try and rig up something out of boxes – the clothes basket that had served them all as a cradle was done long since. He pulled his legs up hastily as Dominic made to pass him on his way to the bedroom.

Mary Ellen called after Dominic, 'Don't lie on that bed with those boots on, mind!' but the only answer she received was the banging of the door.

John settled himself back against the wall: he always felt easier when Dominic was out of the room. He had finished one boot and was preparing the thread by rubbing it with tallow for patching the other when he heard his mother give a startled mutter. She was looking out through the kitchen window, and she exclaimed, 'I don't want them in here!'

As she rubbed the dough off her hands, there came a knock on the kitchen door. Katie was about to open it, but Mary Ellen said, 'Hold on. I'll see to it.' When she opened the door, there stood the old man and the girl.

'Good afternoon, Mrs O'Brien.' It was the old man who spoke, and his voice was as kindly as his smile; but Mary Ellen would not allow it to make any impression on her. She didn't reply, but stared at them fixedly, the door held firmly in her hand, while he went on, 'I thought we would just come round and get acquainted. And also ask you to thank your son for helping my boy last night.'

Mary Ellen's eyes darted to the girl. She was wearing a waterproof coat with a hood attached, and from under it she smiled at Mary Ellen, like a child who was asking to be liked. They were barmy, Mary Ellen thought. Their Mick had nearly done for the lad, and here they were, coming to thank John! They weren't all there, either of them – they couldn't be. She wanted no truck with them. She was aware that the old man was becoming drenched, but that was his lookout; they weren't crossing the doorstep.

She was saying abruptly, 'That's all right. It was our Mick's fault, anyway,' when she felt her hand taken from the door, and John stood there, saying, 'Won't you come in?' It wasn't often she got angry with John, but now it took her all her time not to turn on him.

The old man said, 'Thank you. Thank you. Are you by any chance the Mr O'Brien I owe so much to?'

Pushing two chairs forward John said, 'Take a seat.' He did not look at the girl, but went on, 'It's us should be doing the thanking. Not many people would be taking it like this.' Then he turned to Shane: 'This is my father.'

Shane reluctantly took the proffered hand and muttered something, and his head, which had been still, began to jerk.

The old man, seeming not to notice the lack of cordiality, said, 'My name's Peter Bracken. And this is my granddaughter, Christine.'

Shane nodded, and after a short silence that was broken only by the scraping of chairs, he turned to Mary Ellen, now vigorously pounding the dough, and said, 'I'm off to see if there's anything in.' He pulled his steaming coat off the rod that ran under the mantelshelf, and with a final nod towards Mr Bracken, he went out.

Mary Ellen watched his huge figure slumping down the yard. Off to see if there's anything in at this time of the day! It was just to get out of the way; he hated to talk to strangers at any time. There was a faint wreath of steam still hovering about the shoulders of his coat as he disappeared into the back lane. It brought a tightness to her breast, and she murmured to herself, 'Shane, Shane,' as she was wont to do years ago when her pity was mixed with love. And the feeling made her more resentful towards the pair sitting behind her. Now he'd be wet to the skin, and his twitching would go on all night.

She knew she was being very bad mannered standing with her back to them, but she couldn't help it; yet she found herself listening to the girl talking to Katie. They were talking about the book, Katie's voice sounding broad in comparison with the girl's, which was quiet and even and without dialect. And then she found herself listening to John. He was talking more than she had heard him do so before. He was talking to the old fellow about the docks and the kind of boats that came in and what they brought . . . iron ore from Bilbao, black fine ore from Benisaf, the heavy ore from Sweden that made the steel, esparto grass for paper, prop boats from Russia, with the cargo stacked from one end of the boat to the other to make the tonnage. As if the old fellow would want to know all that! She had never heard him talk so much about the docks before. He went on to speak of the unloading as if he had been down the holds all his life, instead of just two years. What had come over him? Perhaps he was doing it because she was offhand with them. Well, he knew she wanted no truck with them; and they were a thick-skinned pair to sit there knowing, as they must know, that they weren't wanted.

'I suppose you are always kept busy, Mrs O'Brien?'

She started, and was forced to half turn her body and look at the old man, and to answer him civilly: 'Yes, most of the time I'm at it.'

'You must find it very hard looking after such a big family. And I mean big,' he laughed.

'Well, you've got to take what God sends.' Immediately she felt she had said the wrong thing, giving him an opening to start his ranting, but to her surprise he didn't take it.

He stood up, saying, 'Well, we mustn't delay you – I just felt I would like to make your acquaintance, Mrs O'Brien.'

Mary Ellen turned from the dish, again forced to respond, this time with a smile. It was funny, but they seemed all right.

Was this spook business just an idle rumour? People were in the habit of making a lot out of nowt.

She returned the girl's smile too, but when she saw John, silent now, looking at the lass, the smile froze on her face. She didn't want any of that kind of truck, not for John she didn't . . . Dominic could do what he liked.

There was another knock on the front door, and this time she had to tell Katie, who was hanging on to the girl's hand, to go and open it.

Christine spoke directly to Mary Ellen for the first time. 'Will you let Katie come in to tea, Mrs O'Brien? It's rather a special occasion, it's Grandfather's birthday.'

She cast a smile, full of light, on the old man, and he said, 'Sh!'

She answered, 'No, I won't. Do you know how old he is?' She was speaking to John now, looking up into his face.

John's eyes twinkled, and he answered seriously, 'Twenty-six.'

They all laughed, except Mary Ellen.

'You're just sixty years out!' said the girl.

'You're not eighty-six!' Amazement brought the words out of Mary Ellen.

'Yes, that's what I am, Mrs O'Brien.'

Mary Ellen stared at the straight, lean body of Peter Bracken, at his unlined face and deep-set eyes, shining like black coals. The only sign of real age was the white hair, and he was eighty-six. Fear of him overcame her again. You didn't reach eighty-six and be like that, not naturally you didn't. Shane was fifty-seven, and he was old. She had known men live to eighty, but they ended their days in bed, or on sticks. No, her instinct had been right at first . . . there was something funny about them, something beyond her understanding; and she wanted no truck with them.

She was brought from her fear by the sound of footsteps accompanying Katie's through the front room. Who on earth could Katie have let in now!

The small, black-clad figure standing in the open doorway soon informed her. She gasped at the sight of Father O'Malley. His presence always meant a rating for something or other. Today it would be Katie off school and Mick being kept from Mass last Sunday. Oh, she'd had enough for one day! And there were these two still standing there, not smiling now but staring at the priest as if they were struck.

'Good afternoon, Father. Will you take a seat? It's dreadful weather; you must be wet.' Mary Ellen was doing her duty. At the same time, she noticed the half-inch thick soles on the priest's stout boots, and chided herself for thinking: It'll take some water to get through them.

John spoke next: 'Good afternoon, Father.'

'Good afternoon,' said Father O'Malley, in his thin, tight voice; but he looked neither at Mary Ellen nor at John, for his eyes were fixed on those of Peter Bracken.

Noting this, John said, 'Mr Bracken's a new neighbour of ours, Father.'

The priest did not answer, and Peter Bracken said, quietly, 'Father O'Malley and I already know one another.'

'What is this man doing in your house?'

Mary Ellen knew the priest was addressing her, although he did not look at her. She shivered and said hesitantly, 'Well Father . . . '

'Order him to leave at once! And forbid him the door in future.'

Mary Ellen twisted the corner of her apron and turned towards Mr Bracken and the girl. But before she could get the words out, John broke in sharply, 'Hold your hand a minute! Me da's not in, and next to him I'm head of this house, such as it is, and I'm telling no-one to get out, Father.'

The priest swung round on him, his eyes almost lost behind their narrowed lids and the double lenses of his glasses: 'So you are head of the house, are you? And you will take the responsibility on your soul for associating with this man?'

'I know nothing against the man.' John's face was as set as the priest's.

'You don't?' Father O'Malley raised his eyebrows. 'Then you're about the only one in these parts who doesn't. I will enlighten you. This man is an enemy of the Catholic Church.'

'That is not true! I'm an enemy of no church . . . '

Father O'Malley cut short Peter Bracken's protest, and went on: 'Why, I ask you, is a man of his standing living in a quarter like this? Because he makes it his business to live among Catholics so he can turn them against the Church.'

'I live wherever there is fear and poverty, and try to erase it.' The old man's face was no longer placid; it was alight with a force and energy that gave the impression he was towering above them all.

'Do you know what this man has dared to say? Only that he has a power equal to that of Christ!' Father O'Malley's eyes bored into Mary Ellen's and then into John's. 'In fact, he says he is a Christ!'

John, his eyes wide and questioning now, looked to Mr Bracken for denial. But none came.

'You know you are twisting my words!' cried the old man. 'What I maintain is we all have the power to be Christs. If we are made in God's image and likeness, then it stands to reason we are part of Him; our spirit is pure God material. The only difference between my spirit and God's is the size of it – the quality is exactly the same. That is what I preach. And the more I become aware of my spirit, the more I get in touch with it, the more Godlike things I can do . . . And I have done Godlike things—' Mr Bracken pointed at the priest: 'You know I have! And it is this very proof that upsets your slavish doctrine.'

'Silence!' Father O'Malley's voice was like deep and terrible thunder.

Mary Ellen clutched at the neck of her blouse, and Katie hid her face in the folds of her mother's skirt; the bedroom door opened and Dominic came into the kitchen, but no-one took any notice of him.

The priest's voice dropped low in his throat. He addressed himself to John. 'Are you asking for any more proof than that?'

Before John could answer, the girl spoke, 'My grandfather will give him proof – he will show him his own power, and free him from you and your like. It is not God's will, as you preach, that he or anyone else should live in poverty and ignorance all his days. If they were made aware of their own power they would throw all this off.' She flung her arms wide and took a step towards the priest. 'You would stop them from thinking – for once they think, they question. And they mustn't question, must they? They must accept! It wouldn't do for them to realise there's no purgatory or heaven or hell but what they make themselves!'

Before John's eyes there rose the picture of Miss Llewellyn leaning back against the wind, saying, 'Take the heaven you are sure of.' Then his mind was brought back to this slip of a girl facing up to a man like Father O'Malley; not only facing up to him, but attacking him. What she was saying was quite mad, but she had courage.

The thought saddened him; it might be the courage of fanaticism, and she looked too sweet and girlish to be imbued with fanaticism.

The old man drew her back to his side, saying, 'Be serene, Christine. Remember, anger poisons.'

Father O'Malley's voice cast a deadly chill over the room as he said, 'The day is not far hence when you will rot in hell for your blasphemy!'

'The day is not far hence,' took up Peter Bracken, 'when your sect, if it does not throw off its dogmatism and learn toleration, will be fighting for its life; for there are seeds in the wombs of women, at this moment, that in thirty, forty or fifty years' time will shake the foundations of your preaching. The minds of people are moving. They are searching for the truth – they are reading. And what are they reading first? The very books that are forbidden by your Church, for the first question the groping mind asks is: Why have these books been forbidden?'

Father O'Malley looked as if he was about to choke – black anger swamped his face. After a silence, tensed to breaking point, he addressed Mary Ellen, 'I leave you and your conscience to judge. And remember, I am warning you . . . disaster and damnation follow this man. If you wish to save your immortal soul and those of your family, throw him out as you would a snake!' His eyes burned into Mary Ellen's for a second, and then he was gone. And the banging of the front door shook the house.

It occurred to John that Father O'Malley had ignored him because he stood up to him; it was noticeable that the priest concentrated on his mother because she was afraid. He looked towards her. She was leaning on the table with one hand; the other was held under her breast tight against her heart. And she was shivering.

Dominic spoke for the first time: 'Don't take any notice of him; he thinks he's still in Ireland.' His words weren't spoken to his mother, but to the girl. But she did not return his glance, or answer him, for she was staring at Mary Ellen.

Into this tense atmosphere came Mick. He entered the kitchen, his head on one side and his hand over his ear. 'Ma, me ear's runnin' and it's ach . . . ' He stopped short at the sight of Mr Bracken and glanced quickly from him to John.

No-one moved for a second until Peter Bracken exclaimed in an exalted voice, 'Mrs O'Brien, I will show you! Your boy has earache, probably an abscess. I will cure it. Through the great healing power of God I will cure it.'

He made a step towards Mick, and in a moment the kitchen became quickened into life. Mary Ellen flung herself between them, intending to grab Mick to her, but Mick, thinking of last night and taking Peter's cure to mean much the same thing as when his mother boxed his ears, saying, 'I'll cure you!' sprang away from them both. Mary Ellen made a wild grab at the air, overbalanced and twisted herself to clutch at John's hands that were outstretched to her but missed them and fell on her side on to the mat.

Mary Ellen knew, almost as she fell, what had happened. The blinding pain, like a red-hot steel wire, starting in her womb and forcing itself up through her body and out of her head, blotted out even itself in its transit. When next she felt it she was lying on the bed – the pain was filling all her pores and forcing out sweat. She opened her eyes and looked up into John's face. She wanted to say to him, 'Don't worry, lad. Don't worry,' for his face was like death, but she could utter no word.

The hot wire was boring again, identifying itself from the other pains by an intensity that no previous labour had brought to her. It left no room even for fear when she realised that that Bracken man was near her; nor did she feel any element of surprise when she heard him saying, 'I'll go in and work at her head through the wall. Take her hand and don't let go.'

Mary Ellen felt her hand being taken between two soft palms, and she did as she was bidden when his voice came directly to her, as if through a thick fog, saying, 'Hold on to Christine, Mrs O'Brien, and the pain will go.'

As the pain forced her knees up and her head down into her chest, Mary Ellen gripped the girl's hand. And when she next regained consciousness she knew she was not on the bed but above it, lying on a sort of soft platform, and the girl was still by her side, while Hannah Kelly and Nurse Snell were working on somebody lying on the bed. And then the doctor came, not the shilling doctor, but Doctor Davidson from Jarrow, and she wondered vaguely who would pay him. He reached up and took her hand and tried to unloosen it from the girl's, but as he did so Mary Ellen felt herself dropping down into that contorted mass below her, and she clung on like grim death to the soft hand. She heard him say, 'You're Peter Bracken's granddaughter, aren't you?' There followed a silence. Then his voice came again, 'Well, there are stranger things in heaven and earth than this world dreams of; and I won't despise your help, because I'm going to need it.'

She lay for years on the platform with queer sensations passing through her body, and the next voice she heard was that of Shane, muttering, 'Mary Ellen, lass, Mary Ellen.'

She knew he was crying, and she wondered at it. She thought of the time when he loved her and she loved him - it was all so long ago. What had happened since? Nothing. He still loved her, but she loved Katie and John. But they didn't love Shane - he had no-one but her. What would happen to him when she died she didn't know - and it didn't seem to matter.

It was odd, but rather nice, lying here thinking untroubled thoughts. She hadn't to get up and see about the baking or washing or meals, or, what was more important, money. She had an ache somewhere, but she couldn't lay her finger on it. And she was conscious of smiling when the doctor reached up and, lifting her eyelid, exclaimed, 'Odd, very odd.'

The next voice that came to her was Father Bailey's. It was nice to have Father Bailey near; he brought a feeling of comfort. And as he made the sign of the cross and touched her lips, she felt a great happiness. She saw him standing at the foot of the platform and smiling, not at her, but at Mr Bracken, who, she felt, was standing just behind her head. Father Bailey was saying, 'God's ways are many and mysterious. He has made these ways and only He can judge them.' She heaved a great sigh and fell into a kind of sleep, thinking, 'Yes, we are all one.' It was the answer Christine Bracken had given to Father Bailey.

The gas in the kitchen was turned low. It flickered up and down and spurted out of a little hole in the bottom of the mantle. In the dim light John knelt before the fire, taking out the ashes. He raked them slowly and quietly, and was glad of their warmth on his hands, for in spite of a good fire, he felt cold. It was the chill before the dawn, he thought. Was it only twelve hours since all this started? It seemed many lifetimes to him. And what it must be like for Christine, sitting in that one position by the bed, he could not imagine. He thought of her now as Christine – the night had joined them in a relationship that seemed to him to be stronger than any blood tie; he had wrapped a blanket about her and taken off her shoes, and put on her slippers. He had been next door for them, and had to find them himself, for the old man was sitting facing the wall and appeared to be asleep. He had taken her cup after cup of tea, and when, stiff with cramp, she could not hold the cup, he held it for her. Once she leant against him and he supported her with his arm. And an hour ago, he had tried to withdraw her hand gently from his mother's, but the result was the same as when others had attempted to do this – Mary Ellen's fingers became like a vice around those of Christine. His mother had been on the point of death, he knew, her life reduced to a mere flicker, yet whenever her hand was touched it held all the strength of vital life in its grip on Christine's. The doctor had said it was touch and go: 'I've done all I can,' he said. 'I'll be back first thing in the morning.' And looking hard at John, he asked, 'Do you believe in spiritual healing?'

John answered simply, 'I'm a Catholic.'

'So am I,' said the doctor. 'And I'm dead against it professionally and otherwise . . . yet . . . ' He had stopped abruptly, buttoned his coat, and said, 'Goodnight. We'll know more in the morning.'

Father Bailey had left the house without saying anything, his face set and thoughtful.

Shane's reactions when he saw the girl sitting there were surprising to John. He had come back into the kitchen and stood looking down into the fire, his body strangely still. 'I don't care who keeps her alive – it can be the divil himself,' he said, 'as long as she doesn't leave me.'

He had turned and looked quietly at his son, and John realised that beyond the drinking and the fighting there still remained in his father a deep feeling for his mother. It surprised him and at the same time brought him closer to this man, whom at times he almost despised. A little while ago he had managed to persuade him to lie down – Dominic was already in bed, having retired there shortly after twelve. He had stood with the others round his mother when they thought she was breathing her last, but when she continued to breathe he said there was no point in the lot of them staying up, and anyway he'd have to be out early to see if he could get a start.

John knew that he, too, would have to be at the docks by six o'clock. There was a prop boat due in, and he might get set on – not that he liked prop boats, for there was no piecework – you received four shillings a day, and no overtime; but that would certainly be better than nothing, for with his mother bad, money would be needed now more than ever before.

Although he'd had no rest he did not feel tired; the training of working forty-eight hours at a stretch as a young lad when on tipping had hardened him. He thought nothing of working all day and all night to discharge an ore boat, and the men liked him in the gang. He could set the pace, and the pace meant everything when the quicker the discharge was done the sooner the men were paid. He looked at the clock . . . half-past four. There were many things that should be done before he left the house; so he proceeded to tidy the kitchen, shaking the mats and sweeping the floor – his mother would want them to be dependent on neighbours as little as possible, kind as they might be.

He was setting the table for breakfast when Hannah Kelly came from the front room.

'I'll go over home a minute, lad,' she whispered, 'and get our Joe up. Then I'll be back.'

He thanked her, and asked, 'Do you think there's any change?'

'I don't know . . . perhaps there's a little – she seems to be breathing easier. Funny about that lass, isn't it?' She looked questioningly at John. 'Mary Ellen hanging on to her like that after saying she wanted no truck with them.'

John made no reply.

And after a moment she whispered again. 'She's had me scared stiff, sitting so still. 'Tisn't natural. What d'ye make of it? And what are ye going to do if it goes on any longer?'

'I don't know,' he said.

Hannah shook her head: 'It's rum. Makes ye put yer thinking cap on, don't it?'

He nodded slowly, and she said, 'Aye well, there's queer things happen in the world. We'll know this time the morrer, likely.'

After Hannah had gone, he stood staring before him. What would happen to them all if his mother should die? She was the axis around which they revolved. Molly would soon be leaving school, but she would be less than useless to run this turbulent house. He looked down on her, lying in the corner of the couch. Her mouth was open, and even in sleep she looked what she was, feckless. Now if Katie were older . . . What! The thought shocked him. Katie work and slave after the lot of them! No. Let her have a better start than that, even though it be only in service. But his mother wouldn't die. Somehow they wouldn't let her die.

He classed Mr Bracken and Christine as 'they' when he thought of them in their strange and eerie capacity of healers; but as Mr Bracken and Christine, he thought of them as kindly folk, and in Christine's case, as bonny and taking.

When he went quietly from the kitchen into the front room to replenish the fire, he saw them as he had seen them last – his mother, lying straight and still and curiously flat, with one arm outstretched to that of Christine, who was sitting close to the head of the bed; only this time there was a difference – inches separated Mary Ellen's hand from Christine's.

Christine smiled faintly. The smile seemed forced on to the chiselled whiteness of her face, her eyes looked vacant, like the hollowed sockets in a sculptured head.

John bent over her, whispering anxiously, 'Are you all right?'

She tried to broaden her smile, but the effort seemed too much, and she fell against him. He glanced at his mother. She was breathing evenly now, and a faint tinge of colour had crept into the greyness of her face.

Christine whispered, 'She's asleep . . . it's over.' She sighed, and her body pressed with gentle heaviness against him.

'Come into the kitchen,' he said.

'I can't yet. I've . . . I've got cramp. I'm stiff. In a little while.'

She sounded sleepy, and for a moment he thought she had fallen asleep.

Hannah Kelly came into the room again, and exclaimed softly, 'She's let go then.' She peered at Mary Ellen. 'She's better. Ye'd better get away to bed, lass,' she said kindly to Christine.

Christine, in an effort to rise, almost lost her balance, and John put his arm about her and supported her to the kitchen, followed by Hannah's quizzical glance and raised eyebrows. 'Aye, well,' she soliloquised, 'ye never can tell where blisters light. But my God, won't Mary Ellen go mad!'

John sat Christine on a chair by the fire, and stood helplessly watching her as she slowly started to cry. It was a gentle crying; the tears welled up from their source, spilling over the dark, thick fringe of lashes on to her cheeks, then down on to her clasped hands.

'You're all in,' John said. 'Come on, I'll take you in home.'

Like a child, she placed her hand in his, and he drew her to her feet.

'The cramp . . . it's still there,' – she tottered as she stood – 'my legs don't seem to belong to me.'

In the flickering light of the gas, she looked up at him and smiled through the tears. 'It's been a strange night, John.'

He nodded silently. He wanted to thank her for what, in the back of his mind, he felt that she and her grandfather had done, but to say 'Thank you for saving my mother's life' would be to accept the strange and terrible power that was assuredly theirs, and some part of him was afraid. It seemed ridiculous that this slip of a lass could be anything but what she looked . . . a fetching, boyish-looking girl.

Christine sighed and said, 'Everything would have been perfect if the baby had lived. Will your mother be very upset?'

He couldn't answer for his mother . . . nor for himself, for he felt she would be shocked at his thankfulness that it was dead.

She swayed, and again he put his arm about her and led her to the door. Her legs gave way beneath her, and she clung to him saying, 'It's only temporary. In the morning I'll be all right, but now all my strength has gone.'

Stooping swiftly and saying, 'This is the best way then,' he lifted her up into his arms. She offered no resistance, but sank against him, her head on his shoulder. One of his hands was under her breast, and he saw the curve of it as her blouse and petticoat pouched, small, not much bigger than Katie's, and the sight of it brought no more excitement to his blood than the tiny mound of Katie's would have done. Some part of his mind wondered at this. His other hand was below her knees, and his face, as it bent above hers, was close enough for kissing. He could have dropped his mouth on to the lips and told himself it was in gratitude. And she too perhaps would have accepted his excuse. And it would have been a start. It would also have fixed Dominic. But he did nothing, not even press her close. Perhaps it was because he was worried about his mother, but he might have been carrying Katie, for his feelings were not aroused above tenderness. Vaguely, he was irritated by this. The night had brought them together in one way, a way that was deep and would be lasting, he knew, but it wasn't the way of a fellow getting off with a lass; it was a way that had missed his body and touched something beyond.

As he carried her into her own kitchen, she stirred and opened her eyes, and her hand came up and touched his cheek. And she whispered, 'You're so nice, John . . . so good.' And he knew that he would have started something had he kissed her, because she liked him in a way perhaps that hadn't gone past her body.

Chapter Five

The Comic

KATIE MOVED THE parcel on to her other hip. It was heavy; but not as heavy as the weight inside her; the weight was leaden. To go to the pawnshop with any parcel filled her with shame; to walk up the dock bank, under the knowledgeable stares of the men idling there against the railings caused her throat to move in and out; and to meet any of her schoolmates on the journey made her want to die; but when it was John's suit she was carrying every tragedy of the journey was intensified a thousandfold.

When her mother asked, 'Will you go down to "Bob's", hinny?' Katie had stared at her, speechless. She wanted to say, 'Our Molly should go, she's bigger,' but she knew from experience that Molly always got less on the clothes than she did, and generally too, she lost something, the ticket, or worse still, a sixpence. And because her mother looked so thin and white when she asked her she remained silent, and watched Mary Ellen go to the box under the bed and take John's suit out.

It seemed such a shame that it was John's, because he had started work only that morning. They all had, after being off weeks. But there was nothing in the house now to make them a meal, and although they would get subs, her mother was relying on these to pay the three weeks' back rent. Katie felt that once the rent was paid, her mother would look less white.

Going through the arches into Tyne Dock she met Mrs Flaherty.

'Oh, ye're not at school the day?' Peggy greeted her.

'No, I was sick.' Katie stared up into the half-washed face, criss-crossed with wrinkles, and her tone defied disbelief.

'Oh, that's a pity, it is. Ye shouldn't miss your iducation. Some day, when ye're old enough, I'll lend ye one o' me books; they'll iducate ye like nothing else will. When ye're old enough that is.' She snuffled and caught the drop from the end of her nose on the back of her hand.

'Thank you.' For as long as she could remember Katie had been promised one of Mrs Flaherty's books, and the promise meant nothing to her now. She said, 'Ta-ta, Mrs Flaherty,' and walked on, the parcel now pressed against her chest and resting on the top of her stomach.

Although she thought impatiently that Mrs Flaherty was always on about education, she wished her mother was a bit like her. She had almost given up talking to her mother about the examination and what Miss Llewellyn said, for her mother didn't believe Miss Llewellyn meant what she said – last time, she had stopped her talking, saying, 'Oh, hinny, you mustn't take so much notice of things; your teacher's only being nice. The examination she's on about is likely the one you have every year.' And when Katie had sat quietly crying, Mary Ellen said to John, 'Look, lad. I can't go down to the school and see what she keeps on about, I only have me shawl; will you go?'

'What! Me? Not on your life. Now that's a damn silly thing to ask me to do, isn't it! What could I say to the headmistress?'

'Well, will you go and see her teacher, then?'

John had just stared blankly at his mother, then picked up his cap and walked out of the house.

Katie thought the only one who understood was Christine. She liked Christine nearly as much as she liked Miss Llewellyn, but not quite. Life had taken on an added glow since Christine came into it; for Christine made her pinnies and dresses out of her own old ones. She gave her and Molly nice things to eat, too; and she had even given them money, real money, half a crown each. But only twice, for when they took their half-crowns into their mother the second week she made them take them back.

Katie could not understand her mother's attitude of not speaking to Christine and her grandfather. She allowed her and Molly to go next door, but Mr Bracken and Christine had never been into her house since that terrible day some months ago when their mother was taken bad. John and Dominic, too, went next door; and she often sat on John's knee while he and Mr Bracken talked. They talked about funny things, one of which stuck in her mind: Mr Bracken said you could have anything you wanted if you only used your thoughts properly . . . There were so many things she wanted, but she wanted above all to be a teacher. Should she do what Mr Bracken told John, lie on her back with her arms outstretched and think of being a teacher until she felt herself floating away? Eeh no! She'd better not, for there were some people who said Mr Bracken was the devil. He wasn't; but anyway, she'd better not do it.

She always had a queer feeling when Dominic was next door when she would wonder if he were trying to do what he was doing that night she went in unexpectedly. He had Christine pressed in the corner and was trying to kiss her. Her blouse was open, and the ribbon of her camisole was loose. Kate knew that Christine was frightened, for she held on to her until Dominic went out. Then she told her not to mention to John what had happened; and Katie only too readily promised.

At last she reached the dark well of the pawnshop, and listened, her eyes wide and sad, as Bob said, 'Only three-and-six, hinny. It's getting a bit threadbare.' He turned to a woman and asked, 'Will you put it in for her?' And the woman nodded, taking the penny Katie offered her. Katie wished she were fourteen, then if she had to come to the pawn she wouldn't have to pay somebody for putting the stuff in – a whole penny just for signing your name! It was outrageous, and she disliked the woman intensely for being so mean as to take the penny.

As she was leaving the shop with the money tightly grasped in her hand, Bob said, 'I've got something here that might interest one of your brothers. It'll fit nobody else round these parts. It's a topcoat, and it's a bobby-dazzler. Ten shillings, it is. And I only wish I had what it cost when it was new. Tell one of them to have a look in.' Katie said she would.

She went on to the butcher's, and from there to buy a gas mantle. In Mr Powell's, she stood waiting while he hunted for the box which contained the turned-down mantles. His search took him into the back shop, and Katie was left alone standing before an assortment of comics. They were arrayed on a sloping counter: *Rainbow*, *Tiger Tim's Weekly*, *Comic Cuts*, and others. Her eyes dwelt on them longingly. It was weeks and weeks since she was able to buy a comic. She would likely get a penny off John on Saturday. But Saturday was as far away as Christmas, and there stretched before her the rest of the afternoon and the long, long evening. And she daren't ask her mother for even a ha'penny out of the suit money. On the front of *Rainbow,* the Bruin boys were up to their games again: the tiger, the parrot, the elephant, and others, were playing one of their naughty pranks on Mrs Bruin. And inside the comic, Katie knew, would be the story of the little girl who was really a fairy and worked magic. Her eyes darted to the back shop. All she could see was Mr Powell's feet on the top of a pair of steps. Her hand went up and touched the *Rainbow.* It hesitated for a second, then with one swift movement, the *Rainbow* was inside her coat, and for the first time in her life she found herself wetting her knickers. The combined horror was too much for her. She ran out of the shop, down the dock bank to the arches. She did not stop to look inside her coat; her sin had already obliterated the joy of the comic. She was a thief! She had stolen! Mr Powell would miss the comic and put the pollis on her track; her mother would be taken to court and her face would become white again, and all at school would know . . . Miss Llewellyn would know!

Standing over the gutter, under the high, bleak arches, she vomited, and the comic slipped down from beneath her coat and became fouled with the sick.

There was a long row of boys and girls waiting to go into confession, for tomorrow was the first Friday in the month, on which day they all attended communion. They nudged each other and fidgeted whilst bending over in grotesque positions in supposed prayer. They whispered and passed sweets, and showed one another holy pictures; yet there was no noise at all, so practised were they. It was three weeks since Katie was last at confession, the longest period between her confessions she could remember. Although the chill autumn air was filling the church she felt hot and sick. She had been sick a number of times since the day she took John's suit to the pawn – she refused to think of it as the day she stole the comic. But now she had to think of the comic, for she was about to make her confession.

A teacher, not Miss Llewellyn, came and moved a row and a half of children down to the pews opposite Father O'Malley's box, which were singularly bare of penitents. This left Katie the next to go to Father Bailey. She was filled with a mixture of relief and fear, relief that she had escaped Father O'Malley's judgment, and fear that her turn was upon her.

A small, dark shadow emerged from one door of the confessional box, and Katie stumbled in. But for the faint gleam of a candle coming through the mesh from the priest's side the box was black dark inside.

'Please, Father, give me the blessing for I have sinned,' she began. 'It is three weeks since my last confession.'

'Go on, my child.' Father Bailey's voice was like a soft balm falling on her.

'I have missed Mass once.'

'Through your own fault?'

'No, Father. It was me clothes; me ma wouldn't let me come.'

'Go on, my child.'

'I have spoken in church and I have missed me morning and night prayers.'

'How often?'

'Three times . . . no, four . . . perhaps a few more, Father.'

'Why?'

' 'Cos the lino's all cracked and it sticks in me knees when I kneel down.'

The priest made a noise in his throat and said, 'To strengthen your soul it is important that you say your prayers – prayers are the food of the soul like bread is the food of the body . . . You understand, my child?'

'Yes, Father.'

'Then under no circumstances should you starve your soul.'

'No, Father.'

'Go on.'

But Katie couldn't go on. Her clasped hands, pressed against the elbow rest on a level with her face, were stuck together with sweat. The confessional box seemed weighed down with the smell of incense and mustiness.

'Is there anything more?' the priest asked.

'Yes, Father.'

'Well then, what is it?'

Silence followed his question. And after a moment he went on: 'Don't be afraid, my child; there is nothing so terrible that God won't forgive.'

'I stole.'

The priest's hand was taken away from his cheek and his face turned towards the mesh, and Katie looked up into two white bulbs. Then the hand was replaced again.

Katie shivered during the silence that followed; she felt her sin had been a shock even to the priest.

'What did you steal?'

'A *Rainbow.*'

'A what!' The hand was dropped again.

'A comic.'

The priest coughed. 'Now, my child, you know how it hurts our Blessed Lord when you do anything like that.'

'Yes, Father.'

'And will you do it again?'

'No, no. Never, Father.'

'No, I know you won't. And if you could find a way to pay the shopkeeper for the comic it would put everything right, wouldn't it?'

'Yes, Father.'

'Now, for your penance say one Our Father and ten Hail Marys, and tell Our Lord that never again will you hurt Him; and He will forgive you. And don't forget to kneel when you are saying your prayers, in spite of the lino; for remember the nails in the cross.'

The priest made the sign of the cross and said the absolution, whilst Katie murmured, 'Oh, my God, I am very sorry I have sinned against Thee, because Thou art so good and by the help of Thy Holy Grace I will never sin again.'

'Goodnight, my child, and God bless you,' said Father Bailey. 'And worry no more; He understands.'

In a holy daze, Katie walked out of the box, and in the same state she said her penance, kneeling in the corner of the dark church, straining her eyes up to the statue of the Virgin and the Child, knowing that her sin was wiped away. And on walking out of the church, there was John, standing under the lamp. It all seemed part of God's Grace. She ran to him and flung her arms about him, crying, 'Oh John! Oh John!' as if she had not seen him for years. Then she asked, 'Are you going to confession?'

'No,' John said; 'I was passing and I thought I'd wait for you.'

She knew this wasn't true; he never had to pass this way; he had come to meet her because she was crying when she left home. She seemed to have been crying for weeks. She knew that her mother and John were worried about her, for she couldn't tell them why she cried. But now she was free again – the dreadful weight was lifted from her.

John, looking down into her bright face, wondered what had wrought the change. He said teasingly, 'Has Father Bailey given you a pair of wings?'

'Eeh, our John!' She shook his arm as she walked by his side. 'But Father Bailey is nice, isn't he? He's so nice he makes me want to cry.'

'Well, in that case, I'll tell him to go for you the next time I see him, for you've done enough crying lately to last you a lifetime.'

Katie did not speak for a time. And then she said softly, 'I won't be crying any more, John.'

'You won't? Well, that's something to know. Why have you been crying so much lately, anyway?'

There was a longer silence before she replied, 'I stole.'

Her statement came as a shock, stunning him for a while.

'You what, Katie?' he asked.

'I stole, and I was frightened. It was a comic from Mr Powell's. And now I've been to confession and Father Bailey says it's all right.'

'You stole a comic from Mr Powell's?' There was incredulity in John's voice . . . Mick and Molly could thieve; Dominic and himself could lift things from the dock, although his own lifting was a fleabite compared with Dominic's – Dominic filled his trousers from the yorks up with grain, and sold it to anybody who kept hens; the only thing in that line he himself brought home was a few green bananas for the bairns, or an odd bit of fruit from burst boxes. Nevertheless, they all did it; but that Katie should lift anything seemed monstrous to him. It might only be a comic, but everything needed a beginning. 'Have you done it before?' he asked.

'No, only that once!'

'Why did you do it?' The question was ridiculous; as if he didn't know why she had done it!

'I hadn't had a comic for weeks, and I hadn't a ha'penny.'

'If you want a comic, ask me. Don't ever do that again, will you?' He stopped and looked down on her.

Katie couldn't see his face clearly, but she knew by his voice that he was vexed, more vexed than Father Bailey had been. 'Oh no, John, I'll never do it again . . . never.'

Yes, she could say that now, but there would be times, many times, when she would be without a ha'penny . . . and he too. What would happen then?

They walked on in silence, and he told himself it was only a kid's trick . . . Yes, it might be . . . any kid's, but not Katie's. It was this blasted, soul-shrivelling poverty, where a bairn was driven to steal because she hadn't a ha'penny! The thought persisted that because she had done it once she would do it again, and that by the time she left school and was ready for a place she'd be a dab hand at lifting. And then there'd be more scope. Nothing big perhaps; just a few groceries, an odd towel, or a hankie . . . Oh, he knew what would happen . . . Well, it mustn't; not to Katie, anyway. He must try and get more work, or different work, or something. He must see that never again would she be short of a ha'penny. But would that solve the problem?

He slowed his pace, and Katie, silent and apprehensive, glanced up at him. Suddenly he stopped again and said, 'What about this exam your teacher's on about? What have you got to do?'

She peered up at him. 'Miss Llewellyn says that if I pass this examination I can do pupil training after I'm fourteen; and do another examination, and perhaps then I may be able to . . . to go to . . . a college.' The last word was whispered, and John whispered back, 'A college?' He sighed, and they walked on again. It was fantastic . . . College! Yet why should it be? What did Peter Bracken say, not only say but lay down that it was a law? Anything to which you applied your thought you could bring into being. Peter had urged him again and again to put some of his methods to the test, but he had laughed at him, saying, 'No, Peter, I'm a Catholic; a poor one, I admit, but nevertheless that's my religion, and I'm trying nothing else.'

But Peter had said, 'This has nothing to do with religion, John; it's merely using your thought in a proper way.'

Well, here was a test . . . Could he think Katie to a college? It sounded as daft as if he had said he would think her into being the Queen of England. Yet hadn't Peter given him proof of his power of concentrated thought? His mother was living proof. And she was aware of it too; that was why she never spoke of it, or to Peter; to her simple mind it was something too terrible for probing.

Peter said that once you set your mind and heart on something and concentrated on it day after day, things came to your aid in what seemed a mysterious way but which was simply your positive thought reaching out into the realm of all thought and making contact with its own kind.

John did not profess, even to himself, to understand half Peter's words, let alone their meaning, but this much he could, perhaps, believe . . . if you wanted a thing badly enough you could get it. But as Peter warned, beware of what you want, for sometimes that which you felt you wanted most could, in the end, wreck you.

Well, it would certainly be to Katie's good if she became a teacher, and he couldn't see that wrecking anyone. It was a wild and almost impossible dream, yet he would will it. But first he must know what he was up to. He would go and see Miss Llewellyn.

For the third time he stopped. Was he mad? Go and see that lass! She'd scare the yorks off him. Well, he wouldn't wear yorks. No, he wouldn't. To Katie's astonishment, he hurried on again, and now she had to run to keep pace with him.

Only Mary Ellen was in when they got home, and Katie stood listening to John with an astonishment equal to that of her mother's as he said, 'Look, Ma, there's fifteen shillings,' – he placed the money on the table – 'I was saving it up towards a suit. I want you to pay the seven-and-six off that topcoat and get me a new shirt . . . one with a collar.' He did not look at Mary Ellen when saying this, for never before had he asked for a shirt with a collar; it had always been a striped flannelette one and a new muffler. 'Get a good one,' he added, 'about five shillings. And get me a cap too, a grey one, darkish.'

'What's up, lad?' Mary Ellen asked quietly when he had finished.

'Nothing much.' He turned and smiled at Katie, and punched her playfully on the side of the head. 'I'm going to see her teacher about that examination, as you asked me, and I want to be decent.'

Chapter Six

The Visit

John stood sheepishly before Mary Ellen: 'Now if you tell me I look like the silver king I'll not set foot outside the door.'

Mary Ellen didn't proffer to tell him anything, she merely continued to stare at him. Who would have thought that a coat and a collar on his shirt would have made such a difference. He looked like a . . . well, like one of those adverts in the *Shields Daily Gazette* . . . no, better; there's never been a coat like this in Shields, she was sure. And anyway, the name inside the pocket said London. He was big enough, God knew, but the coat made him look even bigger. It was not shaped like those she was used to seeing, but hung full and was as thick as a blanket, with a check lining of fine flannel. A thrill of pride surged through her. Why, he could pass for a 'big pot'. His boots were shining as they had never done before, and the grey cap matched the dark, heather colour of the coat. She said, with a poor effort of offhandedness, 'You'll do. Mind, don't forget to take your cap off when you go in.'

'Now what do you take me for! I'm not a numskull altogether.'

'No, lad, I know,' she said apologetically. 'Anyway, you'll likely not find her in . . . Saturday night and all. Why you couldn't go in the daylight, I don't know.'

'You know fine enough. Imagine me going down the street like this; the place would be out.'

Breaking the silence of her admiration, Katie burst out, 'They would have thought you were going to a wedding and shouted, "Chuck a ha'penny out." '

'Yes, they would that,' he laughed. 'Well, here I go. And if that Miss Llewellyn doesn't fall on me neck and say, "Oh, John, you look lovely," I'll skelp her face for her.'

He left them both laughing, Katie rather hysterically, her face buried in the couch.

Now he was outside in the dark street the jocular ease of manner he had assumed before his mother fell from him. He walked swiftly, passing people he knew but who failed to recognise him, and of whom he felt one or two turn as if puzzled and stare after him.

When he reached the dark stretch of road beyond the sawmill, he slackened his pace and, like a child, fingered the coat. He brought the lapel up to his nostril and sniffed. There was a faint aroma of tobacco mingled with another smell . . . not scent . . . he couldn't place it. He could only think it was a swell of a smell anyway. But now he must forget about the coat and think of what he would say to Miss Llewellyn. God, what an ordeal! Would he be able to speak to her alone, or would her family be there? Had she a family? He supposed so. Anyway, as his mother said, being Saturday night she might be out. Likely with that Culbert fellow. But it was early, not six o'clock yet, so there was a chance he'd catch her. If he didn't he could try again on Monday, which would give him another chance to wear the coat. He chuckled to himself: 'I'm like a bit of a bairn, and as frightened.'

Katie had told him where the house lay on the outskirts of Simonside. She said he would know it, for it had a lawn in front and two gates, and that one of the gates had a wooden arch over it. He found it all too soon; it stood by itself, lying well back from the road. There was a light in an upstairs window, and the only light downstairs came through the stained glass of the front door. He stood at the gate looking towards the house until the sound of approaching footsteps, which had the ominous tread of a policeman, gave him the impetus to walk up the short drive.

His ring was answered by a maid, a little slip of a thing, all starch and black alpaca down to her feet. Very much like Katie would be if this didn't come off, he thought.

The maid spoke first, after having peered at him. 'Mr Llewellyn's not in.'

He almost laughed. They could titivate her up, but they couldn't titivate that accent; it was the broadest of Tyneside.

'Neither is Mrs Llewellyn,' she said, and was on the point of closing the door on him when he found his voice.

'It's Miss Llewellyn I want to see.' He smiled at her; he could be at home with her, anyway.

'Oh.' Her eyes grew wider, and she opened the door further. 'Well, you'd better come in. She's upstairs; she's just got back.'

John stepped past her into the hall, and she went to open a door to the right, then changed her mind, saying, 'Eeh no, you'd better wait in here.' She crossed the hall, passed the foot of the stairs and went down a short passage. And when he followed her she ushered him into a long, narrow room, at the far end of which a fire was burning.

She left him, only to return before he had time to look round. 'I forgot. What's your name?' she asked.

A great desire to laugh came over him. It could be Katie . . . no, Molly; Katie wouldn't have forgotten to ask the name.

'O'Brien.'

'O'Brien.' she repeated. Then, seeing the twinkle in his eye, her face refused to be uniformed like her body and she smiled broadly. 'I'm new, I've only been here a week.' She hunched her shoulders. 'I'm always putting people in the wrong rooms. This is Miss Mary's.'

She disappeared, and he stood, cap in hand, looking around him. Well, he was inside, in Miss Mary's room. So she was a Mary, like his mother. And she had a room to herself . . . not a bedroom either. He thought the Brackens' furniture wonderful. Then what could he say of this room?

As he gazed about him, the room took away the ease and self-possession the little maid had momentarily given him. It was a melody of colour. He had never imagined colour as part of a room - good, strong furniture, yes, but the colour never got beyond a shiny brown. Here there was russet and green, gold and white. The room was carpeted to the walls with green. Green curtains hung across the entire wall at the further end of the room, and a russet-covered chair and couch were standing crosswise before the fire. Half of one long wall was taken up with a low bookcase, on top of which stood a number of china figures, gentlemen in ruffles, ladies in crinolines, their delicate colourings reflected in the dark surface of the wood, on which they endlessly danced or bowed. The yellow tone was supplied by early chrysanthemums, rearing with frosty elegance from a tall glass vase standing on a round table . . . And then the white tone. He found his eyes drawn to this, and he walked a few steps towards it. It was a statuette of a woman, dead white and completely nude. The trailing hair covering part of one breast and falling across her stomach and over her womb only emphasised her nakedness. She was standing on an inlaid box by the side of the green curtains and reached just above his waist. She was about two feet tall, but she filled his entire vision, seeming to become alive before his eyes. In the back of his mind, he knew that she was indecent and should not be in a good Catholic home, especially a schoolteacher's.

As he heard the quick, muffled footsteps descending the stairs, he almost sprang back away from her into the centre of the room again, and faced the door. Mary Llewellyn came in smiling, and as he looked at her he wondered at his nerve in daring to come and see this woman. Never before had he come into contact with anyone like her, and he was struck dumb. She seemed to move in a radiance. Did it emanate from the softness of her eyes or from the tenderness of her lips, or from the quick movements of her hands as she spoke? He did not know – he knew only that she was different.

'Hallo, Mr O'Brien.' Like her eyes, her voice was warm; and a slight catch of huskiness in it added to its charm. 'You wanted to see me? Come up to the fire and sit down.'

He followed her, his eyes fixed on the piled coils of her hair, and his inarticulateness was passed over in the process of sitting down.

He sat, half in the big chair, his cap in his hand, and she sat on the couch, across the hearth from him. She was wearing a blue dress with a dark red belt . . . she was like her room, full of warm, embracing colour.

'I suppose you've come to talk about Katie?' she smiled at him and waited.

'Yes.' The voice didn't sound like his own; it was as if he were shouting in a large, empty hall.

'I'm so glad you have, for I should like to know your plans for her . . . Would you like her to become a teacher?'

'Yes.' Damn! Couldn't he say anything but yes! She would get the impression he was nothing but a numskull.

'I'm glad of that. I know what to do now – I'll speak to the headmistress about her. Even if she only becomes an uncertified teacher, it would be something, wouldn't it?'

'Yes. Oh yes.' Was he a fool altogether? Yes, yes, yes. Why couldn't he be himself and say something, badly as he might express it?

There followed a silence, during which their eyes met and held. Hers were the first to drop away, and he felt she was embarrassed by his staring . . . perhaps annoyed. She leant forward and stirred the fire, and he suddenly began to talk –

to straighten matters, as he put it to himself.

'I'm a poor envoy.' He wasn't sure if this was the right word, but he liked his placing of it; and he went on, 'There is so much I want to say about Katie, and so much to ask you. There's nothing I want more in the world than for her to become a teacher, but . . . Well, it's like this. You can guess how we are . . . ' he substituted the word 'situated' for 'fixed' – 'You can guess how we are situated. It's no good pretending, is it?' Without being aware of the transition, he was at his ease, talking frankly as he would have done to someone who knew all there was to know about him. 'There won't be any money to help her as far as I can see. If it's going to mean money, well, I'm afraid . . . ' He lifted his shoulders expressively. 'If it was left to me and I could earn it I would but I'm rarely on full-time.' This was coming down to earth with a vengeance, he thought. So much for his coat.

Mary was leaning back against the couch now, and she too, as she listened to him, was thinking about his coat. Remembering how she had seen him before, she had expected to find him dressed in much the same way. The coat so altered his appearance that she hardly recognised him as the same person; he looked rather handsome. Well, not handsome. There was something too rugged about his face for it to be handsome. Attractive? Yes, he looked very attractive. His eyes, particularly, were nice, especially when he smiled. It was strange what a difference clothes could make, outwardly at any rate. Yet the first time she saw him, she remembered imagining how he might look if he could dress like Gilbert. It seemed odd now that she should have met him the day she refused Gilbert . . . Suddenly she thought, I like him; he's nice – he's like Katie in a way.

She stood up hastily, saying, 'I haven't had any tea. Perhaps you'll have a cup with me, and then we can talk the whole thing out. Excuse me a moment.'

She gave him no time to refuse, but hurried away; and when

she reached the door she turned, saying, 'Would you care to take off your coat? . . . You'll feel the benefit of it when you go out; it's nippy tonight.'

John stood up, staring down the empty room. This was a contingency for which he hadn't bargained. Against the coat, he knew his suit looked cheaper and shabbier than ever . . . Well, she was no fool to be taken in by the coat – no doubt she had guessed he had come by it second-hand. He took it off and laid it with his cap over the chair. Then he stood on the hearthrug looking down at his suit, and a determination was born in him: this was the last suit he'd ever get from a tallyman. The coat had told him one thing: there were clothes that were made to fit a man. And he'd have them. How? He didn't know; but have them he would. If one rig-out had to last him a lifetime; he'd be dressed decent for once.

And she had asked him to stay and have a cup of tea . . . tea with Miss Llewellyn! It was fantastic.

He ran his finger round the inside of his collar; it felt tight against his neck. He glanced into the mirror over the mantelshelf, and hardly recognised himself; the soft glow of the light seemed to make him look different. Or perhaps it was the collar . . . And that was another thing . . . never again would he wear a muffler at the weekends, and perhaps not at nights either.

He had just sat down again when she came in with a tray; a silver one, with a teapot and jug on it. As he would have done to relieve his mother from carrying anything, he got up and took it from her. She smiled her thanks, and brought a little table, and set it between the chair and the settee, and he placed the tray on it.

The maid came in carrying another tray, which Mary took from her, saying, 'All right, Phyllis, I'll see to it.'

With a sense of unreality, John watched her pour out the tea. She had set a little table at his hand and told him to help himself.

The bread and butter was so thin he could have put the plateful in his mouth at once. He watched Mary double her piece in two, and followed suit, refusing her offer of jam, for that would mean too much palaver.

And so, like one in a dream, he took tea with Miss Llewellyn, and listened with only half his mind while she talked of Katie. He was thinking of this room and of her and of the strangeness of the whole thing . . . They were sitting here alone together, having tea, just as if . . .

He was startled back to the full import of what she was saying by hearing her repeat something he had said weeks ago: 'A day of high winds and far mastheads, and bonny lasses.'

She laughed at his startled expression, and said, 'Now, when I find phrases like that in Katie's composition, although I know she's a clever child, I don't think she's that clever. Nor when she writes this: "The morning sky was massed with white clouds, like brakes ready for a day off." '

He felt the hot colour flooding up from his neck, and she asked, 'Have you tried writing these thoughts down and working them into something?'

'Writing them down?' he repeated. 'Me? Good Go . . . lord, no.'

'Why not?' she said. 'Burns did, and many others. I think you should. I was sorry when I had to make Katie scrap the composition in which she stated that ore on her tongue and sweat in her hair and bleeding nails meant gold on a Saturday and roaming round the market, hemmed in with the smell of tallow and the flapping of skirts.'

Now his face was scarlet, and he said, 'I'll have to be more careful of what I say . . . You see, we go for walks – ' He stopped.

'You should write them up, you know,' she put in; 'a lot of what Katie repeats has poetry in it. Why don't you try?'

He had been leaning back in the chair, quite at ease. He still leant back, but he was no longer at ease. His face drooped into a sadness, which conveyed itself to his voice, together with reproach and stark frankness as he said, 'I can't even speak properly.'

'Oh, please don't say that!'

It was Mary's turn to flush now. She stood up, and taking his cup, refilled it. 'You don't speak differently from anyone else. And that has nothing to do with putting your thoughts to paper.'

'I've been told there's such a thing as grammar.' There was a touch of bitter sarcasm in his voice.

'Yes, but that comes . . . you learn as you go.'

He made no reply, and she, too, became silent, furious with herself for being a tactless fool. He had been so at ease, with quite a charming naturalness, and she had to bring up such a suggestion as him starting to write, of all things! But on the other hand, she was perfectly sincere in all she said, for some of the things Katie repeated were surprising in their poetical content. But be careful of what you are about, she warned herself. Don't put into his head ideas that will make the life he has to lead more obnoxious to him. Remember, you are not talking to Gilbert.

She glanced at the clock . . . half-past six. She hoped Gilbert wouldn't put in one of his friendly visits; visits that were, she knew, manoeuvred by her mother.

John, noting her glance, said rather flatly, 'Well, I'll think over what you've said. I'd better be going now . . . Saturday night isn't a very convenient time to call.'

'No, no,' – she put out her hand as if to press him back into his chair from the distance – 'you haven't finished your tea yet, and I'm not going out again. And anyway,' she laughed in a renewed effort to put him at ease – 'there are many things I want to ask you. Who, for instance, are Mr Bracken and Christine? Oh, Christine's wonderful!' She gave an imitation of Katie, closing her eyes and screwing up her face. 'You see, I get them every morning – while Katie is walking with me to school.'

John laughed with her. 'Our Katie's a chatterer. They are the people who live next door.'

'And Christine has a wonderful house, and cooks wonderful food, and has wonderful clothes . . . Oh, she's wonderful!'

John's laugh rang out, free and unrestrained now – her imitation was so like Katie when describing anyone. 'I'm afraid Katie thinks a number of people are wonderful. Not that she isn't right,' he added hastily, realising that sitting before him was, to Katie, the most wonderful of them all.

Mary, looking intently at him, wondered if he was in love with this Christine, about whom she heard so much. Katie talked of only two people, John and Christine; before, it was only John . . . Our John said this, Our John said that . . . and the child had managed to convey a picture of someone quite out of the ordinary. Mary knew that the O'Briens were poor; not just clothes-poor, but of the poor who did not always eat well, which was a different and more potent kind of poverty; but the child had made this John emerge as someone untouched by poverty, an independent being, living with yet not of them. Then lately, to this worship was added that of this Christine . . . Christine and John, Christine and John.

How was it, Mary wondered, that some girls got men like this to love them, big kind men with a sense of humour as he had. At their first meeting, she'd thought he was to be pitied, but now she saw that she was wrong – he was intelligent and entertaining, the latter without making any effort to be so. He was certainly better company than Gilbert, even if he lacked Gilbert's taste in literature and art . . . or perhaps, because of it. Being a big man, like her father, was he attracted to small women, she wondered. This Christine, according to Katie's description, was apparently small. So was her own mother, small and helpless. Helpless! The word brought a cloud over Mary's eyes, for she had come to recognise that beneath her helpless exterior her mother was pure granite; and to live in peace with anyone like her meant submerging oneself entirely. When she was young, her happy, loving nature did not question her mother's tyranny, and it was easy to accept 'Mother knows best'. How different her life would have been had she stood against her; for now her art study would have been finished. And who knows where it would have taken her – London – even Paris. Because her mother considered it wicked to draw bodies with no clothes on, she obediently put clothes on them. And again, when her mother said she would never make an artist . . . and anyway, artists weren't nice people . . . she subdued her natural talent becoming a schoolteacher, not through necessity, but because her father insisted she should have an occupation. But during these last few years had come a change, until now a state of undeclared war existed between her and her mother. The request to have a room of her own began it, and the refusal to be pushed into marriage with Gilbert Culbert, the son of her mother's old friend, widened the breach. And when, answering some inner urge, she bought the statue, and her mother demanded that it be removed from the house, the breach was further widened.

Lost in her thoughts, she did not notice that they were sitting in silence. How strange. She could never sit in silence with Gilbert. She lifted her gaze from her hands and found John looking at her, not intently, but rather reflectively. She smiled, and he blinked and roused himself.

'Are you interested in boats?' she asked. 'I mean the building of them.'

'Well, I know nothing about the building of them. I only know I get certain feelings when working in them. A feeling of friendliness for some and dislike for others. I suppose it has a lot to do with their cargo . . . and,' he laughed, 'the sweat in my hair.'

She laughed with him and asked, 'Would you like to see some models my father has made?'

'Yes, I would, very much.'

'Come into his workshop, then.'

She rose and went down the length of the room, and John followed her towards the green curtains. Before she drew them aside she gently moved the box and the statue. He watched her steady the statue with her hand, and it occurred to him as being strange that the statue no longer looked indecent but rather lovely . . . very like what she would be . . .

He was red in the face when she looked up at him, and she said hastily, almost apologetically, 'I came across it in an antique shop in Newcastle. It's an octoroon. I don't suppose you know any more than I did what an octoroon is; but, on looking it up, I found that she is the offspring of a quadroon and a white person, and a quadroon is one part negro and three parts white. Sounds very complicated, doesn't it?'

They were standing regarding each other now. Her hand was on the curtain and her face was unsmiling, and in her eyes he fancied he detected an appeal. For what exactly, he didn't know. But he said, 'I think it's very beautiful.' He, too, was unsmiling. And when she answered simply, 'Thank you,' it almost appeared as if the compliment had been meant for her. She turned swiftly and opened the French window, and stepped into the conservatory. He followed, going through a door close by and into the workroom.

It was in darkness, and she said, 'Just a moment. There are matches here, I'll light the gas.'

She gave an impatient exclamation as the box fell from her hand, and when, instinctively, they both stooped to retrieve it, causing them to collide and she to overbalance, his hands naturally were thrust out to steady her, and in the darkness he supported her . . . for one brief second his hands held her arms, and in that second the thing was done – the fuse that might have smouldered and died was fanned.

When the room was plunged into stark light from the double burner, John was still standing near the door. Mary did not speak for a moment, and when she asked, 'What do you think of them?' he moved slowly into the room and began to look round. There were dozens of models of small craft, set in stocks, on the shelves. In amazement, he asked, 'Your father made all these?'

'Yes. And most of them he's built full-size and sold. Do you recognise Mary, the tug?'

It was with genuine astonishment that he exclaimed, 'Your father's Llewellyn the boatbuilder then!'

'Yes. Didn't you know?'

He shook his head. He had never associated Llewellyn, the boatbuilder, with Miss Llewellyn the teacher. He knew Llewellyn by sight, as most of the dock men did. He had a little boat-building yard, tucked away on the side of the river. It still went under the name of Haggart's Yard, and it was known that Llewellyn worked in it as a lad by the side of his father. But that hadn't suited young Llewellyn; and he and his father built a boat on their own and sold it. It was said they built it in their backyard. That was a start, and eventually, when old Haggart died, and his own father too, Llewellyn bought the yard. He was known as a rising man . . . And he was her father!

With this knowledge, she again assumed to him the unapproachableness of an hour ago. How had he the nerve to come here!

When she spoke to him, smiling over her shoulder and saying, 'Come and look at this little yacht, my father hopes to build her some day,' he went to her; but the ease had left him, and he held the model in his hand without making any comment. Her nearness made him uneasy. He suddenly wanted to get away from her and her politeness . . . she would act like this towards anyone, a beggar on the road, even . . . she was made that way, courteous, easy of manner.

'What do you think of it? You have seen lots of boats, but have you seen anything like her?'

She was looking up into his straight face, trying to draw him out again, when a voice from the doorway said, 'Hallo, Mary.'

They both started at the sound of the quiet, even tone.

'Oh! Hallo, Gilbert,' she said, and after a pause, added, 'Come in a minute . . . This is Mr O'Brien. Mr O'Brien, Mr Culbert.'

Neither of the men made the usual gesture to shake hands, but inclined their heads . . . John in an abrupt nod, and Culbert in a more leisurely movement. John knew that he was under Culbert's scrutiny, and after his first concentrated stare, he did not look at the man but at Mary; for he was asking himself how anyone like her could take up with a fellow like Culbert, a weed of a man, narrow all the way up, right to the pointed head, over which his thin hair was meticulously brushed.

When Mary led the way back into her room John made straight for the chair over which his coat and cap lay, and she said nothing to delay his departure.

He nodded again to Culbert in farewell, and Mary escorted him to the front door. The feel of his coat about him did nothing to allay his renewed feeling of gaucheness.

'Well, thanks,' he said awkwardly. 'It's been kind of you to . . . to help me about Katie.'

They stood regarding one another, and she too seemed to have lost some of her ease of manner. 'I'll do all I can for Katie, I'm very fond of her. And she's a clever child . . . Goodnight, Mr O'Brien.'

She held out her hand, and after the merest hesitation he took it. Firm and cool, it gripped his, conveying a sense of breathlessness and urgency. The feeling hung between them; even when their hands parted and he passed through the doorway it was there . . . a breathlessness.

He walked away down the path with her parting words acting like an opiate to his brain. 'If you feel there is anything you would like to know, at any time, please come and see me again.' It was odd, he thought, but she was the kind of person he could ask questions of.

But once out in the cold night air, the old brake of 'Steady your keel' thrust its reality upon him, and he said to himself, 'Well, that's that! It went off all right; Katie's set.'

As he reached the bottom of the Simonside bank, he deliberated whether to go into Shields and the market or walk slowly back home. If he did the latter it would mean thinking and going over every second of the past hour. No. He would go into Shields where there were lights and people . . . But what about being seen in this coat? Well, what about it? It seemed that within the past hour he had lost and regained his self-confidence a number of times, but, each time he regained it, it was stronger, for now he didn't mind being seen in the coat; it was the portent of things to come . . . he would have things . . . his mother and Katie would have things. How, he didn't know; but they would.

His decision to seek company in the shape of crowds did not immediately have the desired effect, and he found himself again thinking of Mary Llewellyn, but with a forced detachment. Fancy a lovely lass like her going to marry that . . . skinnymalink! Well, it was certainly no business of his. She had been very nice to him, more than nice; and she would help Katie; that was the only thing that mattered.

As he entered the first arc of Tyne Dock a well-known figure, shambling towards him, brought him back with a bump to his own world. It was Nancy; and he could hear her snivelling when she was still some distance away.

'Hallo, Nancy. What's the matter?' he asked her. She hesitated, shuffled off the pavement in uncertainty, then shuffled back when she recognised him. 'Eeh, John. Eeh, John.'

'What's the matter?' he asked again.

'It's our Annie. She left me in the market – she run away, and she had me tram fare. An' me ma said she had to look after me and put me on the tram for me place.'

'Have you walked all the way from the market?' he asked her gently.

'Yes . . . It's our Annie. She run away, she did. An' me ma'll skelp me when I get in, she will, cos Mrs Fitzsimmons said I had to be back to clean the shop out when they closed. An' me ma said our Annie had to put me on the tram.'

John put his hand in his pocket and gave her threepence. 'Now stop crying. You'll be back in plenty of time. There's your tram fare and a penny to buy some bullets. Stand over there,' – he pointed back towards the bottom of Simonside Bank – 'the Jarrow tram will be along in a minute.'

'Eeh! I can't get on the tram there, John. There's a bar there an' me ma says I've got to keep away from bars, cos the men come out.'

John could see the tram in the distance swaying towards them. He held out his hand to her: 'Come on, I'll put you on it.'

The tram jolted to a stop, and he helped her up, saying to the conductor, 'Put her off at the corner of Ferry Street, will you?'

As the conductor rang the bell, a figure leant forward from the end of the long wooden seat: 'Why, is that you, John?'

He recognised Mrs Bradley, and answered rather shortly, 'Yes, it's me.'

'Why lad, I hardly knew you . . . Well I never.' The tram rumbled away, and the last John saw was Nancy showing the coins in her hand to Mrs Bradley. The picture did not remain in his mind an instant, but he was to remember it, and, unimportant as it seemed, it was to assume such proportions that although it happened on this day of emancipation, when he had first worn a fine topcoat and taken tea with Miss Llewellyn, its ugly significance was to blot them out.

Chapter Seven

Christmas Eve

MARY ELLEN HUMMED softly . . . it was many, many Christmases ago that she felt as happy as she did now. The morrow was Christmas Eve and she was really looking forward to it. She worked at the table in the middle of the kitchen, cutting out pastry for mince pies. Above her head hung a large, honeycombed paper ball, suspended from the paper chains crisscrossed under the ceiling. The kitchen was quiet and warm with an unusual air of cosiness about it. As she worked she planned for the morrow. She'd get up earlier than usual and blacklead the stove before lighting the fire; and then, after she'd got them all off to work, she'd get done and put everything shipshape; then she'd get the dinner ready, and have the afternoon clear . . . to go and get the coat.

Aye, it was a long time since she'd had a coat, a new shawl would have done her; but no, John had a bee in his bonnet, and she was to have a coat for Christmas . . . What had come over him lately? He was the same lad to her, yet somehow he was altered. It wasn't only the new suit he had, although that made him look fine; no, it was in some other way he'd altered. Well, never mind, he was still her lad, and the best on God's earth. If only the other one was like him.

The thought of Dominic caused her to stop humming. Why hadn't he gone away, as he'd been hinting of doing for some weeks past? Then Christmas would have indeed been grand. She knew he had been enquiring after jobs in both the Liverpool and London Docks; anywhere, he had said, to get away from this hole.

When she came to think of it, Dominic too seemed changed. It was all that lass next door she supposed - he was set on her; but he didn't seem to be making much headway. Was John his stumbling block? This was another thing which puzzled her. John was always in next door, and often she heard his laugh joined with that of the girl's. But there it seemed to end. If he were courting her, he was doing it in a funny way; for he never took her out. Pray God he wouldn't either. No, no, that would be terrible if John really took up with her. Well, she wasn't going to think about it; she was going to enjoy this Christmas. She already had a piece of brisket and an aitchbone, and if John went down to the market last thing the morrow he might pick up a duck or something cheap. They sold them off for next to nothing rather than have them left on their hands. By, it'd be grand if he could get a duck! And on Christmas Day they'd have Christmas cake and the rice loaf she'd made. Nobody knew yet, but she was going to put icing on the cake. By, they'd have a grand do.

A tap on the door broke in on her thoughts and she called, 'Come in,' and Peggy Flaherty, after kicking her boots against the wall, stumbled into the kitchen.

'Oh God above, it's enough to freeze your liver! It's at it again, Mary Ellen - won't be able to stir hand or foot outside the door shortly.'

'It hasn't started to snow again, surely?'

'It has so, Mary Ellen. As if it wasn't bad enough with everywhere frozen solid. God's truth, I've never seen anything like it! We'll have to be after watching the tap in the yard, Mary

Ellen, or it'll be a dry Christmas in one way we'll be having. Oh, ye're lovely and warm in here, lass,' – she wriggled her fat inside her many coats – 'and the smell's good enough to eat. And did ye ever see such a picture of a kitchen, with all those bonny chains!'

'Sit down and warm yourself, and have a pie,' said Mary Ellen.

'I will an' all, for I'm chilled to the bone. I'm just back from Shields. Look,' – she pulled three small packages from her bass bag – 'some bits of things for the bairns' stockings.'

'Now, Peggy,' – Mary Ellen compressed her lips – 'that's madness, that is! You know you haven't got it to go and buy presents.'

'Why haven't I then? I haven't got a bite of sup to buy for Christmas or Boxing Day, because out of the goodness of your heart ye've asked me down . . . so why haven't I? There they are,' – she laid the packages on the mantelpiece – 'we'll say no more about them. There's only one thing I regret, and that is I haven't got it to buy you all something. But business isn't what it used to be; divil the pennorth of advice I've given out this past three weeks. What's the matter with people, Mary Ellen? 'Tisn't as if there were no rows; God alive, they followed each other like flies down at the bottom end last week. If it wasn't for running me clubs I'd be hard set at times; but as long as I get my rent I'm all right. And God's good. There was last weekend I didn't know which way I was going to turn, when, coming up the yard, that blessed lad of yours slipped me sixpence. By, Mary Ellen, I think if ye lost everything in the world and ye'd only him left, ye'd get by . . . Is he courting, Mary Ellen?'

'Courting?' Mary Ellen turned and with a blank face looked at Peggy. 'Not that I know of. Why do you ask?'

'Only I've seen him a number of times, three to be exact, and the last no later than this dinner time, talking to the same lass. And a bonnier piece I've never seen. And mark ye, she wasn't from around these doors either. Today she had a fur coat on, and the tails hanging from the collar alone must have left a number of poor animals feeling cold around their backsides.'

'A fur coat?'

'The same. Tall she was, and strapping looking. And a voice like the gentry, for I heard her as I passed. And it's me that knows how the gentry talk – ye know that, Mary Ellen – for Mr Flaherty spent his life rubbing shoulders with them. And it's the same process, ye know: as ye can't touch pitch without becoming defiled, so ye can't mix among the gentry without picking up their lingo.'

Mary Ellen surveyed Peggy. 'You must have made a mistake.'

'Not a bit of it, Mary Ellen. John called out to me himself. "Hallo there, Peggy," he said, as true as I'm sitting here.'

Mary Ellen turned back to her baking board . . . John talking to a lass with a fur coat on. Who could it be? And three times. He wasn't a one to stand talking to lasses at any time, only that one next door. She turned to Peggy again: 'It wasn't—' she nodded her head towards the fireplace.

'No. I may be short in the sight, but I'm not that bad. This was a big lump of a lass, in fact she was a woman; and twice the size of that scrag end next door, bless ye.'

Mary Ellen could question Peggy no more at the moment, for there was another knock on the door; it was Hannah Kelly.

She had a coat over her head, and she shook the soft snow off it before coming into the kitchen. 'What weather! The only ones enjoying it are the bairns. Hallo, Peggy. Is this where ye are? By! They smell good Mary Ellen.' Hannah nodded towards the pies.

'Help yourself, lass,' said Mary Ellen.

'Not now. Thanks all the same. I only came over to see you a minute . . . about something.'

Peggy, taking the covered hint with the abundance of her good nature, said, 'I'll off up, Mary Ellen, for I must make a start; I'm up to the eyes upstairs.'

'She never said a truer word,' said Hannah, when Peggy had gone. 'How she lives among that junk, God alone knows. I came over to tell ye about our Nancy, Mary Ellen; but I couldn't do it with her sitting there - she'd be offering me advice, and I'm not in the mood to take Peggy's advice the day.'

'Is anything wrong, Hannah?'

'It looks like it; I've had a letter from Mrs Fitzsimmons about her. She says she's getting more queer every day, and she's getting that way she won't work; she just stands staring at her and says she can't. Ye know, Mary Ellen, that isn't like Nancy. As bad as she is she can do the rough work of half a dozen. Mrs Fitzsimmons says I'll have to bring her home if it keeps on . . . Oh, Mary Ellen, there'll be hell to pay again with our Joe if she's in the house all the time.'

'I'm sorry, lass. But perhaps you'll get her in some place else.'

'Not if she won't work. Ye don't mind me coming across and telling ye, Mary Ellen? Ye've got enough on your plate, I know, without my troubles stacked on top, but ye're the only one I seem to be able to talk to about her.'

'Why, lass, I only wish I could help you.'

Hannah sat down by the side of the fire and stared into the glowing coals for a moment. 'It's an awful thing, Mary Ellen, to know that a bairn ye've given birth to isn't all there.'

Mary placed her hand on Hannah's shoulder. 'We all have our loads, lass; if it isn't one thing it's another.'

Hannah gnawed at her lower lip. 'You and John are the only two who treat her like a human being. I know I don't. Sometimes I can't stand the sight of her. Oh, ye don't know, Mary Ellen, it's awful. But then, when I hear Joe going for her, I get a sort of feeling and want to protect her somehow.' She shook her head sadly. 'Well, the only thing I hope is she doesn't come home till after the new year. Joe's banking on a little bit of a do on New Year's Eve, but it'll be knocked completely on the head if she's home; he'll do nothing then; likely stay out most of the time.'

'She'll be all right,' Mary Ellen persisted, 'don't worry. Look, let's have a cup of tea.'

Mary Ellen bustled about making tea. In the face of the tragedy of having a partly imbecile daughter her load seemed very light. She had poverty and drink to put up with, but not that, thank God. Hers were all right up there.

The two women drank their tea and talked on . . . about Bella now. Hannah wasn't speaking to Bella, for whenever she did Bella made some excuse to come downstairs and ferret out her business. And Bella's constant presence in the house maddened Joe. Mary Ellen could well understand this, for she had no use for Bella Bradley, who was never happy unless someone else was in trouble . . .

As the snow thickened and the light vanished earlier than usual the kitchen was lit only by the glow of the fire – through necessity the gas was never lit until it was almost impossible to see, and Mary Ellen worked on, after Hannah had gone, more by feel than anything else. She began to sing softly to herself – her mother and grandmother had sung the song before her – the simple words expressing the tragedy of at least one phase of their love:

> Love, it is teasing,
> Love, it is pleasing,
> Love is a pleasure when it is new;
> But as it grows older and the days grow colder
> It fades away like the morning dew.

Mary Ellen wasn't thinking of the words, or how they applied to her own life, but that she had much for which to be thankful: Shane had not been really drunk since she was bad that time, and his twitching had eased. There had been no row in the house for months either. Well, they said it was a long road that had no turning, and hers had turned.

On these pleasant thoughts the kitchen door was thrust open again. She turned towards it, but could not distinguish who was standing there. It could have been John, Shane or Dominic; but she was expecting none of them for another hour.

'Why can't you light the bloody gas!'

Mary Ellen groped for a piece of paper, which she lit in the fire and put to the mantle, then turned and looked at Dominic. She had seen his face portraying many moods, contorted with passion or anger, drawn tight with cunning; but his expression now was one she had never seen; his eyes were wide and hard, and to her mind, had the thick, dull shine of a beer bottle. He seemed to be spread in a new kind of anger, wide and high with it.

'I want me tea now. I'm going out!'

'Well, get in first, can't you! It isn't ready yet. Can't you get changed and have it with the others?'

'No, I can't! And anyway, you wouldn't expect God Almighty to sit down with me, would you?'

She stared at him. Had he gone off his head? She watched him fling his cap across the table on to the couch, pull off his coat and fling it after the cap. The coat, in its flight, whipped a number of pies on to the floor and sent a cloud of flour off the board.

'Here!' Mary Ellen cried, 'What's up with you?'

He did not answer, but grabbed the kettle from the hob and emptied it of hot water. He also emptied the pail of cold water, and proceeded to wash, the water splashing over the side of the dish and up the wall as he did so.

Mary Ellen cleaned up the mess from the floor; then picked up the kettle and pail and went cautiously down the backyard. The ashes on top of the ice were already covered with a layer of snow. The tap was running in a thin trickle and she stood on the fringe of ice and water, steadying herself against the wall as she filled the pail . . . Always something to spoil things. What was it now?

She hunted around in her mind, but could find nothing. Whatever it was was connected with his work, for he was home early. And him saying, 'You wouldn't expect God Almighty to sit down with me.' Did he mean John? She couldn't fathom it.

When she returned to the kitchen, Dominic was in the bedroom, and she hurriedly cleared the table and set some bread and dripping and mince pies out.

When he eventually came to the table he stared down at the food. 'That's a fine meal for a man, isn't it!' His voice seemed to be torn from his throat.

'Well, you wouldn't wait. I'm going to fry.'

'You're going to fry!' he mimicked raspingly. 'Well, see that you do plenty of it; the big pot'll need it to fill his swelled head.'

Then his anger had to do with John. But how? What could have happened at work?

After having eaten all Mary Ellen had placed before him, Dominic left the house by the front way. As soon as the door banged behind him Mary Ellen went hastily into the room, and stood listening. Then, as she expected, came the muffled knock. He was next door.

She sang or hummed no more but, filled with the old dread, waited for John coming in – she had spoken too soon about her road turning. There was something afoot, and from the appearance of Dominic it was bad.

Katie and Molly rushed in, their hands blue and their noses red. 'Oh, Ma, is the tea ready?' 'And, Ma, our Katie's dirtied her knickers,' cried Molly.

'What!'

Both Katie and Molly burst out laughing at their mother's expression. Molly bringing her head down to Katie's and the two of them pressing their faces together in their mirth.

'Not that way. She slipped on a slide and ended up in some broken ice and slush,' Molly giggled.

'Are you wet?' Mary Ellen asked Katie.

'No, Ma, it dried.'

'Tea won't be for some time yet,' said Mary Ellen. 'Here take a bit of bread and get yourselves out again.'

Mary Ellen pushed a slice of bread at each of them. 'You can stay out for another half-hour or so. Hunt up Mick and bring him back with you.' It would be better, she thought, if she had the house to herself when John came in.

When at last she heard the clanking footsteps in the yard, she stood still facing the door. It might be Shane. The feet kicked against the wall, and the door opened. It was John, not with brows drawn and lips tight, but with an almost childish expression of pleasure on his face. He wasn't smiling – with an effort he was keeping his face straight – but the light in his eyes danced at her. She turned from him, puzzled. It couldn't be that lass with the fur coat. No, how could that affect Dominic?

'Is it still snowing?' she asked, as she bent over the pan on the fire.

John didn't answer, but came and stood by her. 'Anybody in?'

'No,' she said.

He took her by the shoulders and pulled her round to face him, so close that her head had to go back to look up at him. 'I'll give you three guesses . . . What do you think's happened?'

'Why, lad, how should I know?'

'Go on.'

'You've been set on the Benisaf boat.'

John flung his head back and laughed out loud.

'Aye, lad, how should I know? Tell us.'

He stepped back, thrust his thumbs into the lapel of his coat, drew himself up to his fullest height with mock dignity, and said, in the deepest tones of his voice, 'Mrs O'Brien, behold . . . a gaffer!'

A gaffer . . . Mary Ellen could make no comment. Had he gone mad too? A gaffer. Her lad, and him only twenty-two. Why, there was something wrong somewhere. There was only one gaffer over the boats, and he must be a man steady in his years. The old gaffer had died a couple of days ago, she knew, but they couldn't have picked John. It was fantastic. Her face expressed her feelings, and John laughed and said, 'You don't believe it?'

'Well, lad . . . '

'Yes, I know it's hard to take in.' He was suddenly serious. 'I haven't taken it right in meself yet. I couldn't, for the life of me, believe they meant it.'

'Did the men pick you?'

'Yes, they voted for me to take old Reville's place.'

It was customary for the dock men who unloaded the boats to choose their own boss. They also paid him so much a head out of their wages. Most of the unloading was paid on tonnage, and the gaffer's job was to select men for the boat and at the end of discharging collect the money from the dock office, subtract his due and pay out the men. But this alone did not cover his duties, which often entailed taking off his coat and fighting it out with any man who thought he was not getting a square deal, and who said so forcibly. Another thing expected of the gaffer was to provide subs for men who were out of work and advances to those just being set on again.

This was in Mary Ellen's mind when she said, 'But lad, how can you do it? . . . The subs.'

'I've got over that. You know McCabe in the dock office. Well, when I went to tell him he seemed to know how I was fixed, and offered to lend me a few pounds to make a start . . . I'll be able to pay it back in a few weeks. And I won't forget him for it.'

'Lad, don't start on borrowed money. There's the twenty-five shillings for that coat. I don't need a coat; I've made . . . '

'Here . . . that's enough. You're getting that coat.'

'Were all the men for you?' She gazed up into his face; she was smiling now and her heart was racing within her breast. To think her lad had been picked for a gaffer. Oh, the road had turned all right.

'Not all. But the ones that mattered were.' He turned away and took off his coat. She knew he was referring to Dominic, and perhaps Shane.

'Does your da know?'

'Yes. He took it all right.'

She heaved a sigh of relief. Now perhaps Shane would get set on more often. No. She could quieten her hopes on that score – John would more likely be fair to the other extreme.

'Was none of the others after it?' she asked.

'Yes. But none of them were steady.'

Her eyes became misted. They had picked him, despite his years, because he was . . . steady. Her John a gaffer. And Katie set on the road to be a teacher. Oh, God was good.

The tears, gathering in her throat, threatened to choke her, and she turned away and put her apron to her face.

'Here! Here!' John pulled her round, and as his great arms pressed her gently to him a dam burst within her: No sorrow could have broken it; but this happiness was overwhelming, and she sobbed it out, leaning against him.

An hour later, when John saw Christine, he knew that she was already aware of what he had come to tell her; and after she exclaimed, 'Oh, John, what wonderful news! And at Christmas too,' he looked at her closely and asked, 'What's the matter? Aren't you well?'

'Yes. Yes, I'm all right,' she said hastily.

'No you're not, you're as white as a sheet. Has . . . ?'

She turned away and picked up a half-dressed doll from the table. 'Dominic's just gone. He told me about you being made a gaffer,' she said.

'Yes, I bet he did; and he'll likely be the first one I'll have to take my coat off to. But that didn't make you look like this.'

Christine sat down by the fire with the doll on her knee, and proceeded to pull a filled silk dress over its head.

'Look. If he's been up to any of his tricks . . . '

Christine cut him short with unusual curtness: 'He asked me to marry him.' She said it while looking John full in the face; the look was almost a challenge, and he experienced a feeling of guilt. Why, he couldn't fathom; but it was so strong that it swamped his indignation at Dominic's audacity.

'He wants me to go to Liverpool with him; then perhaps abroad.'

'Abroad?'

'Yes.'

'Are you going to marry him?'

'No.' She was still looking at him, the dress was only half over the doll's head. He blinked, and looked away from her down at his feet; and she sighed faintly and resumed the fitting of the dress.

John looked at her again. She was so sweet sitting there dressing the doll; why couldn't he go to her and put his arms about her and kiss her, just as often before he'd had the desire to kiss her? But he knew that, whereas for him it would merely be a kiss, to her it would be the absolute symbol of love. How he became possessed of this knowledge he didn't know, for, as he had asked himself on previous occasions, what did he know about lasses? If she were Jenny Carey or Lily McDonald he would perhaps have kissed her by now and let things take their course, but with Christine he couldn't, it wouldn't be fair. Was it even fair to come in so often? He supposed not, but he liked talking to her and Peter.

The strain that had fallen on them was relieved by David appearing. After glancing round, he asked, 'Has he gone then?'

'If you're staying in take your coat off, dear,' said Christine.

John knew to whom David was referring, he also guessed that Dominic had shooed David out.

'I'm getting a sculler for Christmas, John . . . a real one.'

'No!'

'Yes. Aren't I, Christine?'

The boy's large, dark eyes, glowing in his pale face, always aroused a tenderness in John. He was so thin, and almost girlish in his fragility.

John asked Christine, 'He doesn't mean a real one?'

'Yes. Grandfather has already bought it – it's at the quay corner. David's going to paint it himself and get it ready for the fine weather. Aren't you?'

The brother and sister smiled at each other. John realised that this was another of Peter's ways to eliminate yet another fear from his grandson. The child was highly strung and nervous, and had never quite got over the shock of seeing his parents killed in a collision between a tram and a cab when he was five years old. The episode at the gut no doubt added the fear that the boat was to erase. And the thought came to John, as it had often done lately, that Peter was a splendid man. How could anyone mock at him? By! He wished he'd been there when that crowd of hooligans burnt his hut down. They would have gone along with it.

He looked at the boy standing by Christine's side watching her put the bonnet on the doll . . . They were like a little family of saints, tender with each other, kind to everyone, and forgiving beyond his power to understand. He sat for a while longer watching Christine finishing the doll. Then he said he must get indoors and give a hand, for there were still more decorations to be hung around the walls.

Christine smiled at him as he left: 'I'm glad about your job, John.'

'Thanks. I knew you'd be . . . Tell Peter, will you?'

Christine nodded; and David cried suddenly, 'I'm going to stand at the corner, Christine, and wait for Grandfather.'

The boy chattered loudly as he and John walked down the

yard, but outside, in the back lane, he pulled at John's arm and whispered, 'John, can I . . . I want to tell you something.'

'Yes, what is it, David?' John stooped to him.

'It's Dominic - Christine's frightened of him . . . she's always frightened of him. He made me go out and he said to Christine you wouldn't get her, but he would, some way. You won't let him, will you?'

John remained silent for a moment, looking at the blur that was the boy's white face, which stood out even against the newly fallen snow. It was straining up to him, appealing, pleading. 'Don't you worry, David. Christine will be all right; I'll see to that.'

'Will you, John? Will you?'

'Yes—' John patted David's hand, and the boy seemed satisfied and ran off in evident relief; and John turned thoughtfully into the backyard, to meet Katie coming out of the lavatory.

'Come in here a minute,' he said to her, drawing her into the wash-house and closing the door; 'I want you to do something for me.'

'Yes, John?'

He knew by her voice that her face was eager. 'Look; whenever you hear Dominic go in next door, you run in the other way, will you?'

'Yes, John. But if me ma . . . ?'

'You can tell her you are going to return something of David's, a picture book or something.'

'Yes, John.'

'And no matter what he says, don't leave him alone with her. If he makes you and I'm in, come and tell me. You've got that now?'

'Yes, John.'

'Has he ever chased you out?'

Remembering Christine's warning, Katie merely answered, 'Sometimes.'

'Have you ever seen him . . . ?' John stopped. 'Well, never mind. You know what to do, don't you?'

'Yes, John.'

Neither Katie nor Molly could remember a Christmas Eve like this one. They had faint memories of being excited at the prospect of hanging up their stockings, and a memory, not so faint, of disappointment at the meagreness of their contents when they opened them; but tonight was different. In the cupboard at the side of the fireplace were parcels, some that John brought in last night, some from Christine, and others. Katie and Molly would make running dives at the lower door of the cupboard, calling, 'I'm gonna open it, Ma! I am! I am!'

Apart from saying, 'You dare,' Mary Ellen took no notice of them. Her face wore a faint smile and her body seemed settled in contentment as her needles flew on the toe of a sock. They were the last few rows of a pair she was knitting for Shane. Why had she thought of knitting him socks for Christmas she didn't know – she could not remember ever giving him anything at Christmas, except the first Christmas they were married. She wouldn't, of course, say that these were for a Christmas box; she would just put them out with his change of clean underclothes. Perhaps he would notice them, perhaps he wouldn't.

She glanced up as John came out of the bedroom, and she had to say to Katie, 'Leave John be, hinny, he's got to go out . . . Stop clambering! You'll dirty his suit.'

'Give me a shuggy before you go. Come on, John, just one,' Katie coaxed.

'Well mind, just one . . . that's all.'

'You're worse than she is,' said Mary Ellen as John sat down and crossed his knees and stuck a foot out.

Katie clambered on to the foot, and he held her hands as he hoisted her up and down. And she giggled and shouted, 'But say it! You're not saying it!'

'Give over, Katie, John's got to go out! You'll be packed off to bed, mind . . . Oh, what's the good! You're worse than she is,' Mary Ellen exclaimed, as John began to chant with each movement of his foot:

> Father Christmas soon will come
> Laden with all treasures.
> I would like a boat to sail,
> A rocky horse with a bushy tail,
> A farthing or a spade and pail;
> Katie wants a big, fat . . . dol-ly.

After the final heave, Katie fell off his foot, laughing, and John's eyes were drawn, for a moment to Molly. She was standing to one side, smiling, yet wistful. He suddenly realised he'd never had much time for Molly, and, scatterbrain as she was, she felt it. He saw it in her face now as she stood there. Impulsively, his hand went out and he pulled her to him, saying, 'Come on, you big soft lass,' and, laughing and giggling, she sat on his foot.

'Well I never. What next, I wonder!' Mary Ellen's tone was half laughing, half derisive.

Molly wasn't so easy to lift as Katie, and before John was halfway through the rhyme she had tumbled off on to the floor, where she lay, clasping Katie, helpless with laughter.

Mary Ellen, trying not to allow her gaze to linger on this son of hers, who was looking so grand, said, 'Get yourself away, lad, or else I'll not get them to sleep the night. And if you should see Mick, send him in.'

John put on his coat, saying, 'Well, expect me when you see me – I may have to follow the men to Newcastle to get the ducks. It's six you want, isn't it?'

He left the house with his mother joining in with the laughter of the children. The sound made him happy. There was something different about this Christmas . . . Well, so there should be. A gaffer! He breathed deep of the icy air. But it wasn't that alone. There was a difference both inside and outside the house. Perhaps the difference lay in himself; life at last seemed to be opening.

He walked briskly to Tyne Dock, and stood waiting for the Shields tram. The snow plough had been out, and the space opposite the dock gates had the appearance of land on which the grab had been at work; pale grey mounds lined the pavement, and the hurrying figures, passing in and out of the lamplight and the light from the bars, looked jet black against them. Some iron ore men, still in their working clothes, came out of a bar and hailed John: 'Why, man, you look as if you've had some money left you. Pinched our wages already? Or has the North-Eastern left you a prop boat?'

'Aye, they offered me one for Christmas, but I told them what to do with it: "A Benisaf or nothing" I said.'

There was loud laughter at this. 'I bet you did too! Well, a happy Christmas, and many of them,' they called as they moved away. 'And see we have full shifts for full bellies next year, mind.'

'Many of them,' John answered.

As he watched their unwieldy figures disappear into the darkness, he felt a thousand miles removed from them. They were good enough fellows in their way, but with one thought dominating them all . . . plenty of work, which meant plenty to eat and drink, or the reverse process. But somehow he didn't feel of them. It wasn't just since he had been made a gaffer, he had been feeling like this for some time past. Was it since he had got this coat? He didn't know; something had changed him . . .

The aisles of the open market were congested with buyers, and the shouts of the stallholders were deafening. John saw that it would be hours yet before the stuff was sold at anywhere near his price. Ten or eleven would be the time to come back. So he walked down King Street, debating whether he should go to the second house at the Empire or the Tivoli. To whichever place he went, he couldn't go in the threepennies, not in this rig-out. It would mean the sixpennies, or even the ninepennies. That was one drawback of being dressed-up.

'Hallo, Mr O'Brien.' Mary Llewellyn stood in front of him, her arms laden with parcels.

'Good evening, Miss Llewellyn.'

They were blocking each other's path and that of the other pedestrians as, after the greeting, they stood mutely surveying each other, surprise showing in both their faces, as if this was the last place one would have expected to find the other.

'Did you ever see such a crowd?'

'No, I never have.'

John hadn't noticed the crush before, but now they seemed to be hemmed in on all sides.

'Are you doing your last-minute shopping?' she asked him.

'No . . . yes . . . Well,' – his eyes twinkled – 'I'm hanging around until they give the ducks away in the market.' And as he said it, he wondered why it cost him nothing in pride to admit such things to her.

They laughed together, and one irritated shopper exclaimed, 'If you want to stand laughing your heads off clear off the flags and let people pass.'

They pulled long faces at each other, and Mary said, 'I suppose she's right.'

'Can I carry some of your parcels to the tram?' John asked.

'Well, I wasn't going home yet. But it would be a help if you'd relieve me of some of them for a time; I have a little more shopping to do.'

He took the boxes from her and stacked them under his arm. Then they turned towards the market again, John walking slightly ahead of her to make a way.

Laughing gaily, she left him outside while she went into a linen shop, and he stood gazing into the window, seeing nothing. He knew that this night was different. There was magic about it; in the cold and the snow, in people's faces, and in meeting her. Strange, up till a few months ago, he had never set eyes on her. But since that night he had been to see her they had run into each other a number of times, mostly when he was coming from work; yet she didn't seem to mind his working clothes. The first time they met, it was she who stopped and talked, just as if he were all got up instead of being covered from head to foot with splatters of wet clay. He had been working on a boat from Sweden, and the ore was embedded in lumps of clay, which made the digging and picking heavy and dirty.

After these meetings, he never allowed himself to think, using his mother's formula . . . thinking got you nowhere. She was interested in Katie, and through Katie, kind to him. That was that. But this meeting, like everything else on this Christmas Eve, was different. She had asked him to carry her parcels, and he was standing waiting for her as if he was her . . .

'I won't ask you to carry this one.' She was standing by his side, and he stared at her, not speaking; her face, under her fur-trimmed hat, shone at him like a star. For one brief second, the street and the hurrying crowds vanished, and she was alone in a vast emptiness, shining, and for him.

His face was unsmiling and his voice deep in his throat as he asked, 'Have you time . . . would you care to go to a variety show or the pantomime?'

He waited, tense and unthinking as her smile faded. The expression in her eyes changed a number of times in as many seconds, but not once did they portray annoyance or amusement.

'I should love to.' She turned away from him, and he fell into step by her side, thinking now, as he had never thought before: Had he gone mad? What of the Mr Culbert? It was Christmas Eve and perhaps she was expected at home for a party or something. What in the name of God had made him ask her!

And what about money? He had five shillings of his own . . . would that do? . . . Yes. Somehow, he knew she wouldn't expect too much. But again, what in the name of God had made him do it! It was the last thing on earth he would have thought of doing . . . Or was it? Hadn't he often wondered what it would be like to take someone of her stamp out? Yes, but just as one dreamt dreams, never for one moment expecting them to happen. The funny thing was she hadn't refused. She hadn't been merely polite, either; she seemed quite sincere when she said, 'I'd love to.' Well, now he must put his thinking cap on. They would have to go in the very best seats, and she'd have to have some bullets. Bullets! He repeated scornfully . . . chocolates. Get a little box . . . A box! No need to go mad altogether. She wouldn't expect it anyway. He pushed his shoulders back. Expected or not, he'd get a box.

'Do you think there's time for me to make a telephone call?'

They were standing outside the Empire, and for a moment she drifted from him into the class that made telephone calls.

'Where do you have to go? The post office?' he asked.

'Yes; I won't be more than five minutes.'

'Of course. Come on.' He shouldered his way through the crowd. Class or no class, she was going out with him, this once anyway. And he'd do the thing properly; it would be something to remember.

In spite of her fur coat and rinking boots, Mary shivered as she waited in the telephone box. It had happened as she hoped it might. But where would it lead? . . . There was time enough to ask that later, she told herself. What she had to do now was to smooth things over with those at home.

She gave a gentle sigh when she heard her father's voice say, 'Yes. Who is it?'

'It's me, Mary.'

'Mary? Why, where are you? What's up? You should be home by now; we're nearly ready.'

'Look, dear. I won't be home . . . not until . . . quite late.'

'But where are you? You know you can't do that, Mary; we're going to Gilbert's! Look lass,' – he cut her short as she was about to speak – 'it's Christmas, and we want things to go peaceable like. Where are you, anyway?'

'Shields Post Office.'

'What's made you change your mind?'

'I . . . Well, I met a friend.'

'But it isn't right. You know what a state this will put your mother in.'

'I never wanted to go. I've told her so all along. She shouldn't have accepted for me . . . Look, Father, can't you see what Mother is trying to do?'

'Yes. I know, I know.'

'Well then, why should you want me to go? And anyway, it isn't fair to Gilbert. She's giving him the idea that I can be coaxed round, and I can't.'

'Who's your friend?'

'Oh, you . . . you don't know him.'

'It's a man then?'

'Yes, it's a man.'

'Well, this is going to be a lovely evening for me.'

Mary laughed softly. 'It's yourself you're thinking about.'

'Well partly.' There was a chuckle. 'You'll be for it tomorrow, mind. And somehow I did think this was going to be a peaceful Christmas.'

'It's the loveliest Christmas I've ever known. Goodbye, dear.'

'Here! Mary . . . look, who's this fellow?'

'We may talk about him later.'

'Mary . . . you'll go to Midnight Mass? For God's sake don't miss that, or there'll be hell to pay.'

'We'll see. Goodbye. Wait. Do you want to know something?'

'What is it?'

'I like you, Mr Llewellyn.'

Laughing, she hung up the phone, and almost ran to join John.

Mary Ellen yawned. She wished John was in, and then she'd go to bed. She leaned back and glanced up at the clock . . . ten-past eleven. Had he managed to get a duck?

She sat with her chair drawn up close to the fire, her feet on the fender, her skirt tucked up on to her lap, exposing her short legs to the dying ashes. The house was quiet, only Shane's and Dominic's snores alternating with each other's from the rooms. Behind her, the girls lay curled up under the thin brown blankets and a heap of coats; and, at each end of the mantelpiece hung their packed stockings, together with one for Mick.

As she yawned again, she heard the muffled pad of footsteps on the yard, and, pulling down her skirt, she got up to open the scullery door as John quietly lifted the latch of the back door.

Stupefied, Mary Ellen gazed at him; then, in a whispered exclamation, said, 'In the name of God! Have you bought the market?'

John laughed softly as he lowered a great parcel on to the table, followed by a stone brown paper bag and a square box. 'You'll never guess what it is . . . it's a turkey! And this is a bag of fruit. And there's bullets in that box.' He spoke softly and rapidly.

'A turkey! But where'd you get the money, lad?' Mary Ellen looked closely at him. If she didn't know differently she'd have thought he'd had a drop – his eyes were shining, like coals . . . Perhaps it was the frost.

'We . . . I waited till the last thing, and I got him for four bob.'

'But what's all this other?'

'Fruit.'

'A stone bag of it!' Mary Ellen looked amazed. 'Are they specked?'

'No, I should say not.'

John did not look at her. He had taken off his cap and was

combing his hair. 'Miss Llewellyn sent them for the bairns.'

Mary Ellen stared silently at his profile. Miss Llewellyn.

John turned to her, putting on his cap again. 'I'm going to Midnight Mass at Jarrow. I'm getting the last tram up.'

Miss Llewellyn and Midnight Mass. Her lad going to Midnight Mass with Miss Llewellyn! It was funny but she'd been thinking about Midnight Mass earlier on this evening, feeling the need to give thanks for all her good fortune at this Christmas time. It was years since she had been to Midnight Mass, and in spite of her tiredness, she'd thought: For two pins I'd go to Midnight Mass if John was in. She would have worn her new coat, although it wouldn't have mattered about going in her shawl; there'd be mostly shawls and mufflers there anyway. And she'd imagined herself kneeling as she used to do in the aisle, or even on the altar steps, wrapped about in the thick, incensed air, full of hushed rustle, so full would the church be. And for a brief hour she would really feel the Child was being born and be one with Mary in her travail.

But John was going to Midnight Mass, and he was going with Miss Llewellyn. She knew now the reason for the light in his eyes.

John tried not to show undue haste, but there was only a few minutes before the tram would pass the bottom of the street, and she would be on it. Already it was late, and perhaps they'd not get in the church. He did not want this to happen, for he had the desire to kneel at Mass with her, not only because it would mean being with her another hour or more, but because to go to Mass with a lass had a subtle meaning, which neither needed nor could be defined by words.

The four hours they had been together seemed to spread back down his lifetime. There seemed no moment when he had not watched the expressions dancing over her face like shadows in a garden, nor a moment when he had not been carrying her parcels or buying her chocolates, or when he was not sitting with her in the dark and laughing with her at a pantomime; or when there was a second in his life when she did not urge him to remain quiet while the stallholder, in desperation, brought his final and unmovable price of eight shillings a turkey down to four shillings! Or when had he not watched her taking her choice of fruit, bananas, pomegranates, oranges, apples, pears and nuts. And now they were going to Midnight Mass, and there would be no tram back. They would have to walk all the way from Dee Street, in the centre of Jarrow, to the heart of Simonside. It would be a long way for her, and difficult walking, for the pavements were sheets of knobbly grey ice; and it would be a long way to walk without touching each other. She might have to take his arm – he thought of it as 'link' – Miss Llewellyn and him linking!

A surge of feeling that demanded some form of expression swept through him, and, stooping, he kissed Mary Ellen swiftly on the side of the brow. Without a word, he was gone. And Mary Ellen stood fingering the place his lips had brushed . . . Her lad had kissed her . . . for the first time since he was a tiny bairn. And because he was in love.

She had been worried lately, thinking he was struck on her next door, and had wondered where it would lead, for she doubted, if he took her, there'd be much happiness for him; not that she had anything really against the lass, only that terrifying religion of hers. God knew there was no happiness came out of a mixed marriage. With a Church of England one it would be bad enough, but with a Spiritualist! . . . And yet, as awful as that possibility seemed, he would have had a little show of happiness in a way, whereas now there was none for him that she could see. For what was the obstacle of religion compared with the obstacle of class? Had he gone mad? And that Llewellyn lass, too? Where did they think it would lead? Her da was a boatbuilder; and a docker, even a gaffer, would be so much midden muck to him. They had a fancy house, with even a lavatory inside, so Katie said, and kept a parlourmaid and cook. Was the lass mad? There was no-one better than her lad, no-one in the wide world, but he was a docker and from the fifteen streets. And that lass must know nothing could come of it . . . She was struck by his size and his ways, and she would shelve him when the novelty wore off. And what would it do to him? She thought of his eyes when he had come in, and slowly she sat down by the fire again and stared into its rose-grey embers.

Chapter Eight

New Year's Eve

It was a good thing New Year's Eve fell on a Saturday, John thought, for it meant one day less holiday. They would start work on Tuesday, the ones, anyway, who were sober enough. He wanted work, and more work. If he had his own way he'd carry on, night and day, for three parts of the week; he'd make them throw the stuff out of those holds as it had never been thrown out before. He wanted money. God, how he wanted money.

He sat before the fire, dressed in his working clothes, tense with thinking. Shane sat opposite him, sober and sullen; he'd been drunk only once during the holidays. This was a record. Was he turning over a new leaf? John wondered, or was it because he was forced to realise that the more he drank the more he twitched? But twitching or not, tonight he'd likely have a skinful. What would she say to this house and the lot of them? Would she take them as she took him? That was too much to ask. Whereas last Saturday night he thought he'd never known a moment in his life without her, now, across the vast space of time since he last saw her, he could not even recall her face clearly. Again and again he tried to visualise her; but always her face ran into a blur. Even when he attempted to recapture the wonder and the ecstatic feeling of achievement as, with her on his arm, he walked past the fifteen streets, huddled and sleeping under the star-carpeted sky, the feeling would slither away. It was strange, too, but he could not actually remember how he left her. What did they say to each other? Nothing much. They were quiet on the journey back; all the laughter and fun had been left in Shields market. As they walked up Simonside Bank, he had asked if she were tired, and she had replied that she'd never felt less tired. Yet she sounded sort of sleepy when she said it . . . But there must have been more than that said. One thing he knew he hadn't said: 'Can I see you again?'

Why hadn't he, when it was foremost in his mind during those last few minutes with her? But foremost, too, had been the thought of money. He couldn't really ask her out unless he intended taking her somewhere. Well, he could have taken her out tonight.

All this morning he was hoping he would run into her as he came home from work. And when he didn't, he told himself it was the best thing that could have happened; there were many things he could do with those extra few shillings – his mother would know what to do with them. So perhaps it was all for the best – he moved impatiently in his chair. Perhaps . . . there was no perhaps about it. What was he aiming at, anyway? Was his brain softening, just because of that one night? If he were to see her again, what would it lead to? So intense was the urgency of the question that he almost spoke aloud. You are going stark, staring mad! Look around, and ask yourself what you and she can ever be to each other . . . even if she does like you . . . He was on his feet, staring down into the fire; she likes me all right, I know it. She more than likes me . . . she feels the same as I do.

Mary Ellen could remain silent no longer; John's drawn, twisted face was wringing her heart. Shane was dozing now, and she whispered, 'What's up, lad?'

'Nothing. I'm going to have a wash.'

He went quickly into the scullery, and as he washed himself

Mary Ellen gazed sadly at his back. She knew this would happen – she knew there'd be no happiness in it for him. She wanted to go to him and in some way comfort him; but her mind was lifted from him to Molly.

Molly's screeching voice came from the back lane, and Mary Ellen knew she was fighting again, for she was hurling rhymes at someone's head:

> Annie Kelly's got a big fat belly,
> And her belly wobbles like jelly.

My God! That lass nearly fourteen and yelling things out like that. Mary Ellen pushed past John and opened the back door.

'You, Molly! Come in here!'

Molly was having her last word: 'You wouldn't do much for God if the divil was dead, Annie Kelly. You're mean, so you are. Poor Nancy!'

'Come in here!' Mary Ellen hauled Molly over the step. 'You can thank your lucky stars your da's dozing,' she whispered fiercely, 'or I'd bray you!'

'Well, I was only sticking up for Nancy,' Molly snivelled. 'She's been sent back from her place, Mrs Fitzsimmons won't have her. And Annie wouldn't let her play with us; she punched her.'

'Sent back from her place,' Mary Ellen repeated to John. 'That means the do's off.'

'Damn good thing, too,' John answered shortly. 'They'll be yelling out for the money before the new year's in a week.'

'It'll likely be spent now, lad, in any case.'

The door opened again, and Katie rushed in breathless.

Mary Ellen hushed her: 'Be quiet, hinny! And close that door, the cold's enough to cut you in two.'

'Ma, can I go with Christine? And Molly too? There's a big stretch frozen hard, past Cleveland Place, and everybody's going there to slide . . . proper sliding. Christine's got proper sliding skates with knives on the bottom. And there's a man there with a fire selling roast taties . . . Oh, Ma, can we go?'

'Go on, Ma, let's.' Molly joined her plea to Katie's.

'What about it cracking?' Mary Ellen asked John. 'Will it be deep?'

'It won't crack in this frost.'

He was drying himself, and asked Katie, 'How does Christine know there's skating? Has she been?' He hadn't seen Christine since Christmas Day, and then only to wish her a happy Christmas and to thank her rather sheepishly for the tie. He knew now why he hadn't kissed Christine, and the knowledge made him strangely embarrassed in her presence.

'Yes,' answered Katie. 'She was there yesterday, her and David. She says they're going to have a big fire on the bank the night to light the ice up.'

'How far past Cleveland Place is it?'

'It's in Roper's Field.'

'You'd better give it a miss,' said Mary Ellen; 'you'll slide the boots off your feet.'

'Not any sooner than with sliding in the streets,' said John.

'But it's them falling through I'm afraid of.'

'Don't worry,' he said; 'I'll take a walk up and have a look.'

He went into the bedroom and started to change hastily. Roper's Field . . . off the Simonside Road. There was just a chance she might be there.

In the kitchen of Cumberland Villa, the two maids were standing near the partly open door, straining their ears.

'Hear anything?' asked the cook.

'Not a word,' replied Phyllis. 'And the way the missis looked I thought she was going to explode. I bet you anything you like though she'd heard about that fellow.'

'I wouldn't believe a word of it,' said Cook. 'And I'd be careful what I was saying if I was you. Miss Mary walking out with one of the O'Briens! Huh! I'll believe that when I see it.'

'I tell you our Doris saw them in the market, and our Doris knows them both as well as I know you. She was standing behind them, and she said they were laughing and talking together like . . . well, like a couple who was walking out . . . Sh! Listen.'

Phyllis' elbow stopped the cook's retort. 'There!' she hissed. 'Get an earful of that. Have you ever heard the missis go off like that before? What did I tell you?'

In the drawing room, James Llewellyn was appealing to his wife: 'Look, Beatrice, leave this to me.' He spoke gently and soothingly; the jocular brusqueness, which was his usual defence against her, was gone from his tone.

'Too much has been left to you, and look at the result!' She turned from him, and again addressed her daughter, with quiet tenseness now. 'No wonder you wouldn't tell me who you were with on Christmas Eve! It is to your credit that you were ashamed.'

Mary stood with her elbow resting on the mantelpiece; her face was half turned from her mother, and she stared unseeing into the fire, her attitude belying the anger that was filling her body.

'You must have lost every spark of decency. You never, at any time, had a proper sense of what is correct. But this! Have you any idea how I felt when Florence Dudley told me they saw you in the Empire with a . . . docker?' Beatrice Llewellyn spat out the last word, her thin nose and delicately chiselled mouth almost meeting over it. Her large pale blue eyes showed depths of purple, and her expression was weighed with actual hate as she looked at this girl whom she had come to think of as being by her but not of her. This last disgusting episode proved only too conclusively from which side she had inherited her qualities. 'Will Dudley says he comes from the fifteen streets and the family are notorious,' she ended.

Mary faced her mother, and her tone was infuriatingly quiet

when she said, 'Of course they are. Anyone within a three-miles radius of the fifteen streets knows that. If you didn't shut out every unpleasantness from your life you would have heard it before . . . One of the main things for which they are notorious is hunger. Dwell upon that the next time you're preparing for the Dudleys coming to dinner.'

Beatrice Llewellyn stood aghast – never before had Mary dared to address her so. 'They are poor because they drink and gamble. And you! You are a slut! You were out with that man until three o'clock in the morning. Do you think it won't be all round Jarrow and Shields by now?'

'I hope so.'

Mary's stillness seemed to lift the tension to breaking point. Her father cried, 'Here, lass! Here, that's enough!' and Beatrice Llewellyn perpetrated what was to her mind unforgivable . . . she screamed. 'You low creature!' The words seemed to emerge from the top of her head. 'You're utterly debased. I shall have Father O'Malley to you. Yes. Yes. I shall . . . Leave me alone!' – she tore her arm from her husband's soothing hand, and flung like a small tornado out of the room.

During their twenty-six years of married life, James Llewellyn had never seen his wife lose control; this was the first show of sincere passion he had witnessed, and it left him, not only shaken, but worried. Usually she tried gentle tears and studied silences, alternated with the persistent reiteration of her point. But for Beatrice to lose her dignity meant this affair had indeed struck home.

'You've done it this time.' He came to the fireplace and knocked out his pipe against the bars. 'You know, lass, it was a bit of a shock.'

'To you too?' Mary asked sharply.

'Aye . . . yes. It's no good saying one thing and thinking another. But when Will Dudley got on about seeing you with one of the Big O'Briens I could have punched him in the face.

Although he put it very nicely, I could tell it had afforded them a good topic of conversation all the week, and that was why Florence Dudley was so anxious for us to drop in this morning. When your mother came downstairs with her I thought she'd collapse . . . How long has it been going on, lass?'

'It hasn't been going on, as you call it; that was the only time.'

'Oh . . . Well,' – there was a measure of relief in her father's voice – 'and are you . . . Well, is it finished?'

'I don't know.'

'You don't know! What do you mean, lass?'

'I mean that if it rests with me it won't be finished.' Mary turned towards him, nervously rubbing the palms of her hands together. 'I haven't seen him since, because he never asked me.'

James Llewellyn stared at his daughter. His lass, who was the best-looking lass for miles, and who could have her pick, was in love. Even had she not practically put it unashamedly into words, he could see it in her eyes. She was in love with this dock worker, John O'Brien; and not in the light-hearted way that lassies fell in love, but in an earnest, stubborn, painful way, a way that would leave a mark on her, however things went. Well, he wasn't going to stand by and see her make a hash of her life, and say nothing. This was one time her mother was right. 'Now see here,' – he planted his feet firmly apart and pointed his finger at her – 'you know which side I've always been on, don't you? You know that life would have been much easier for me if I'd taken your mother's part all along.'

As his fingers wagged at her, Mary thought: he's nearly as big as John, and he has the same clumsy movements, a sort of endearing gaucheness. All the money in the world won't polish him. Anyway, he was once a dock worker himself, so why can't he understand about this?

'But I want you to understand, lass,' James Llewellyn went on, 'that I'm with your mother in this.'

'You'd rather see me married to Gilbert then?'

'I don't want you to marry anyone you don't fancy . . . But yes,' – he thrust out his head – 'yes, I'd rather see you married to Gilbert than carrying on with this business. At least you wouldn't starve . . . Oh, Mary,' – his large leathery face crumpled – 'stop while there's time. You don't know what you're running yourself into. Lass, I hate to say it, but I've seen those O'Briens rolling from one side of the arches to the other. I even remember the mother, years ago, a little body, standing outside the bars with the bairns clinging round her, trying to get a few shillings out of her man before he blued the lot. I tell you, lass, they're noted.'

'He doesn't drink.'

'That's what he says.'

'He doesn't, Father.' There was a fierce ring in her voice. 'And he's not just a docker either; he's been made a gaffer.'

'What! Did he tell you that? How old is he?'

'Twenty-two.' Her head was thrust up in defiance, daring him to say, 'So he's younger than you.'

But what he said was, 'He's a damned liar! There's no fellow could be made a gaffer at twenty-two. Thirty-two would be more like it. He's stuffing you, lass. Can't you see?' He was angry for her.

'No, he's not. Anyway, it should be easy for you to find out.'

'Yes. Quite easy. But even so, if he is a gaffer, what's that?'

Mary did not reply but stood looking at him, her eyes wide and sad, for she too, was asking herself the same question . . . He was worth something better than that.

To James Llewellyn, she looked at this moment pathetic, and he could never remember his joyous, laughter-loving daughter looking this way. Taking her by the hand, he said, 'Hinny,' – using the endearing word that was banned in the house because of its commonness – 'I only want your happiness. What do you think I've worked for all these years? To leave you comfortable. Look, my dear, tell me you'll drop this.'

The tears gathering in her eyes obscured her vision. Why, oh why, did they think money could buy off or replace a feeling that was made of intangible stuff? Money and love were on two different planes . . . Yet were they so divided? Love needed money for its existence. Without it, more often than not it died, as the body, wherein it was housed, fought and struggled for life. Yet if the chance were given her, would she risk the survival of this love that seemed to be eating her away? Oh yes, yes. The tears spilled on to her face. 'I can't. If he asks me out again, I'll go.'

She watched her father leave the room and close the door after him with painful slowness . . .

Mary was sitting in her own room, crouched over the fire, when the dinner bell rang. She made no move to carry out its summons. Nor, as the time went on, did anyone come to enquire why. Never before had she felt so unhappy, and she couldn't see the unhappiness lifting; it stretched on and on into the future, for the only person capable of dispelling it was as class-conscious as her mother. She felt now that Christmas Eve had been merely a lapse of John's, and that during the quiet walk back from Jarrow he was already regretting it; he had left her with scarcely a word. Every dinner time and teatime of this past week she had fought with herself not to stroll casually down through the arches, presumably on her way to Shields, in the hope of encountering him. But some hard core of pride said no . . . she wouldn't scheme to trap him into asking her out; if he wanted to see her he would find a way; and there was always the post.

What a New Year's Eve! She got up and wandered about the room. If only she could see him for a moment, run into him accidentally, as she had done last Saturday night . . . But wouldn't it have been better had they not met at all – not last Saturday, but in the first instance. He attracted her that first night he sat in this room, and she had been unable to get him out of her mind since.

The memory of that meeting brought back the niggling envy of Christine . . . Was that girl something to him? Was she the reason why he hadn't asked her to repeat the evening? She didn't know . . .

She went upstairs and put on her outdoor things, for she felt that were she to stay indoors any longer she would scream, as her mother had done this morning. Remembering her mother's voice and look, she realised that whether she pursued this business to its height or it merely fizzled out, the last supports of the barrier that had been erecting itself for years between them were hammered home today, and their combined lifetimes would not be long enough to break it down.

Standing on the bank at the edge of the field, John looked down in amazement on the scene. He had witnessed nothing like it before. The field, which dipped into a shallow valley, had every appearance of a lake, and there was scarcely a yard of its surface which had not its moving figure. Very few had skates; the main sport seemed to be concentrated on the long single and double slides. On the double slides young men and girls crossed hands, skimming away with enviable balance towards the centre of the ice. Children had their slides nearer the edge, and were watched by spectators, who outnumbered the skaters. Some of the young lads were already getting the bonfire going. The air was filled with laughter and shouting, the smell of burning wood, and the thick, comforting smell of roasting potatoes. The faces of the crowd seemed alight with a newborn joy.

The feeling of mass gaiety puzzled John. It was this whiteness; it had gone to their heads and caused a madness. The drabness of life was lost under the spell of its gleaming sparkle, and the people seemed to be deluded into thinking this clean, white world would remain – their house roofs were white, their window sills, their doorsteps. The docks and the ships, too, lay buried under the clean illusion – even on the top of the highest mast there was a virgin white cap of snow, fast and secure and promising to remain for ever. There would be no tomorrow, or the next day, when the gutters would be choked with brown slush, the roads become rivers, and the houses grey again, and they themselves grey and blue, feet wet, bodies shivering. It was cold now; but this was a dry cold, which quickened the blood, freed the perception and brought all the instincts to the surface, giving to each person an awareness of his existence, which demanded of the body that it be used, now, at this very time.

As he stood there John began to feel something of this mass joy. The whole scene, which seemed to have been dropped from another world, where only light laughter existed, bewildered him, and part of him realised that it was out of place in the realistic grimness of this area.

He watched Christine gliding gracefully in small circles near where Katie, Molly and David were sliding with other children. She looked little more than a child herself, a dark, elfin, slip of a child.

Christine caught sight of him, and waved and beckoned him on to the ice; but he shook his head and waved his hand in refusal. And after a while, she glided to where he stood on the bank.

'Isn't it wonderful! Come on . . . I'll pull you.'

'Not on your life,' he laughed.

He was relieved that there was no stiffness in her manner, for it must have been evident to her that he had avoided seeing her during this past week. She looked very fetching, standing below him with a red tam-o'-shanter on the back of her head, and for a fleeting second he felt a regret that it was not she who was filling his mind and body at this moment, for then things would have been plain sailing.

'A big thing like you afraid of the ice!' she called up to him, teasingly.

'You'd be more afraid if you got me on there and I fell on you.'

'I'll risk it. Come on. Come on, John,' – the pleading was in her eyes and voice.

He shook his head: 'I've a number of other ways of making a fool of myself besides that.'

Christine saw that it was no use trying to coax him; nevertheless, she stood for a time gazing up at him. Then, without further words, she turned and skimmed away again.

John continued to watch her and the children, but between times his eyes would search the field. Although the light was fading he could still see the further bank, and he thought it would have to be very dark to prevent him from picking her out from the crowd. He noticed Katie leave the long line of sliders and walk quickly towards him.

'What's the matter?' he asked. 'Are you tired, or after a hot tatie?'

'Our Dominic's along there, John. He's watching Christine.'

John remained silent, and did not turn to the spot Katie indicated but looked to where Christine was still whirling unconcerned. 'Is he all right?' he asked; which meant, was he sober.

'Yes, he looks it . . . and . . . and he's got a collar and tie on too.' Katie's eyes fell to John's collar and tie, then to his new coat; and she added, with awe in her voice, 'He's got a new coat an' all, John.' Her eyes were round in amazement – the advent of any new clothes in the house was something to dwell upon, for in most cases their approach was awaited for weeks. As late as last night Dominic had no new clothes, yet here he was, all dressed up.

John's mouth moved into a twisted grin. Dominic wasn't to be outdone then. The buying of new clothes would be all to the good if it kept him off the drink; but John knew only too well that someone would have to whistle for the money for the coat. He glanced casually now in Dominic's direction. Yes, there he was, practically head and shoulders above the crowd, and even from this distance and the little John could see of him, the difference in his appearance was noticeable.

Momentarily John's attitude towards his brother softened, and he wondered if Dominic's feeling for Christine was anything like his own for Mary. But his wondering was definitely only momentary . . . He would have gone about it in a different way if it was . . . and he still paid visits to 'Lady Pansy'. Moreover, his love for Christine, if it could be called such, had instilled her with nothing but fear.

He bent down to Katie: 'Don't forget what I told you about keeping with Christine.'

'No, John, I won't.'

'No matter what he says on the way home, don't you leave her, mind.'

'No, John.'

'Go on then, on your slide; I'll be here for some time yet.'

Groups of lads and lassies on the banks had started singing. 'Keep your feet still, Geordie, hinny' vied with 'Cushy Butterfield', and 'Bleydon Races' with 'Auld Lang Syne'. But now the careless mad pleasure of the scene was dispelled for John, for Dominic was there. His presence acted like a pressure forcing out the ease from his body and the quietness from his mind, and replacing it with antipathy, which was the only true bond between them.

As the daylight of the last day of the year faded, the twilight seemed to urge on the gaiety. The bonfire was well alight now, sending up showers of sparks through the grey dusk into the far-reaching blue beyond. John found that after looking towards the fire for a time the skaters on the ice appeared like dark, scribbled lines on a white canvas. He closed his eyes and pressed his eyeballs with his fingers. And when he opened them, there she was, standing not a yard from him.

When he was a child, his mother, if she had a piece of toffee for him, would say, 'Shut your eyes and open your mouth and see what God will send you.' He had shut his eyes, and look what God had sent him.

He took a slow step towards her – Dominic and all he stood for was gone, and the magic and madness of the scene was upon him fully now. No subterfuge need be used on a night like this; truth was easy, and desirable.

'I wondered if you would be here.'

At his words, her face, which had been set and strained, fell into a smile; not her usual, light-flashing smile, but one holding a tinge of sadness.

John did not detect the sadness . . . sadness and this girl were as apart as the earth and the sky. To his mind, she spelt radiance, to his body, magnetism; she was ecstasy and joy. But he had only plain words with which to speak: 'Have you ever seen anything to equal this around these parts?' He did not take his eyes from her face, but indicated the ice with a movement of his head.

'Never. It's like something you'd see in Switzerland.'

Her eyes, playing over his face, made him drunk with feeling; all the barriers between them were being swept away on a swift moving tide. The need was upon him to touch her, if only her hand.

'Have you been sliding?' he asked.

'I haven't any skates.'

'What about using our feet? It seems popular.'

'Here?' She pointed to the entwined throng below them.

'No. Let's go round to the other side; there are fewer people there, and if we fall there'll be less to laugh at us.'

Mary made an almost imperceptible motion with her head. The action was more pointed than words in its acquiescence.

They turned together. Then stopped. It was the red tam-o'-shanter that brought itself to John's notice. Without it, Christine, at that moment, would have been merely another face – even Katie was just part of the crowd.

Christine and Katie stood hand in hand below them, silent and staring.

'Why! Hallo, Katie.'

'Hallo, Miss Llewellyn.' Katie's fat, rosy cheeks were very like the proverbial apples as she smiled.

'Are you having a lovely time?'

'Yes, Miss Llewellyn.'

'And did you have a nice Christmas?'

'Oh yes, Miss Llewellyn. Oh, lovely! And thank you, Miss Llewellyn, for the presents and all the lovely fruit.'

Mary's eyes were forced from Katie's to the girl in the red hat. The girl was staring at her; her eyes, dark and enormous, seemed to glow with a purple gleam. Even in the dusk, their light was penetrating, and Mary felt it stripping her. It was an odd sensation. It was almost as if the girl was looking into the very depths of her heart and finding there things of which even she herself was not aware.

When John said, 'This is Christine,' the girl, with a lightning movement, whirled Katie round and away, and in a moment they were lost in the moving figures and the dimness.

The situation had suddenly become awkward. Why had Christine dashed off like that? He knew fine well why! His neck became hot. Then a surge of relief swept over him . . . thank God he had never made up to her! He was free in that sense, anyway . . . free for Mary. Oh, the daring, the audacity, the madness of it!

He turned towards her again, and this time the sadness in her face was clear to him. She too then had seen how Christine felt. He must make it clear to her that there was nothing in it.

'What about the slide?' he said.

Without answering, she turned from him, and they threaded their way among the crowd.

'Christine's a nice girl,' he began lamely.

'Yes, she looks it.'

They were forced to step apart to make way for a group of running children, and when they came together again, he continued, 'I don't think she'll ever grow up though. She's . . . well, she's just like Katie.'

She looked at him and smiled, a small, understanding smile. He smiled back at her, and they walked on in silence.

The far bank was almost deserted, the crowds having been drawn to the light of the bonfire and the man with the brazier and the roasting potatoes. The ice, too, was not so smooth here, for tufts of grass broke the surface.

'Shall we chance it?' He held out his hand, and she took it and stepped from the bank on to the ice. 'Single or double?'

'Single I think, for a start . . . You go first, I haven't been on the ice for two years.'

'Two years! It must be at least eight since I was on a slide . . . Well, here goes.' He ran and started to slide; wobbled, steadied himself, and wobbled again; then, with a suddenness that found every bone in his body, he sat down on the ice with a heavy plop.

With a sureness that spoke of past schooling, she reached him as he was getting to his feet. He was laughing, and said, 'Good job you weren't behind me.' And when he felt her hands gently dusting his shoulders he prolonged his own banging of his clothes to shake off the loose snow.

'Shall we try again?' he asked.

'If you like,' she said; but there was little enthusiasm in her voice.

'Do you want to slide?' He was facing her now, their breaths were mingling and their eyes holding. The words were a question that did not mean what it asked, and she answered with a candour that seemed to be of the very essence of the day.

'No.'

He reached out and took her hand, and they walked carefully towards the bank again.

'Would you . . . would you like to go for a walk? Or what about Shields?'

'Not Shields. Let's go for a walk.'

They walked down the narrow lane and on to the main road without speaking. Being a country road it was unlit, and in spite of the snow covering it, it appeared black after the glare of the fire-lit field. The darkness gave him courage, and he unclasped her hand and drew her arm through his, entwining his fingers through hers and holding them close to his coat. They walked on in step, and as he felt her hip moving against his he became conscious of the stillness between them, a stillness that seemed to be waiting only for the right moment to burst into sound . . . sound that would bewitch and delight him, because it would be her voice telling him what he wanted, above all things, to know. But as they walked on, it seemed to him as if the silence would never be broken.

When, of one mind, they turned down a side lane and stopped and faced each other, he told himself that never before had any man felt for a woman as he felt for her. But now the moment had come he seemed paralysed, and even the potency of his feeling could not lift him over the barrier to her. It was she who opened the way, with such words that flung barriers, prejudices and classes into oblivion: 'Oh, John, if you don't tell me I won't be able to bear it.'

There was a second of wonder-filled time before his arms went about her, not gently, as he had imagined them so often doing, but savagely, crushing her into him until he could feel her racing heart pounding against him. He did not kiss her immediately. His lips travelled the whole surface of her face before they reached hers, but when they did, their bodies merged and rose, above the snow and ice, above their separate lives, away from this earth to some ethereal place where time is not. When, swaying together, their lips parted, it seemed to them both as if they had actually fallen into another era of time, so much did they know of each other.

'Mary.'

She did not answer but leaned upon him, moving her face against his.

'I love you.'

Her arms tightened about him.

'I'm mad . . . I shouldn't say that.'

'Oh beloved.'

Beloved . . . a woman had called him beloved . . . him! This beautiful woman, this girl, this . . .

'How is it you can care for a fellow like me? Mary! Oh, Mary!'

Her reply was smothered against him. And when he would have again begun deprecating himself her fingers covered his mouth. 'You're the finest person I know – there is no-one to come up to you.'

She cut short his protest: 'John, let nothing ever separate us, will you?' Her voice was earnest. 'Nothing nor no-one. Promise. Never.'

The urgency in her voice stilled him – it was almost as if she was pleading with him. That she should be asking to let nothing separate them seemed fantastic.

Taking her hand gently from his lips he said, 'It's me should be putting that to you. What do you think will be said when this gets about? Will you be able to stand it?'

Her answer was the covering of his mouth by hers with such passion that all the longing, all the loneliness of his life, all that was drab and tawdry, vanished. Her love for him raised him to a new level of self-esteem.

'Oh, Mary, my love . . . my dear . . . do you know what you mean to me? Do you know what you stand for?' He was gentle now, holding her face between his large hands, peering at her, seeing each feature in his mind's eye: 'You're beautiful.'

'I couldn't be too beautiful for you.'

Her words were like notes of tender music, borne on the white wings of the snow. He shook his head slowly at the wonder of them. 'I don't know how you can love me . . . you who have everything. I'm ignorant, and I'm ashamed of it. Mary,' – his voice was shy – 'will you teach me?'

'Oh, my dear, you don't need . . . '

He stopped her, 'Yes, I do need. And you know I do. I never want you to be ashamed of me.'

'John . . . John, don't.'

His humility brought the tears to her eyes, as he went on, 'And there's my folk. it isn't that I'm ashamed, only . . . well, I suppose you've heard of our family. There hasn't been much chance for any of us; my mother slaved all her days, and . . . and my father and brother . . . '

'Sh!' She leaned gently against him, stroking his cheek as a mother would soothe a child.

She murmured something, and he whispered in awe, 'What?'

And she repeated, 'It's a case of Ruth and Naomi.'

But still he did not understand, yet although the words held no meaning for him, her tone conveyed a deep humility, and he was filled with wonder.

CHAPTER NINE

NANCY

THE HOME-MADE paper chains lay in a jumbled heap on one side of the table, the three bought ones lying neatly concertinaed by themselves together with the honeycomb ball. These would do for another year, Mary Ellen decided, if she could hide them somewhere. She had never before been so late in taking down the decorations; it was 5th January, and she was just escaping bad luck by taking them down today, the morrow would be too late. But it had been nice to leave them up till the last minute, for they carried on the feeling of this wonderful Christmas and New Year. By! – She stopped in her work to look out of the kitchen window to the roofs beyond, where the last of the snow was sliding in a grey mass into the gutter – she had never known such a time. The stuff they'd had to eat! And Shane being sober, even on New Year's Eve; and no rows in the house. There was Dominic's surliness, of course, but she was used to that and had not allowed it to spoil things. And anyway, he was out most of the time . . . all night, once.

This business of John's troubled her at times; but what could she do, for he said nothing. He was going about looking like a cat with nine tails. She hoped to God something would happen to make it last. But how could it – him and Miss Llewellyn!

Where would it end? . . . Well, she wouldn't worry – everything else was going fine; the coal house was full of coal and the bairns were rightly set up with clothes, the last, thanks to them next door – the thought of thanks took shape before she could stop it – well, anyway, they had been good, no matter what they were. She'd wished time and again she could go and thank them, but she was unable to bring herself to do so. The fear of them still held her, and she couldn't face them, so she had sent her thanks by the bairns and John. The fear had strengthened in an odd way too during these past weeks, for Mick's ear had stopped running for the first time in two years, and Shane . . . Why was it, after all these years, Shane had eased off the drink and his twitching had lessened? Did he find himself lying on a platform above the bed with Peter Bracken's hands moving over him? My God! She shuddered. It was the first time she had admitted to herself the influence of Peter Bracken on her the night the child was born. She put her hand inside her blouse and felt for her rosary, which she had taken to wearing round her neck of late.

Staring out of the window, she said her beads: Hail, Mary, full of grace, the Lord is with thee. Blessed art thou amongst women, and blessed is the fruit of thy womb, Jesus . . . She had gone through two decades, when she saw the backyard door open and Hannah Kelly enter the yard.

Hastily, she fastened her blouse.

What did Hannah want so early in the morning? . . . There was something curious about her walk: she couldn't have had a drop already, surely. She watched Hannah fumble with the latch of the kitchen door, and when she came in and closed the door, and stood with her back to it, Mary Ellen exclaimed, 'Why, lass, you're bad! Come and sit down.'

Hannah shook her head and murmured, 'Oh, Mary Ellen!'

'What is it? Is it Joe?'

Hannah again shook her head. She tried to speak but the

words refused to come, her mouth opening and shutting like that of a fish.

'What is it then? Nancy?'

Hannah's eyes drooped and her head fell on her chest.

'Tell me, lass. What is it?'

'Dear God, dear God,' Hannah said, and her voice sounded small and lost, and she looked like a bewildered child in spite of her long, bony frame.

'I may be wrong. Will you come over with me, Mary Ellen, and see? I came the back way, for Bella Bradley's on the lookout.'

'Is Nancy ill?' Mary Ellen asked, taking her shawl from the back of the door.

Hannah made no reply but went out, and Mary Ellen followed closely after her . . .

Nancy was in bed, lying well down under the clothes, and Mary Ellen, as she entered the bedroom, could see only her eyes. They held an odd look, a mixture of wariness and cunning, an expression not usual to their dullness.

'Hallo, Nancy,' said Mary Ellen.

But Nancy did not reply with her usual normal address; she just stared from one to the other.

Hannah, stripping the clothes from her, said, 'Lift up your nightie!'

With her eyes still darting from one to the other of the two women, Nancy complied. The nightdress was short and tight, and she had to drag it over her hips.

Mary Ellen gazed at Nancy's stomach. She knew now what Hannah suspected, and she exclaimed to herself. 'Oh, Jesus, don't let it be.' Nevertheless, to her eyes there was nothing really to justify Hannah's suspicions, and she looked across the bed to Hannah: 'Lass, what makes you think . . . ?' she said.

'She's past her time, and I've seen nothing; and I think that's what Mrs Fitzsimmons twigged. And her being sick and not working.' She spoke as if Nancy wasn't there. 'Stand up!'

she said harshly to her daughter.

Nancy lumbered out of the bed, still with her nightdress held above her stomach. And now Mary Ellen thought she could detect a small rise. But still she would not believe this thing possible; nobody in their right senses would dream of taking a lass like this.

'Look, lass,' – she turned to Hannah – 'it may only be wind. Or perhaps a growth,' she said hopefully.

Hannah, her eyes dead in her large, round face, turned away and walked into the kitchen.

'Put your clothes on, hinny,' Mary Ellen said to Nancy; and the girl immediately pulled her nightdress over her head and began to dress.

In the kitchen, Hannah was sitting dejectedly at the table, and Mary Ellen said, 'Get her to the doctor's lass. Take her now. It may not be what you think, and it'll set your mind at rest . . . Anyway, it can't be that.'

Hannah, in dismay, turned and stared into the distances beyond the kitchen walls: 'It's that all right. I'll take her, but I know.'

'Have you asked her anything?'

'Yes, I asked her if a man had touched her, and she wouldn't answer. And that's a funny thing in itself, for she always says right away, "No, Ma, when men speak to me I run away." And then again, twice last week she disappeared. I had Annie out looking for her for three hours on New Year's night, and she found her round by St Bede's Church. She had come across the salt grass, but she wouldn't say where she'd been . . . Oh, Christ . . . Christ Jesus!' Hannah burst out. 'What's going to happen? Joe will kill her. And if he finds out who it is there'll be murder done. Oh, Mary Ellen, what am I going to do?'

'Here, steady yourself, lass. Come on, get up and put your coat on and take her now.' She pulled Hannah to her feet. 'You'll catch him if you go now.'

While Hannah was putting on her coat, Mary Ellen went into the bedroom where Nancy was still laboriously dressing: 'Hurry up, hinny, your ma's waiting.'

Mary Ellen found she couldn't look at the girl . . . If she were going to have a bairn and had kept quiet about the man, then there was some part in her that was sensible, Mary Ellen reasoned. Unless, of course, she was too afraid to say anything. But now that she came to look at her, the lass looked less afraid than she had ever done.

She bustled Nancy into the kitchen: 'There you are then, lass,' – she was addressing herself to Hannah – 'get yourself off . . . And remember, whichever way it goes, don't worry. You can't help it; the blame can't be laid at your door, you've done your best.'

She watched them walking down the street, wide apart, like strangers, Nancy humped and shuffling, Hannah as stiff as a ramrod; and a sadness settled on Mary Ellen, the beginning of a long, long sadness.

John hurried out of the docks . . . Friday night and the first week of the new year over, and six boats discharging at the same time. He had just come from the weigh beam after paying off half the men. It was a strange sensation standing at the weigh beam with his pockets full of money and handing each man his due, and feeling that although he was young enough to be a son to three parts of the men they liked him, and trusted him to give them a square deal. As he left the last arch and passed the bottom of Simonside Bank he glanced through the darkness to the curving incline, and the thought that within the next hour he would be hurrying up there brought a leaping and tingling to his blood. The nights of the past week had been like glimpses of paradise – was there anyone in the world as beautiful and as sweet as her? Where was there a woman of her standing who would take him as he was? He had no notions about himself. Eight years in the docks had not filed him down, but roughened him. The only saving grace, he told himself, was that he was aware of it and would do his best to remedy it. He would have to if he were ever to feel worthy of her, even to the smallest degree. Moreover, another thing he would have to do was to find a better job. It was impossible for him to remain in the docks . . . even as a gaffer, for it would take more than a gaffer's wages to support her in the way to which she was used. Almost every night of the past week, after he had left her, his main thought had been that he must better himself; and he had worked it out that there was no chance for him in the North, nor yet in England . . . America . . . the Mecca of the Tyneside Irish loomed before him like a lodestar. If she would have him he would go there. Perhaps she would go with him right away . . . No; not for a moment would he consider that. When he had made enough money he would send for her. Not for one day of her life would she live differently because of him . . . And then there was his mother and Katie. If he went to America he'd be able to send them money too. For look at the wages you earned out there! And it wasn't all moonshine. The Hogans from High Jarrow were doing fine, he'd heard; the father and four lads all in regular work, and sending for the rest of them this year. And there was that young Stanley Tapp, who went out and had his lass follow him. So why shouldn't he, with his strength and fitness, make a go of it! There was no job he couldn't tackle. Yes, that's what he'd do. But he'd have to wait a while before he put it to her; he couldn't ask her anything yet; it was too soon. Had he been loving her for only a week? It seemed now as though it had been going on for years. And each time they met the knowledge grew stronger that she loved him with an intensity that almost matched his own. This coloured his life, and lifted him to the heights whereon he saw himself wrestling a mighty living out of the world and giving her, not only the things that she was used to, but such things to which even she had not aspired.

He was whistling as he walked up the backyard, but stopped before he entered the house; his mother wouldn't have whistling in the house, it was unlucky. She was standing by the table, and before her, on the mat, stood his father and Dominic with their bait tins still in their hands. Shane's lower lip was thrust out, and he was saying, 'The swine should be crucified!'

'What's up?' asked John, loosening his muffler.

'It's Nancy,' said Mary Ellen, looking down at her feet.

'Nancy? What's wrong with her?' John took off his coat and rolled up his sleeves before reaching for the kettle from the hob.

'She's going to have a bairn.'

John's hands stayed in mid-air. 'She's going to what!' His brows met over the exclamation.

'It's true. Hannah's had her to the doctor. She's nearly out of her mind.'

Turning slowly, John looked from his father to Dominic, and back to his mother again. Nancy Kelly going to have a bairn! It was utterly incredible. He thought of her face as it really was without the veil of his pity covering it . . . the loose, repulsive mouth, the beady eyes, and the pushed-in nose. How could any man touch her, unless he too 'wasn't all there'.

Mary Ellen was saying, 'And the funny thing is, she's gone . . . odder,' – she couldn't say 'brazen' to the men – 'I can't keep her out of the house.'

Although Mary Ellen was filled with pity for Hannah and the girl, she had found the day trying beyond description, for when Nancy wasn't standing leaning against the stanchion of her own front door, staring across the street towards the house, she was knocking at either the back or the front door. Mary Ellen felt she could not say anything to Hannah as yet, for Hannah was distraught, not only with her daughter going to have a child, but at the change in her. It was as if now, with life moving within her, some part of Nancy had become activated into normality . . . a crude and shocking normality to the women, for she seemed proud of her achievement and was determined to show it to her world. Subconsciously through the years, she must have taken in, with perhaps a feeling of envy, the arrogance of the pregnant women standing at their doors, their arms folded across the bulks of moving life. And she may have laughed unknowingly at their jokes as they patted the tiny flutterings of their aprons, saying with raw wit the old, threadworn joke, 'Lie down, yer father's not workin'!'

Whatever had happened, she was now . . . brazened, and Mary Ellen's pity was turning to irritation.

Dominic sat down by the fire – he hadn't spoken – and Shane and John still stood regarding Mary Ellen.

'This'll send the little bantam clean off his head.' It was Shane who spoke, and he was referring to Joe.

As Mary Ellen was about to make some reply, the back door opened and Nancy sidled in.

'Look, Nancy!' Mary Ellen exclaimed sharply; 'get yourself away home.'

But Nancy, who never to Mary Ellen's knowledge had disobeyed a command in her life, simply ignored her. Instead, she came well into the kitchen and stood looking from one to the other of the men. They all stared at her, Dominic out of the corner of his eye. And when Nancy met his gaze, she flung herself round from him, showing him her back, like a child in the huff, and amidst silence, she walked towards John, and smiled her grotesque smile as she placed her hand on his sleeve.

'John.'

Tears almost came into John's eyes as he looked at her: God, but it was awful! Yet above his pity there arose a feeling of revulsion against her. Some subtle change in her was making itself felt – she was no longer the child.

She said again, 'John,' and he was about to say something to her when his head was jerked up by the sound of choking.

It was Dominic; he had risen from his chair, his body quivering with waves of shut-in laughter. Mary Ellen and Shane were staring at him. He lumbered past them and threw himself on to the couch, where he sat leaning back, facing them, his face working with glee.

Staring wide-eyed and questioningly at her son's contorted face, Mary Ellen was wondering what in the name of God had come over him.

Suddenly Dominic could control himself no longer, and his laughter filled the house. Bellow rolled on top of bellow. But as he rocked himself back and forth his eyes never left John's, and the implication was lost on none of them. He waved a helpless hand, encompassing Nancy and John. And John's voice rose above Dominic's laughter, almost deafening them, as he cried, 'You bloody swine!'

'With one movement he flung Nancy aside and sprang for Dominic. At the same moment, Shane and Mary Ellen threw themselves on him. Dominic got up, his laughter gone now: 'Let him fight, the dirty bastard! Come on!' He tore off his coat and made for the back door.

John's rage sent Shane and Mary Ellen spinning away from him, and he was after Dominic; but as he crossed the step, Dominic's fist shot out and caught him full in the face: yet so little did it affect John in his rage, it could have been Katie's hand.

After the light of the kitchen, the backyard appeared black, and for a time they struck at each other blindly. But soon their fists met the other's body with quickening and sickening thuds.

'For God's sake, stop them!' Mary Ellen cried to Shane. She tried to push past him into the yard, but he barred her way, saying, 'Let them have it out.'

'No! No! He'll kill him. John'll kill him! For God's sake stop them!'

A small crowd was now gathering at the yard door, and the windows on the far side of the back lane were being thrown up – the cry had gone round, 'The O'Briens are at it.'

The one showing the least concern was Nancy; she stood against the kitchen table her arms folded on her stomach and a silly smile flicking her face.

The sight of her thus was too much for Mary Ellen. She darted back into the kitchen, and taking Nancy by the shoulders, pushed her through the front room and out into the street shouting, 'Go on! Go on, you young trollop, you! And don't darken these doors again!'

Back in the kitchen she tried once more to push past Shane, for blood was flowing freely now. it was running from John's mouth and from Dominic's eyebrow, and their shirts were wet with it.

Peggy Flaherty's voice came from the upstairs window, crying, 'Stop it! Stop it, you lads! Stop it, the pair of you. John, where's your sense gone? Do you want to break your mother's heart? Behave like a gentleman, can't you! Oh, if only Mr Flaherty was alive!'

Mary Ellen, through Shane's arm, could see the dark bulk of Peggy hanging half out of the window.

Peggy cried down to her: 'Mary Ellen, are you there? Will I throw some slops over them?'

Mary Ellen made no answer, for she was now staring at the lass from next door. Christine had come into the suffused light, paused for a moment near the battling figures, then walked right between them.

John's fist was travelling towards Dominic's body, and Mary Ellen closed her eyes tightly, for the girl's face, as she confronted John, was in line with it.

Only the sound of gasping breaths came to Mary Ellen. She opened her eyes slowly, and they were apart, with the girl standing untouched between them.

Christine lifted her hands and pushed John towards the kitchen door, where Mary Ellen pulled him over the threshold.

Then Christine turned to Dominic. He was leaning against the wash-house wall now, wiping his face with his shirt sleeve. He paused and looked at her, and said pointedly, 'This is one time I'm fighting in the right.'

'Fighting was never in the right.'

'No? Huh!' – he spat out some blood, then went on wiping his face – 'not even when your wonderful John gives Nancy Kelly a bairn?'

There was a rustle among the crowd about the yard door. The whispers linked, forming a wave; then broke again, as one person after another darted away into the blackness . . . John O'Brien had given Nancy Kelly a bairn!

When John at last arrived at their meeting place, Mary wasn't there, and his feelings became a mixture of sick disappointment and relief . . . relief because of the uncertainty of her reaction when she saw his face. She would, he knew, be full of sympathy, but would she think that he was indeed one of the 'Fighting O'Briens', fighting for fighting's sake? – he'd be unable to explain why he had fought. So he walked towards her house, keeping on the far side of the road, and when he came opposite the gate he stood well back in the shadow of a hedge, and waited, wondering what construction she had put on his non-appearance.

The house was lit up, and occasionally a shadow darkened the blinds, but the shadow could have belonged to anyone.

How long he stood there he did not know, but a clock somewhere in the distance, struck the hour, and he guessed it was nine o'clock. And as he was making up his mind to move away, the front door opened, and she was there, silhouetted against the light. But not alone; a man was with her, and from his thinness, John knew him to be Culbert.

John's nerves tensed as he watched them standing talking, and his teeth grated when he saw Culbert's hand take hers. But she remained still and Culbert moved away, and the door was closed.

After standing for a while longer, John walked slowly away. He was cold, and his eye was paining, and the whole of his face was stiff and sore. Now the import of Dominic's wild laughter rose to the fore of his mind again; and with it came a paralysing sense of fear. Fear was the least of John's emotions – he could not remember ever having known real fear; he had been scared, but being scared had no connection with this weakening feeling of fear. 'What if it got around, what Dominic had suggested? God! He couldn't stand it. Anyway, people wouldn't believe it. Him take Nancy Kelly! . . . But wouldn't they? The lot around the fifteen streets would accuse Jesus Christ himself of it, if they were in the mood to do so. At times, it would appear they were utterly devoid of reason or sense, the rumours they believed and passed on.

As he neared the corner of Fadden Street, the huddled darker blur standing out against the wall told him the men were there. it was usual for them to gather at the corner and crack, and it was their voices which generally proclaimed them. But tonight they were quiet. And as he passed them he knew a mounting of his fear, which almost reached the point of terror when he realised the rumour was already let loose.

A figure stepped from the group and walked for a few steps by his side, then stopped. John stopped too, and the two men peered at each other.

'I want a word with you,' said Joe Kelly.

John did not answer him, for the fear was drying his mouth. He waited, and Joe seemed to be waiting too.

Then Joe brought out thickly, 'What have you got to say?'

'What about?' John parried.

'Come off it, you know bloody fine!'

John made a desperate effort to bring reason and calmness to the fore: 'Look, Joe,' he appealed to the little man, whose face, even through the darkness, conveyed its trouble to him, 'do you, for a moment, think I would do such a thing? For God's sake, man, have some sense! Nancy's always made a set for me because I've been kind to her . . . What do you think I am? I mean no offence, Joe, but I'm not that hard up for a woman.'

'Then why did you take her up the country?'

'Take her up the country? Me?'

'Aye, you! And give her money . . . You might be big, John O'Brien, but I'm going to kick the guts out of you!'

Before Joe could spring to carry out his intention, John's hands gripped his shoulders and pinned him against the wall, while he kept his body bent out of reach of Joe's legs.

'Listen here, Joe Kelly: if there's any guts to be kicked out, I can do a bit of it myself. But before we start that, let's get this straight. The whole thing's a pack of damned lies from beginning to end. You bring me the one that saw me up the country with Nancy; and let's get Nancy herself and ask her.'

'That's the ticket,' said a voice from the group of men; 'give him a fair crack o' the whip. I told you you were up the pole to believe it. Now, if it had been the other big sod . . . '

Another voice was added to that of the first: 'Aye, Joe . . . Ask your lass, and get Bella Flabbygob to face him and tell him herself.'

Joe's writhing body was stilled. 'All right then,' he growled. 'If you've got the face, come and clear yourself.'

John, walking swiftly and tensely by Joe's side, said, 'I don't need to have any face, I've done nothing that I'm ashamed of.'

Thrusting open his back door, Joe cried to the startled Hannah, 'Get her up!'

After one bewildered glance towards John, Hannah went into the bedroom, and in a few minutes returned, pushing Nancy, half awake, before her.

Nancy had a coat about her shoulders, and her long, thick legs stuck out, like mottled props, below her short nightgown. Her feet were bare and not very clean, and the whole picture of her was revolting to John . . . That anyone should imagine he could touch a thing like this! The thought made him angry, and momentarily banished his fear. He confronted Nancy.

'Look, Nancy. Have I ever taken you up the country?'

Still only half awake, she blinked at him.

'Have I?' he persisted.

'No, John.'

John cast a quick glance at Joe.

'Now,' he went on, 'have I ever given you money?' She blinked again. She was a child once more; her new-found self was lost in bewilderment and sleep. 'Yes,' she answered simply.

Joe scraped his feet on the floor as John said, 'Listen carefully now. When did I give you the money?'

She thought a while, then said, 'Up Simonside.'

They all stood silent. Simonside was the country. It was the place for lovers and courting. Hannah drew in her breath, and Joe bit out, 'Want to know any more?'

'Yes. How much did I give you?' John bent towards Nancy.

'Threepence.'

'And what did I give it to you for?'

'For being a good girl.'

Joe snorted and John turned on him. 'I know the night I gave it to her. I met her crying under the arches. Annie had left her in the market and she hadn't her tram fare. She was afraid to stand outside the bar, and I put her on the tram, and,' – the face of Bella Bradley peering at him came back to John – 'Bella Bradley was on that tram. it was her who put this into your head.'

'I've no use for that 'un,' Joe said, indicating Bella with a lift of his eyes towards the ceiling, 'but she said she saw you coming down the Simonside bank with her.'

'How the hell could she,' burst out John, 'if she was in the tram and it black dark!'

Joe had no answer to this. He turned from John to Nancy, his look indicating his detestation. Then he flung a question at her that made Hannah cry out and John wince.

Nancy stared back at her father, unmoved by the question itself. She was wide awake now, and she wriggled and flung her head to the side with a new defiance. As Joe, all restraint gone, went to hit her, she screamed and jumped aside like a grotesque animal.

Hannah caught her husband's arm, crying, 'Leave her be, man!'

Then Joe, Hannah and John were struck speechless, for Nancy, standing in the corner, her coat lying at her feet, her long neck thrust forward, was yelling at Joe: 'Leave me alone . . . see, you! You hit me if you dare, see! I'm gonna have a bairn; I am, an' be married . . . Yes, I am. I'm gonna be married when the bairn's born I am.' She tugged her tight nightgown back and forward around her hips, then turned her face towards John: 'Aren't I, John?'

John stood gazing at her; he was dumb and sick. Had she remained the half-imbecile child he could have dealt with her, but this new Nancy, full of craft and cunning, filled him with horror. When she came boldly towards him, her hand outstretched, he yelled at her, 'Take your hands off me!' and like someone possessed, he rushed from the house and started to run, with Joe's voice bellowing after him, 'You won't get off with it like that!'

Chapter Ten

Mary Llewellyn

Her home had always appeared a place of warmth and comfort to Mary, but not up to now had she looked upon it as one of the tentacles of her mother's possessiveness. Mary knew that, in her gentle way, her mother clung like a leech and sucked at one's individuality; and one of her sucking tentacles was the creating of comfort . . . good food, warmth, even the seductive fire in one's bedroom.

After Mary's victory of claiming a room to herself the creature comforts were diminished for a time; if she wanted a fire in this room she had to light it. Yet after a while, Beatrice Llewellyn saw that by pandering to her daughter's ridiculous idea of privacy, a new tentacle could be affixed. But since New Year's Eve, much to Mary's discomfort, this tentacle had been released. No fire had been lit in the sitting room for a fortnight, let alone in the bedroom, and Mary's enquiry of Phyllis had been answered by, 'The mistress says there are fires in the drawing room and dining room, Miss Mary.'

For the first week of the new year it had not irked her, for her evenings were spent with John; and the fireless room was merely something that showed up her mother's pettiness. But for six days now she had seen John only once, and that under such circumstances, she would rather not have seen him at all. Added to this, the striking cold of her fireless rooms seemed to have brought her up against life with a vengeance.

Last night, after having gone fruitlessly to their meeting place, she wrote John a letter . . . a letter bare of pride. She had thrown pride over from the first night he failed to keep their appointment, for each dinner time since, she had taken a roundabout way home, walking slowly through the arches, hoping against hope to meet him. Then today she saw him; but unfortunately only after she had met her mother and father almost at the dock gates. After her father's kindly greeting and her mother's fixed stare, they were walking on abreast, past the gates themselves, when John came out. His abrupt stopping brought them all to a halt; but before she even had time to speak, he was gone, across the road and into the Jarrow tram.

It was only by using all her control that she did not follow him. In the brief moment of meeting she could see something was wrong. He was in trouble, and he had been fighting. His eye was discoloured, and there was a scar across his lip. But it was the look in his eyes that shocked her. They were not the brown, kindly eyes of her John, they looked haunted . . . even frightened.

It was disastrous that her mother should see him like this. Mary knew, by her mother's tilted chin and stiff profile, that she recognised him and was showing her disgust. And her father's repeated short coughs spoke, too, of his embarrassment.

Mary stood now in her bedroom, recalling the incident. There was another hour and a half before she would know if her letter had broken this estrangement for which she could find no cause. She pulled her fur coat tighter about her as she sat down by the window and looked out into the black garden. If he did not come tonight what would she do? Her life seemed barren and futile without him, and he had toppled her standards overboard. Up to a few months ago she was sure she knew what she wanted from life: culture, travel, and of course a lovely home. It was true she had never loved Gilbert Culbert, but it was his profession, she thought, had weighed her feelings against him; for she could not see herself going out to work when married, and thirty-seven shillings a week wasn't going to enable her to do the things she had planned, although she knew if she were to make this match there would be considerable help forthcoming from her mother. Yet, compared with John, Culbert was a man of means. But here she was, willing to forgo everything she valued for this man, who would hardly be able to feed her, as her father had so strongly pointed out, apart from supporting her in the smallest comfort.

She was helpless before the power of her feeling. No clear thinking would touch it. Nor did she want it to be touched, for she realised she had found something given to few, a love strong enough to defy convention. And not in the ordinary way; but to defy convention by living under its nose. For that's what it would mean if she, Mary Llewellyn, the boatbuilder's daughter, married John O'Brien, the docker.

'Miss Mary!'

Mary started. 'Yes?'

'Your mother says she wants . . . she would like to see you in the drawing room. '

'Very well.'

Mary turned from Phyllis, whose bright eyes were greedy for more scandal. Mary guessed her own doings were the high spot of conversation in the kitchen, and knew that, because she was associating with one whom they considered to be below their class, she was unworthy of their respect. It showed covertly in their manner, and she upbraided herself for being hurt by it. For this, she told herself as she went downstairs, was nothing to what she would have to put up with - she must get used to scorn, and the scorn of the poor was scorn indeed.

Her mother was sitting in her wing chair to one side of the large log fire, the heat of which met Mary as she entered the room.

Beatrice Llewellyn looked smaller and younger and more fragile at this moment than ever before.

'You wanted me?' Mary halted in the centre of the room.

'Yes.' Beatrice Llewellyn paused, adjusted the lace cover on the arm of her chair, then went on, 'I would just like to ask you, Mary, to conform to the rules of this house if it is your intention to stay in it.'

Mary remained silent; it was like the ultimatum to a lodger.

'You know your meals are served in the dining room! If you do not deign to have them there with us, then I'm afraid you'll have to eat out, for I'm not having them taken to your room.'

Anyone but Mary would have been deceived by her mother's tone into thinking that behind its evenness lay forbearance and toleration, but to Mary its studied calmness, in itself, was a danger signal.

'Is that all you wanted me for?' she asked.

'No, it is not all I wanted you for.' Beatrice Llewellyn lifted her eyes from the contemplation of the lace cover and looked straight at her daughter. 'You astound me, Mary. I cannot begin to understand you . . . '

'No?' Mary raised her eyebrows slightly and waited.

'I can't think that one, even with your liberal tastes, can have sunk so low as to continue to associate with a man who is the father of an imbecile girl's child!'

The words glanced off the surface of Mary's mind. She was prepared to hear something against John, she hadn't thought her mother would speak otherwise, and at this moment she was feeling sick with cold and worry; so until, like a boomerang, their meaning rebounded back at her she just continued to return her mother's stare. There was a cause then for the six empty nights and his avoidance of her at dinner time . . . there was a reason; someone was going to have a baby by him.

What! - Her mind jumped clear of its numbness - her John who was clean and loving and kind, whose love, so full of desire, was yet restrained, whose hands, even in their loving, were not the probing, groping hands of Gilbert . . . her John going to father a what!

She repeated aloud, 'What! What did you say?'

'You heard what I said.'

'And you expect me to believe you?'

'No,' – her mother's voice took on a note of resignation – 'No, all Tyneside could believe it, but not you. You are so obsessed by that . . . that man, that individual with the brutalised, battered face, whose licentiousness drives him to take a poor imbecile.'

'Be quiet! How dare you!'

'Don't speak to me like that, Mary!'

'I will! You sit there taking a man's character away . . . damning him . . . you, who know nothing . . . !'

'I take his character away! Can a man have any character who would touch that dreadful Kelly girl?'

'Kelly. You mean Nancy Kelly?'

'Yes, I mean Nancy Kelly.'

'You're mad! No man would . . . would go with that girl.'

'She's going to have a child, and you don't for a moment imagine it's an immaculate conception, do you?' Her mother was being unconsciously funny; if only the implications for John were not so terrible Mary would have laughed.

There was scorn in her mother's smile and maliciousness in her voice when she said, 'His exalted position of being a gaffer is in jeopardy too, I understand. For even certain dock men have standards of morals.'

The desire of her mother to hurt her was so palpably evident that Mary was stung to reply, 'Yes, for your sake, I should hope so, seeing that my father worked in the docks until he was twenty. You seem to forget that, don't you. I, in my way, am doing exactly what you did . . . taking up with a dock worker.'

Beatrice Llewellyn rose swiftly from her chair – she was no longer calm; Mary had touched a vulnerable spot, and she hated to be reminded that her prosperous husband had ever been other than what he was now. 'There's a coarseness in you, Mary, that disgusts me,' she said sibilantly. 'Your father was never a dock worker; he was apprenticed to a trade, as you well know.'

'What difference does it make?' Mary found she wanted to argue, to keep talking, so that she would not have to think.

But her mother ended the interview by leaving the room. She walked past Mary, her face tight and her blue eyes flashing with vexation, causing the air seemingly to vibrate with her displeasure. Mary did not move – she stood nervously tapping her lips with her fingers . . . Nancy Kelly was going to have a child . . . that dreadful-looking girl who was no more than a child herself. And they were saying John was responsible. So that was why he looked as he did. And that, too, was why he had been fighting. How had he come to be accused of such a thing?

The old saying: There's no smoke without fire, came to her. But she refuted it with her mind and body; and she swung round and rushed upstairs. Yet the thought persisted; why had he been named?

Mary reached their meeting place half an hour before the appointed time. In the darkness of the lane she waited, each moment dragging itself out into seeming hours, filled with dread and anxiety. Twice she heard footsteps on the main road, but they didn't turn into the lane.

When at last she heard the heavy tread of feet coming towards her, she pressed back into the hedge, fearing lest it was not him. But as the dark bulk drew to a halt, she whispered softly, 'John.'

No answer came to her, and she moved slowly forward, and again she said, 'John.'

In the centre of the lane, he stood out against the starlit night, and she could feel the tense unhappiness holding him down. She reached out her hands and again spoke his name. This time he answered her. His arms went about her, and she was lifted into his embrace and held tightly against him in an unhappy silence. He did not kiss her, but bent his head and buried it against her neck; and his mental anguish engulfed her.

'What is it, my dear?' She purposely asked the question, for she felt he must tell her himself, and in the telling perhaps the strain would ease.

But he said nothing. And so they stood, wrapped close in an embrace that was full of questioning and stress. Then, as if his words had journeyed through many doors before finding a way out and were now tremulous in their release, he asked, 'Mary . . . would you marry me if I had enough money?'

The proposal was so unexpected – it was the last thing she had thought of hearing at this moment. She had imagined he would give some reason for their separation, if not speak of this dreadful other thing. For perhaps a second she remained still. Then she gently took his head between her hands and raised it. His face was indistinguishable in the darkness, but so well did she know each feature that his expression seemed at this moment to be outlined in light.

'Oh, my dear, I'd marry you now, just as you are.'

The question of Nancy Kelly flashed like a falling star across her mind, only to disappear into nothingness; its dreadful import could not possibly touch this man.

'No, no. Never that.' John's arms fell from her, but she held his face tightly, saying, 'Why not, my darling? Why not?'

'Because,' – his head moved restlessly between her hands – 'I'll never take you while I'm in the docks.'

'But, my dear . . . '

'It's no use.'

He gently released his face from her hands, and held them tightly: 'I couldn't do it . . . Mary, I'm going away. Will you wait for me?'

'Where are you going?'

'America.'

'America! But John! Oh, my dear,' —she pulled him towards her – 'I can't let you go . . . not all that way, not without me . . . John, take me with you. Let's start together,' – she was pleading as if for her very life – 'if we are together nothing matters.' She had her arms about him now, and he stood still within their circle, steeling himself against her offer, which for the moment had lifted him out of the terrifying depths of despair and revulsion to life that had almost overwhelmed him during these past few days, and which during that one brief moment had erased the picture of Nancy Kelly from his mind, so that he could no longer see her waiting for him at the corner of the street, or watching the house from her door or front window. His whole life had been coloured darkly by her. He would see her face reflected in the expression of the dock men's covert glances and in the too friendly overtures of a section of the men, who wanted him to know they didn't believe the rumour. The house that, during the holidays took on a semblance of happiness, was now a place of dread, and his mother seemed to have become bent under the load of it. Time and again he had found her watching Nancy from behind the curtains as she, in her turn, watched the house . . . What would his mother do when he was gone?

He jerked his head as if to throw off this additional worry, and answered Mary, rejecting her offer, as he knew he must, but crying out internally at the necessity that drove him to it: 'No, it wouldn't work. I've got to go there and get a start, and make enough money to set up.'

The term set up and all that it implied lifted him back to a week ago, when there was no fear in his life, only the ecstatic feeling of loving her. He pulled her to him blindly and kissed her, and so was lost for a time, until she murmured, 'John . . . listen to me. Now don't get wild at what I'm going to say. But I've got a little money . . . only a little,' – she felt his withdrawal and clung on to him – 'Listen, darling, don't be foolish. It isn't much, for

I've never bothered to save. It's what my grandfather left me. There's two hundred pounds. We could . . .'

'Mary . . . do you love me enough to wait a year, perhaps two?'

It was as if she had never made her offer. She answered, 'Yes . . . for as long as you wish.'

'That's all right then.'

He kissed her again. Then said, 'I've been making enquiries; I'm going as soon as I can. I went up to see some people called Hogan in Jarrow last night. They've told me what to do.'

'Oh, John,' – the huskiness of her voice was deepened by the catch of tears – 'why . . . why all this rush?' And as she asked the question, Nancy Kelly came back into her mind. It was because of this he was going more than anything else. He was running away.

'John, what is it? What's worrying you? Tell me.'

He remained quiet, and she felt the stiffening of his body again. Then he put her thoughts into his own words: 'I'm running away . . . I've been accused of something, and I can't face it . . . Mary,' – the muscles of his arms hardened against her soft flesh – 'if you heard something bad about me would you believe it? I can't prove to you that I'm innocent, I can only tell you I am . . . It's about . . . I'm . . . ' He stopped and a shiver passed through his body. He could not bring himself to say, 'I'm accused of giving Nancy Kelly a bairn,' nor could he say, 'I'm as innocent as Christ himself, for I've never had a woman; nor will have until I have you, be it in two years or twenty.'

The cold dark bleakness of the night pressed down on them. They stood slightly apart, and Mary waited for him to go on and voice his misery. But he remained silent. The silence seemed to fill the lane and to widen the distance between them. At last she could bear it no longer, for now she was with him she knew without doubt that he was incapable of committing that of which he was accused, and she cried out, 'You would never do anything bad. Never! Oh, my dear, don't let this thing cause you to make hasty decisions. Don't let it drive you away. Stay and see it out.'

'You don't know what it is they are saying.'

'Yes, I do. I know all about it.'

The silence fell on them again, softly now, filled with reverence.

She knew all about it and she was here! He whispered, 'You know about Nancy Kelly?'

'Yes.'

The wonder of her love and faith coursed like a mountain stream through him, sweeping before it the fear and dread that had been intensified by the thought of her revulsion towards him should the rumour ever reach her. Her name burst from him on a broken laugh that could scarcely be identified from a sob.

She was in his arms, crushed tightly against him, and he was pouring words over her: 'Nothing matters now. I can face anything. I'll make money. We'll start a new life together . . . Oh, Mary, my love, I'm as innocent of what they say as . . . as Katie is. I've always been sorry for the girl. I used to mind her when she was a bairn, and she would come to me when she was frightened . . . She's changed; she's different now. But somehow, I think she's still frightened, and that's why she's made a dead set for me. And it's made them think . . . But what does it matter now? Nothing matters, only you. We'll start life in a new land; and you'll teach me, as you were going to, and make a new man of me.'

She tightened her arms about him . . . She teach him! What could she teach him but the superficialities, whereas he could teach her all there was to know of life.

Chapter Eleven

Ask and Ye Shall Receive

THE FEBRUARY STORM had raged for three days, during which hail, snow and rain was driven against the houses with such force as to almost penetrate the walls. It succeeded through many windows, and some of the people found it as dangerous to stay indoors as to go out and risk the flying slates and toppling chimney pots. But today the storm was lashing itself out. The streets were dry and the sun shone fitfully through the racing clouds.

It shone now on Nancy standing in her doorway. It showed her up vividly to Mary Ellen as she watched from behind her curtains. For the past three days Mary Ellen had seen Nancy only dimly, and appearing more grotesque than ever through the two rain-streaked windows. But now, there she was, as vivid as the picture that was seared on Mary Ellen's mind.

The girl, Mary Ellen knew, was possessed of a devil. This was the only way to account for her laying the blame of the bairn on John without actually saying so, and for her turning on Hannah and standing up to Joe. Mary Ellen knew that she, too, had become possessed of a devil. It entered into her the night Dominic and John fought, and when John stayed out all night, wandering the streets, after Joe Kelly had followed him into the house, demanding to know what he was going to do about supporting Nancy. The devil had frightened Mary Ellen, for he urged her to do Nancy a physical injury, and she prayed constantly to be relieved of all temptation. But from the night her lad told her he was going to America, she prayed no more, and the devil took full possession of her. She watched Nancy at every available moment, and there were times when she actually lifted the sneck of the front door with the intention of making a dash at the girl and tearing her limb from limb.

Nancy stood now scratching her head. She was doing it systematically, working over first one section then another; and Mary Ellen wondered for the countless time how anyone in their right senses could imagine her lad touching that thing . . . But they not only imagined it, they voiced it. Since Bella Bradley had set the ball rolling, at least half the fifteen streets would swear to having seen John with Nancy Kelly in some questionable place.

She could have borne it all, Mary Ellen thought, if only it wasn't driving her lad away. What would she do without him? The day he left the house, it would be as if she were laying him in his coffin, for she would never see him again. It was all right him saying he would send her money . . . he'd want all his money if he was going to marry that lass. And anyway, she didn't want money, she only wanted him. What would life be like when, cooking, washing and mending, she wasn't doing it for him?

She moved from the window and leaned against the wall, and pressed her nose tightly between finger and thumb, meanwhile taking great gulps of air – she mustn't start crying now, it was close on twelve o'clock, and John and Shane would be in soon, it being Saturday. Dominic was already in, sitting over the fire, picking his toes.

In spite of her efforts, tears started to flow. Unless Dominic got that job in Liverpool she'd be left with him and his beastly ways. John never sat over the fire, picking his toes . . . he washed his feet in the scullery. But not Dominic; he'd sit picking at the hard skin on the soles of his feet, or lifting the dirt from his toenails with his fingernails. There was nothing so ugly, Mary Ellen thought, as feet and none so repulsive as Dominic's, big and broad and well-shaped as they were. She knew, with an overpowering certainty, that once John was gone and she was left to suffer Dominic, the devil would have his way. And there would be no door standing between her and Dominic, as there was between her and Nancy, acting as a deterrent to her uplifted hand. And the devil alone knew what she would have in her uplifted hand. Oh, if only her lad wasn't going to that America. Oh, God, if only something would happen to prevent him! She groaned and rocked her body . . . Ask and Ye Shall Receive. Yes, but there were so many things she had asked of God, and had she ever received them? Perhaps she hadn't asked properly. Or she may not have wanted them as she wanted this one thing. If there was only somewhere she could be alone and kneel down, she'd pray to Him and ask Him. But the minutes alone were few and far between, especially at the weekend . . . But she was alone now. She moved swiftly to the room door and closed it. Self-consciously she knelt down close by it so that she wouldn't be taken unawares if Dominic made to enter, and should anyone happen to glance in the window through the narrow aperture of the curtains it would look as if she were scrubbing.

Almighty God, she began, Almighty Lord of Heaven and earth, grant me this one prayer and I swear unto You that never until the day I die will I miss Mass. Almighty and powerful God, grant me this plea . . . She did not at once voice the plea, even mentally, but searched about in her mind for other words to denote power with which to adorn the name of God. But she could think only of Great and Almighty. She discarded the set prayers – she wanted something more powerful with which to contact Him. So she began again . . . Great and Almighty God,

Ruler of our lives, You who can do all things, do this for me I beseech Thee . . . don't let my lad go to America. Make something happen to stop him. Only You can do this, Almighty God . . . only You.

Her joined hands were pressed tightly between her breasts and her chin above them quivered with emotion. As she rose trembling from her knees, Katie's voice called from the scullery, 'Ma! Ma, I want you.'

Mary Ellen smoothed down her hair and rubbed her face over with a corner of her apron before going into the kitchen. She knew Katie must have seen Dominic and would not pass him, fearing lest his fingers were pushed beneath her nose.

Katie was standing in the scullery, trying to tidy her windblown hair before replacing her hat.

'What is it, hinny?' Mary Ellen asked heavily.

Katie whispered, 'Sh!' and pointed towards the kitchen. She pulled the door to, before going on in hushed tones, 'I just wanted to tell you I'm going to the slipway with Christine.'

'The slipway?' said Mary Ellen. And Katie again cautioned her. 'Sh! Ma.'

'What are you going to do there?' asked Mary Ellen softly.

'The boat's there . . . Mr Bracken had it fetched from the quay this morning on a cart. It's all painted up. David did it all himself. Oh, it looks lovely, Ma.'

'It's too windy, hinny, you'll get blown off the wall.'

'I won't go on the wall, Ma. The boat won't be on the wall,' – Katie chuckled at her mother's ignorance – 'it'll be in the water!'

After a pause during which Mary Ellen adjusted Katie's hat, she asked, 'Who'll be there?'

'Only Christine and David.'

'Not Mr Bracken?'

'No.'

'Then you'd better not go, hinny. There should be no messing around with boats unless a man's knocking about.'

'But Christine knows all about boats . . . she can row! But anyway, Ma, it's tied up, and Christine's not going out in it, she says it's too windy. She says, maybe the morrow if the wind goes down we'll have a sail . . . there's a sail in it too, Ma!' She looked up at her mother with a mischievous smile. 'We'll take you out for a sail, Ma . . . right to where the big ships are. And the boat'll rock, and you'll be sick.'

The picture of her mother being seasick tickled Katie, and she leaned against her, and put her arms round her mother's ample waist, and shook with laughter as she moved her from side to side, imitating the rocking of a boat.

'Stop it, hinny!' Mary Ellen felt far from laughter, but she smiled at this canny bairn of hers, and she had the desire to fondle her. She took off Katie's hat again and reached for the broken comb lying on the scullery window sill, and began to comb the top of her plaits.

Katie made a protest, 'Ma, Christine's waiting!' But she still leaned against her mother, and the pressure of her arms tightened about her.

When Mary Ellen replaced the hat she patted Katie's cheek. Then, awkwardly, she stooped and kissed her. Katie's arms came up swiftly about her neck, and she returned the kiss with an ardour that seemed strange in one so young. Kissing was an uncommon ritual in the house, and Mary Ellen said, 'There, there. Now off you go.'

But although she told Katie to go, she still held on to her, buttoning her coat, lifting her plaits from off her shoulders, and yet again straightening her hat. When at last she closed the door after Katie, she stood for a time thinking of her, and the thoughts brought her a modicum of comfort . . . she'd always have Katie. For years and years yet she'd have Katie, and they'd cleave together even more so when John was gone . . . That was another thing . . . Katie had to be told that John was going. What would her reactions be, for John was to her as a god?

A new fear entered into Mary Ellen . . . Would it create an aim in Katie's life, and that aim to be to go to America to join John? She shook herself. This was going too far . . . this is what came of thinking . . . Let God's will be done.

She steeled herself to go into the kitchen and to the oven where a hotpot was cooking, for Dominic would be still on with his poking – she knew he prolonged it merely to tantalise her. But when she entered the kitchen he wasn't there; and further to her surprise, he came out of the bedroom, pulling on his old mackintosh. He had changed his trousers and was wearing his good boots. And he passed her without a word and went out, slamming the door after him.

Where was he off to in such a hurry? Surely he couldn't have heard what Katie said. If he did hear, he was off now to corner the lass at the slipway. it was quiet there, and nobody to stop him . . . only Katie. Well, Katie was as good as any.

Dominic's chase of Christine had aroused little interest in Mary Ellen of late. Under other circumstances the fact that Peter Bracken had forbidden him the house would perhaps have aroused in her a feeling of shame that a son of hers should have acted in a way to merit such treatment. At times, she did wonder at Dominic's persistence, and wondered too what it was about the lass that made him half demented for her. These past few weeks he had been drinking more than he had done since the Brackens came to live next door; not getting blind drunk, but just enough to arouse his temper and make him more detestable still. He was close on that stage now, having spent the best part of the morning in the bars.

Shane came in, and to her surprise spoke first.

'Lashing itself out,' he said gruffly.

It was some time before she answered, 'Yes, and about time too.' There was a change in Shane that bewildered her; he had almost dropped the drink, and he sat with her at nights instead of going to the corner. It began, she felt, when she was ill . . .

or was it when John was made the gaffer? She knew that in his own way Shane was proud of that. And the change was more evident still since this trouble of John's. She felt dimly that he was trying to comfort her for what she was suffering on account of the lad, and dimly also, she felt a bigness in him for doing this, for it was John who had the affection that should have been his.

'Will you have it now or wait for John?' she asked, indicating the dinner.

'I'll wait.'

It was strange that she should ask him this and that he should comply. Not long ago he would have bellowed, 'Who the hell's boss, him or me?'

When John came in she did not glance towards him, for she knew how he would look – his face would be straight and lean; the flesh had dropped from the bones these past weeks; the brown of his eyes would be darker, and in their depths would be a look she could not bear to see.

Mary Ellen's heart lifted towards Shane when, seated at the table, he said to John. 'We got her out in time all right, didn't we?' He was referring to the unloading, and her emotion almost choked Mary Ellen as she realised that her husband was trying to get on a friendly footing with his son; for never before could she remember him speaking in such a way, not only acknowledging John as an equal, but as his superior . . . it was how a man spoke to his gaffer; it was also how a father tried to convey his faith in his son.

John looked hard at Shane, then said quietly, 'You did that.'

They ate on in silence, and Mary Ellen went into the scullery to try to suppress the choking in her throat. As she stood, her hands pressed tightly against her neck, Molly's voice came screaming from the back lane. 'Ma! Oh, Ma! . . . Ma!'

What could she do with that lass? Would she never grow up?

'Ma! Ma!' Molly's voice came nearer.

Was she mad, screaming like that! By, she'd box her lugs for her when she got her inside.

Molly's cries effectively suppressed Mary Ellen's emotion, and she pulled open the back door with an angry jerk . . . She'd give it to her; she'd swipe the hunger off her!

'Ma! Oh, Ma!' Molly tore up the backyard and flung herself on her mother, ignoring the upraised hand: 'Ma! It's Katie . . . Katie and Christine.'

She stopped and gasped for breath as Mary Ellen gripped her shoulders.

'What's happened?' Mary Ellen asked with strange quietness; then called over her shoulder, 'John!'

As John reached the door Molly was gasping out, 'They're in the boat; they haven't any oars . . . It's going round and round down the gut. It was our Dominic; he tried to get in the boat with Christine, and she pushed him back and Katie loosened the rope . . . I was behind the railings watching. Katie wouldn't let me go with her, but I sneaked down, and I saw our Dominic come. Oh, Ma! And David's screaming in the slipway.'

John was running down the yard with Shane on his heels, calling, 'Make straight for the slacks; don't go down the slipway, it'll be in the main gut by now.'

Mary Ellen, with Molly at her side, followed them, whispering as she ran, 'What is this now? What has come upon us now?'

On the main road, passers-by stopped and gaped at the two great men in shirt sleeves tearing along as if the devil was after them, the old man behind the young one, and the little woman and the lass behind the old man.

Someone called, 'What's up? Is it a fire?' But the running men took no heed, and one after another, the passers-by appealed to the woman and girl. And sometimes the girl answered, 'It's me sister . . . she's in a boat an' being carried down the gut.'

Children tacked themselves on to Mary Ellen and Molly, and

men turned in their tracks to run back down the road towards the slacks.

When John came to the open space of the slacks his heart almost stopped. Without looking towards the gut he knew the boat was there, for the bank was lined with people. At this end of the slacks was the double tram line, where one tramcar had to wait for the other to pass. They were both standing empty, and their drivers were calling to the people, 'We'll have to go'; but none of the passengers attempted to leave the bank.

As John ran down the pavement towards the middle of the slacks where the gangway of timbers led from the bank to the edge of the mud, he had to push his way through the people now pouring out from the streets known as the New Buildings that faced a part of the slacks. He thrust at them with his arms, knocking them aside and calling forth hot exclamations. Those standing on the gangway jumped clear of him, and he took the timbers four at a time. The noise from the bank died down and there was only the wind, on which was borne thin wails, and the squelch of the water between the timbers beneath his pounding feet. Automatically he paused at the cabin, which was mounted on a platform of lashed timbers in the centre of the great square, and grabbed up a long pole with a hook on its end that the timber man used for pulling the timbers together. Now the race was to reach the end of the timbers bordering the gut before the boat came abreast of him. He could see it was being held stationary at the moment; but by what he couldn't tell. If it was stuck on the other side of the gut on the great mud flat that extended to the river then it was almost a certainty that it would be sucked into this oozing morass.

Arrived at the end of the roped timbers, he had to take to the narrow planks that formed a precarious gangway to the gut. Here, he couldn't run, but had to pick his way over the green slimy wood. The pole impeded him still further; and once he slipped and the water swirled about his thighs before he could pull himself up again. He had managed to retain his grip on the pole; and as he regained his footing a great 'Oh!' came to him from the bank. The sight of the boat speeding towards him lent wings of sureness to his feet, and within a matter of seconds he reached the gut.

Clinging to the great post that was the last support of the foot timbers he shouted madly to the approaching boat, 'Grab the pole!' But the wind tore at his voice, carrying his words away from him and them.

The boat was now making swift circles; one second, he would see Katie's face over the gunwale, her eyes staring in terror, the next he would be looking at the back of her head, her hat still on it. Christine was sitting in the middle of the boat, her arms stretched taut, her hands gripping the sides in a pitifully vain endeavour to steady the tiny craft. She had seen John, for each time she fronted him her eyes held his for the second before they were torn away again.

It was not the wind that was driving the boat down the gut so much as the tide which was in full ebb; the locked waters between the floats of timbers were rushing madly back into the gut to meet the water draining from the mud flat beyond. Added to this, the suction of the cross channel, bordering the sawmill on the far side of the slacks, made the main gut a frothing, boiling mass of water.

As the boat came abreast of him, John bellowed, to the very limit of his lungs, 'Catch the hook, Christine!'

Perhaps she heard him and was afraid to loosen her grip on the sides of the boat, or perhaps his voice became only part of the wind, for when he cast the crooked end of the pole towards the boat it fell close to it, and anyone on the alert could have grabbed it; but the fraction of time during which this could have happened was lost. The boat gave another mad turn and was away, past him. He saw Katie stand up. She seemed to stand perfectly straight and still, and he experienced the odd sensation that her face was floating to him . . . imagination! But it was not imagination when he heard her voice coming to him against the wind . . . 'John! Oh, John!'

The boat was now flung into the vortex of water where the channels of the gut crossed. It heaved and whirled. Then like a ball, held by some mighty hand, it became still, and John saw clearly the two figures, their arms wound tightly about each other, crouched together; the hand was lifted, and the boat like a ball, was thrown up and over.

As John raised his arms to dive, two hands clawed at him and grabbed his belt. He half turned, screaming at the man behind him, but in wrenching himself free he overbalanced and toppled into the water. When his head broke the surface Peter Bracken grabbed his hair, and Peter's agonised voice screamed at him, 'It's no use! It's no use! They've gone. Don't make another.'

Two more hands stretched out and, gripping John's braces, they hauled him on to the plank again, where he lay still with Peter Bracken bending over him. A great stillness was pressing down on him. It was the stillness of the dead of all time. In it there was no regret, no pondering, no desire, no recrimination, no feeling whatever; it was void, because it held no thought.

He looked towards the upturned boat; he watched Katie's hat, mounted on a crest of frothing bubbles, rise and fall, bobbing round and round the swirling boat, like the earth round the sun. Peter Bracken's tearing sobs came to him, and he did not wonder at them. Nor, when he turned towards him was he surprised to see a very old man. Time passed and the receding tide showed the shining mud about the planks on which they stood.

Men were walking cautiously along the planks now. First, Peter Bracken was helped back, and when the men said, 'Come, lad,' John allowed himself to be led back to the timbers, one going before him and one behind, steadying him as though he were a child.

The timbers were thick with men, soundless men. John walked alone now, and they made a path for him. Closing in again after him, they followed him to the bank, where the sobbing and wailing rose and fell like the waves of the wind.

Three people were standing apart at the foot of the bank, and when John stopped and looked at them, the stillness began to lift from him. The first impression to penetrate it was that his father had his tick back worse than ever. This was followed by the painful realisation that his mother was a little old woman, and her not yet fifty, and that Molly would never be Katie. They looked at him, and the sobbing on the bank seemed hushed.

Then from the middle of a group of women, David's voice rose, crying, 'Christine! I want Christine!' and the stillness was lifted completely from John; and a name passed through his brain like a tearing flame . . . Dominic!

He threw up his head as if sniffing a scent, and his eyes swept the crowded bank from one end to the other. But from where he was standing below it, it was impossible to seek out anyone from the broken front line of the crowd.

A path was miraculously cleared for him when, turning suddenly from the agonised stare of his parents, he rushed up the gangway. Across the main road was a rise of grassy ground bordering the New Buildings. He made straight for it. Now he was looking down on the congested road, and there in the far distance, on the very outskirts of the crowd, he saw Dominic's head. It was hatless, and the fitful sunshine was turning the hair to gold. Whether Dominic had seen him John did not know, but as he tore along the comparatively clear ground Dominic's head disappeared; and when John reached the spot, Dominic was gone.

To a woman of the fifteen streets, John said only one word, 'Dominic?' and she pointed to the disused workmen's hall: 'He went round by the back of there, lad.'

When he reached the back of the hall John caught sight of

Dominic . . . he was running across the middle of the field used by the chemical works as a dumping ground for their foul-smelling residue. The field was a mass of small mounds, and Dominic was leaping like a kangaroo over them.

As John raced over the field the distance between them lessened appreciably, and when he came out on to the Cleveland Place road, there was Dominic, not twenty yards ahead, disappearing round the corner of the tram sheds.

They were both on the main road now, and the people struggling back to the fifteen streets called to John, 'Stop lad!' 'Give up, lad! . . . ' 'What's done's done . . . think of your mother.' And when men's arms went out and tried to hold him he brushed them off like flies.

As they neared the fifteen streets Dominic was lost in the dense crowd awaiting news from those who had been down to the slacks. But John knew that Dominic would make for the stack-yard at the top of the streets; here, in the maze of stacked timber he would hope to escape. He was right; he saw Dominic mount the wall and disappear.

John did not jump the wall, but stood on its top – his desire was teaching him cunning. He could not tell which way Dominic had taken, and once on the ground it would be like searching for a needle in a haystack; but from up here he should see Dominic's head as he moved between the stacks.

It was some minutes before John detected it, for Dominic's hair was in tone with the seasoning wood. Dominic had paused to glance behind, and John was off the wall, running swiftly and noiselessly, not in Dominic's direction but to the right of him. Dominic was making for the railway line at the end of the yard and he'd get him there.

John reached the end of the stacks and waited, his eyes darting back and forth to the last three openings – it would be from one of these that Dominic would emerge. He came out of the middle one, running swiftly; and pulled up a few yards from John. His mouth was open and his jaw was moving from side to side. The brothers surveyed each other, John's eyes sending out streams of diabolical hate, while in Dominic's the hate was mixed with fear.

John did not say, 'You killed them . . . Katie and Christine, and now I'm going to kill you,' nor did Dominic say, 'It was an accident'; without any word they closed, and John, like a raving bull, smashed his fists into Dominic's face. From the start, Dominic was handicapped by his raincoat, but fear made him hit back desperately. It also made him aware that he could not stand up to the blows being levelled at him; so he used his knee. Bringing it up sharply, he rammed it into the lower part of John's stomach, and as John bent double Dominic ran back down the opening through which he had come, only to be brought to a stop by the cries of men coming through the jumbled stacks. Assuming that the men were after him, he decided to carry out his first intention of taking to the railway. But when he turned once more there was John, at the opening of the stacks.

Blindly, Dominic rushed at him, using his fists and his feet; but it was as if John had set up a guard of flaying hammers, and soon all Dominic could do was to protect his face with his crossed forearms. He was pinned against a stack, and long after he ceased to fight John's fists pounded him, and he seemed to be kept on his feet only by the succession of lifting blows. At last, Dominic's knees gave way and he slid on to his side. John stood above him, gasping; then, using his foot, he pushed Dominic on to his back, and only then did he become aware of the crowd gathered about them.

Exclamations came from all sides. 'My God!' 'Leave him be, lad; he's had enough.' 'God Almighty, I think he's done for him!'

On hearing the last remark, John wiped the blood from his face with a sweep of his hand, and stared down on Dominic . . . Was he dead? No, he mustn't be dead . . . Not this way, this easy way. He was going to die in the gut. He would drag him there, to the spot where they went down, where Katie's straw hat went round and round. The tide would be low, so he'd throw him down the steep incline of mud. He would be conscious and would claw at the mud as it slowly sucked him in. But – he looked up from Dominic and stared glassily at the faces of the men – they would stop him. Yes, if he attempted to do it now. Well, he would beat them; he would take this thing home. He moved Dominic again with his foot . . . He wouldn't let him out of his sight, and in the night he'd get him to the gut. If he had to drag him every inch of the way he'd get him to the gut.

The exclamations came to him again, more shrill now, for the women had joined the men, after forcing open the stack-yard gates.

'Oh, Jesus, have mercy on us! He's killed him. God Almighty, it'll be a hanging job!'

It'll be a hanging job! . . . The cry reached Mary Ellen, standing on the outskirts of the crowd, surrounded by a group of women, all with tear-stained faces, and all urging her, in one way or another, to return home . . . 'You can do no good, Mary Ellen.'

'You must think of yourself and Shane.'

'Yes, Shane's lying back there bad, the shock's been too much for him . . . Come on lass.'

Mary Ellen stood quiet in the centre of them. She wasn't crying, there was no liquid left in her body to form tears. Her body was dry, it had been burnt up, and the flame was now going to her head . . . If these women didn't get out of her way, she'd scream. She must get to her lad. He had killed Dominic, so she must be with him. To her, this seemed to be the end of a long waiting – Katie was gone; Dominic was dead; and there was only John . . . He had done what he said he would do – John always meant what he said. Now there was nothing else to wait for.

Mary Ellen knew that the agony within her was screaming to be set free. The agony was wide and deep, reaching into the bowels of the earth. In an odd way, she felt herself one with the earth . . . the dirt, the mire, and the richness. The scream of agony was tearing around in the dry emptiness of her body, and swiftly, in a spiral, it was mounting to her head. Once it was there, she would be free, for when it escaped from her lips she would feel no more . . . at least, not with any feeling she would recognise; once she screamed, she would be changed for all time, for madness would possess her.

As her mind ran to meet the scream, she heard it. It seemed to lift her and the women from the very ground. But it wasn't her scream; it was Nancy Kelly's. And it was mixed with laughter . . . the terrible laughter. The women covered their ears, but Mary Ellen stood listening. Then she thrust wildly at the bodies hemming her in, and forced her way through the men to the space where John stood, and Dominic lay with Nancy Kelly kneeling by him, pulling at his torn and bloodstained clothes, and crying, 'Dominic! Dominic! Don't be dead! I've kept me mouth shut, Dominic . . . I did what you told me.' She pulled at him, trying to shake life into him again. 'Dominic, you must marry me when the bairn's born . . . I've been a good girl, Dominic, I did what you told me.'

Nothing but her screeching voice could be heard; the crowd was as silent as the stacked piles of wood.

The blood pounded into John's head. Dominic, the father of the bairn! The swine! The goddamn, dirty swine! Reaching down, he grabbed Nancy and flung her to one side. Then he was on top of Dominic, crying out as he beat his fists into the inert, blood-covered face, 'You dirty swine! And you put the blame on . . . '

His words were lost as the men tore him aside. Fighting, they bore him to the ground, and so many held him that only his eyes were free to move.

As one of the men shouted to the others, 'Look slippy there! Get him away, can't yer!' John heaved in an effort to free himself . . . If they got Dominic away they'd hide him. Why didn't he finish him off when he had the chance! He writhed and struggled until the uselessness of his efforts was borne upon him, and he suddenly became still. Well, wherever they took Dominic he'd find him! Oh, Katie! Katie! – he closed his eyes to shut out the men's faces as sorrow overwhelmed him.

When the men released him and he got to his feet, he saw his mother. She was picking at a button of her blouse, her eyes, dead in her white face, staring at him.

When he said, 'I'll find him,' she remained silent; then she turned and walked slowly away, and he followed her; and the crowd closed in behind, like a gigantic funeral.

Chapter Twelve

The Aftermath

There was no door in the fifteen streets that was closed to John; for three days he had walked in and out of the houses, into bedrooms, some tidy in their bareness, some a mass of jumbled old clothing and mattresses, and some indescribable in their squalor. He saw nothing of the conditions, he looked only for a concealed form; under beds, in cupboards, in rooms where the sick were lying, and where weary hands would reach out in a vain effort to give him comfort. He spoke to no-one, and he trusted no-one; he knew that in this time of trouble the people of the fifteen streets were united in one huge family to protect him, as they thought, from himself. So he did not search systematically, but after searching the houses at the lower end, he would suddenly double back to the top or middle streets, and houses he had searched but a short time before would be gone over again. No harsh word met him; even if he stalked in on a family eating he would be greeted soothingly.

He had one assistant in his search: Peggy Flaherty. Her fat, wobbling body hugged by coats, she would accompany him at odd hours of the day, most of the time talking away at him: 'Never give up, John. We'll get him yet. By God! We will an' all . . . He needn't run off with the idea he can escape you, can he lad? And he'll not get out of these buildings.'

Often, in his darting from one place to another, he would leave her behind; but she would be guided to the house where he was. And again she would tag along after him, nodding knowingly to the groups of people gathered in the street. Only at night did she leave him alone for any length of time, for then he paraded the main road.

John knew that Dominic would be in no fit condition for days and that it was practically impossible for him, up to now, to have made his escape by the stack-yard, for since the breakthrough, the gates were doubly locked, and there remained only the wall as a means of exit that way. So for two nights now he had watched from the main road. The night policeman, on his beat, would stop and talk to him, the darkness wiping away his officialdom: 'Is it worth it, lad? You know what will happen, don't you? You'll get time, if not the other. Anyway, how do you know he's not already gone? By what I hear, he's likely in hospital. If it hadn't been for your sister saying the little lass loosened the boat, we should have been on to him ourselves. And you can count yourself lucky, you know, one of us wasn't on the scene when you got at him. So don't look for trouble, lad, and get yourself home to bed.'

No words had penetrated John's mind since those spoken by the men when they were holding him; and it might have been that he did not hear this advice, for he made no reply. It was as though his mind, so packed with the weight of his sorrow and hate, could take in nothing more. During the first two days he did not actively think of Katie and Christine, nor yet of Mary, whom he felt to be part of his sorrow for all time, for she, in some strange way, was a partner in the guilt he was laying on himself. Because he had allowed the madness of his love to possess him, he ignored the danger in which Christine stood, and did nothing to protect her beyond ordering Katie to act as a buffer to Dominic's advances.

On this, the third day of the search, when the strain was telling on him, in the leaden weight of his limbs and his unsteady walk, and in his burning eyes that would close whenever he stood still for a moment, his mind, strangely enough, was beginning to sort itself out; thoughts were separating and presenting themselves, as it were, before him. He was standing leaning against the wall on the waste ground at the top of one of the streets, where he had paused for a moment during his search; and his hand moved over the three days' growth on his face. His body felt dirty, his inside empty, and his head light. But the thoughts came, one after the other, isolated yet joined: I must stop sometime . . . if only they find them before they're carried out to sea; if I could see Katie once again it might not be so bad. Oh! Katie! Katie . . . My father's done for, he'll not work again. Why am I not with my mother, she needs me! But she understands I've got to find him. She wants me to find him; she hates him as much as I do . . . Why doesn't Peter Bracken look for him instead of yapping, 'Forgive us our trespasses'. Father O'Malley says Peter is the cause of all this, and if my mother and me had done as he commanded this would never have happened.

As if his thoughts had conjured up the priest, Father O'Malley, accompanied by Peggy Flaherty, appeared before him.

'Oh, there you are, lad,' Peggy said. 'And here he is himself, Father . . . Away with you now!' she added to the children who were following them.

Father O'Malley confronted John: 'Come into the house,' he ordered. 'I want to talk you.'

John blinked slowly and made no reply.

'Did you hear me?' demanded the priest.

And after a short silence, during which Father O'Malley waited, and the children sniffed, and a few women added themselves to the group at a respectful distance, the priest went on, 'This has got to stop! Who are you to take God's work into your own hands? He will seek vengeance without your help. He has already shown you what He thinks of you going against His Holy Will – I cannot repeat too often, that had you kept that man Bracken from your house this state of affairs would never have come about.'

'It's hopeless,' Peggy Flaherty broke in. 'Time and again I've told him to give up the search. Oh! It's no use at all.' She proceeded to rattle on, in spite of the priest's gimlet eyes demanding her silence and John's blurred and bewildered stare as slowly the fact forced its way into his mind that she, and she alone, had urged him in his search.

There were murmurs from the women: 'The priest's right. There's been no luck about the doors since that Bracken man came.'

'No! Nor will there be!' Father O'Malley threw at them, effectually drowning the more considerate comment: 'Aye, but he's lost his lass too.'

'Come!' Father O'Malley commanded John.

John stood for a while longer . . . the priest and Peggy, and the women, were becoming blurred: he must rest and have something to eat if he intended going on. And so, in the eyes of the women and children, strength was added to the priest's power when John turned and obediently followed him . . .

In contrast to John's ceaseless moving Mary Ellen sat almost immobile in the kitchen. At odd times she would go to the front room and attend to Shane; but she cooked nothing, nor cleaned, and, like John, she did not speak. And if at times she stared at Molly, her face did not show any surprise or wonderment at the change in this daughter of hers; for Molly was 'running the house'. She had screwed her plaits into a tight little bun at the back of her head and she wore her mother's holland apron, rolled up at the band. Overnight, Molly threw off her prolonged childhood; she was not now a girl, but a little woman. And she was spurred on by the praise of the neighbours: 'That's it, hinny, you be your mother's right hand. You must take Katie's place now.' They talked as though Katie had been an elder sister.

Sometimes Molly would stand in the scullery and cry for Katie, while at the same time experiencing a feeling of relief that Katie was gone; for she would never have been needed had Katie still been here; and she was needed – they couldn't do without her. Why, she told herself, she was the only one in the house who hadn't lost her mind . . . except Mick; and he was no help, one way or the other. All he could do was to stand among awestruck groups of lads, bragging that he knew where Dominic was hiding . . . He didn't! She tucked her apron more firmly about her as she thought that, of all the youngsters, she was the only one who really knew – Dominic was taken into a house at the top of the street when they carried him from the stack-yard; but when John started to search they moved him. It was Peggy Flaherty's idea. They did it in the night and John hadn't found Dominic yet.

Thinking of John, Molly looked again at the screwed piece of paper in her palm . . . After attending her father, the doctor had said, 'Look, my dear; take heed of what I'm going to say to you. Now do you think you can make your brother John some tea when he comes in and put these two tablets in without him seeing you? Be very careful of them; they are strong and will soon put him to sleep.'

She felt very proud it was she who was asked, for her mother was sitting there and he never asked her to do it. So there was a rising of excitement in Molly when she saw John and Father O'Malley coming up the backyard. She'd make the tea now, and offer a cup to the priest; and perhaps he would bless her and say she was a gift of God to her mother and them all at this time.

But the priest did not bless Molly, nor speak to Mary Ellen, but continued to talk to John, who was sitting with his elbows resting on the table and his hand covering his eyes.

Mary Ellen listened while she looked into the fire. Did he

never tire? Would he never stop? Why did he persist that the Bracken man was accountable for all this, when it was she herself who had brought it about? Hadn't she prayed on her bended knees to God, and asked Him to make something happen to stop her lad from going to America? Well, He had made something happen . . . John would never go to America now. God was laughing out of the side of His mouth at her, she felt, and He was waiting for the climax between John and Dominic. The regret she felt in the stack-yard when she knew that Dominic was not dead had soon changed to a dread that John would find him. By now, he must have been in every house in the place bar one, and if he were not half demented, that one would surely soon present itself to him. She cast her eyes towards the ceiling . . . How much longer would Dominic remain there, hidden amongst the old furniture, the crocodile, and the poss tubs? She felt like his jailer, sitting outside the prison door, protecting him from a vengeance that hunted him. Had the hunter been anyone but John she would have let him in to do his work.

She turned to look at the priest drinking his cup of tea, and she wondered what she would do if he should propose that they kneel down and say the Rosary, for she was feeling hostile towards a God who had done this to her . . . using her own prayers to bring her to grief! Her eyes moved slowly to John – he was drinking his tea at one go. Soon he would be asleep, if Molly had done what the doctor told her. How long would he sleep? Long enough to get the other one away? And when would he go back to work? There would be only him to work now, for it was doubtful whether Shane would do a hand's turn again . . . No, John would never now go to America.

She turned to the fire once more, and her old dominant self made an effort to oust the apathy . . . Get up and see to Shane, it ordered. And that lass is wasting the food trying to cook it. You can't expect neighbours to go on bringing stuff in . . . But the apathy lay heavily on her and she allowed it to settle about her again as a protection.

The priest's voice was going on and on, and she was listening again. He was saying, 'You've been godless for years, and then you wonder why tribulation like this comes upon you. Can't you see, man, you can't defy God and get away with it; the ignoring of His Holy Mass Sunday after Sunday brings its tribulation. Make up your mind to turn over a new leaf . . . Throw off all undesirable companions, and come to Mass.'

The priest's voice was falling to an almost sympathetic tone, it was quiet and even; and, as Mary Ellen listened, the wonder was born in her that he could be capable of such gentleness. As his voice became slower still, she turned to look at him. His eyes half closed, he was leaning across the table, for all the world like someone drunk, and he was emphasising each laboured word with a wobbly shake of his finger.

Mary Ellen rose sharply to her feet, staring at the priest, her eyes wide and her mouth open. As Father O'Malley lifted his head and slowly comprehended her astonished look, he pulled himself upright . . . What in the name of God had come upon him! This great, great tiredness. He shook his head in an endeavour to throw it off. Holy Mother of mothers, had he caught something? . . . But what could he have caught? Where had he been today? . . . The Flannagans . . . and the child with the suspected sleeping sickness . . . In the name of God, it couldn't be! God wouldn't let his faithful servant suffer such a thing. But he had surely caught something – never before in his life had he felt so tired.

As Mary Ellen began to laugh, the priest rose slowly to his feet. These people! What were they? Ignorant hooligans, who could be driven to do the right thing only by fear . . . Oh, God, don't let this thing fall upon me, he appealed. By the use of my strong will I will bring these people to You . . . Only take this from me . . . that woman laughing! She was mad! . . . He must get home and to bed. He turned and staggered through the front room, with the terrified Molly behind him and Shane, half raised up in bed, following his erratic course in bewilderment and Mary Ellen's laughter becoming dimmer in his ears.

Mary Ellen had no power to stop the laughter; it swelled inside her, like the fire did a few days ago . . . or was it years? It shook every fibre of her body. She held one hand tightly against her stomach and a forearm across her wobbling breasts. John was standing over her, his glazed eyes blinking, and saying, 'Stop it, Ma! Look; steady on.' He was holding her by the shoulders, and her wide-open mouth and grimacing face were doing more to bring back his mind to normality than all the reasoning in the world. It only wanted his mother to go mad to complete the whole thing. 'Look, be quiet!' His voice cracked hoarsely on the words.

'I . . . I can't, lad.' She moved her hands to her sides, where the pain of her laughter was rearing at her. 'The . . . the pills! She p-put them in the wrong . . . c-cup.'

John could not understand what her words were meant to imply. He shook her again: 'Ma! Ma! Stop it, I tell you!'

Shane's voice came weakly from the front room, calling, 'What is it? What is it out there? Why are you laughing? For God's sake!'

Slowly Mary Ellen's laughter subsided, and she gazed up into John's dirty, stubbly face, and for a second her own smoothed out into an expressionless mask before crumpling under the release of her tears; and her broken words, 'Oh, me bairn! Me bairn! Me bonny bairn!' cut through John, and completed his awakening.

He put his arms about her, holding her tightly, and her emotion rocked its way through him, and the burning of his eyes became unbearable. Like the rush of water when the main dock gates were opened to admit a ship, the tears came to him too. Silently flowing, they fell on Mary Ellen's brow; and their raining, more than her own, restored her, and set her once again in her rightful place as pivot of the house. And so, as always, they balanced each other.

Mary Ellen's body still shaking and her tears still falling, she drew away from John, and taking his arm, saying, 'Come, lad,' she led him to the bedroom. When he sat on the bedside she lifted up his feet, and as she unloosened his boots he groaned and, turning his face into the pillow, sobbed, with the tearing, heart-rending sobs that only a man in sorrow can cry.

As Father Bailey hurried up Fadden Street he kept telling himself that this was not the time to be amused; tragedy had stalked this street, and was still doing so. But, nevertheless, only the darkness hid the twinkle in his eye and the quirk on his lips. The story the child Molly had brought to him was fantastic . . . giving Father O'Malley the tea with the drug in! And him staggering out into the street to be confronted by Peter Bracken, of all people. And then to be taken into Bracken's house! Oh, it was the limit of limits. In the wildest stretches of imagination, Father Bailey could not see his pastor allowing himself to be even touched by the hand of Peter Bracken, apart from being led into his house.

When Peter Bracken opened his door, Father Bailey said, 'You sent for me?'

'I did,' said Peter. 'Will you come in?'

Nothing more was said until they reached the kitchen, and even then not immediately; for the sight of Father O'Malley stretched out on the mat, with his head on a pillow and a blanket covering him, was almost too much for Father Bailey. Father O'Malley looked less prepossessing in sleep than he did awake. He looked, Father Bailey thought whimsically, as though he might be dictating to the sender of dreams as to their type and quality.

Father Bailey suppressed his mirth and left till later the relish this situation would provide, particularly for those times when his superior would be most overbearing . . . Oh, the laughs he would get from this would last him a lifetime!

'How did it come about?' he asked Peter, without daring to raise his eyes from the floor in case this man who was also in sorrow, should detect his mirth.

'I happened to be coming up the street,' replied Peter, 'and found him slumped against the wall near my door. Molly was with him and she told me what she had done. There was no-one about at the time, but I knew that should anyone see him it would be said immediately that I'd put the evil eye on him.'

Without looking up, Father Bailey nodded.

'Or should he have been seen staggering about,' went on Peter, 'some people would have said . . . well, that he was drunk. People only need to see a shadow to create the substance.'

Father Bailey slowly brought his gaze up to this man . . . How many terrible substances had been created from shadows for him! And not a few by the priest at his feet. And yet he had endeavoured to save Father O'Malley from the stigma of drunkenness!

'You can get a cab and take him home,' Peter Bracken went on: 'Or you can leave him here till he wakes.'

Yes, he could get a cab, Father Bailey thought, and take him home. But then again, should he be seen being carried from the house, this man would be blamed for putting some influence on him . . . No; he would leave him here. And please God, he'd be here to see him wake . . . he wouldn't miss that for a bucketful of sovereigns.

'Would it be putting you out,' he asked, 'if he stayed?'

'Not at all,' said Peter Bracken quietly.

'And myself too?' added Father Bailey. 'I have some things to attend to, but I'll come back later if I may . . . And I'd better look in on the doctor who issued those tablets.'

'There's something I'd better tell you,' said Peter . . . 'It was important that John should have taken those tablets,' – he nodded down at the sleeping priest – 'for tonight it is arranged that . . . that,' – he couldn't bring himself to speak Dominic's name – 'the other one is to be got away.'

'You know where he is then?' said Father Bailey, with interest.

'Yes. But he can't remain there much longer. John will shortly regain his senses, and he will surely guess; for he's upstairs above him in the only house he hasn't searched.'

'Good God!'

'John is too good a man to suffer . . . for him. He must be got away!'

The priest nodded again, and asked, 'Where is he going?'

'I can't tell you that. I can only tell you he'll be put aboard a tramp steamer.'

'Will he be fit to work his passage?'

'Not for a time; but that has been arranged.' Peter Bracken said no more, but Father Bailey knew that sick men weren't taken, even on tramp steamers, for nothing. And the man before him was the only one around these parts who could supply the money and arrange the whole thing.

He shook his head . . . Here, indeed, was a good Samaritan; and under such circumstances as to make the act heroic. He looked at Peter's shrunken figure and at the face, which during the last three days had drooped into deep lines of age, and he said: 'I think you're a very brave and forgiving man.'

The old man turned away, his lips trembling: 'I am not brave; it is that I can bear my sorrow easier than the others, for my child is near me. Death to them,' – he nodded towards the wall – 'even with their religion, is a severance that only death can join again. But to me there has been no parting, the main part of her is still with me.'

For the moment, the priest experienced a tinge of envy for this man's faith . . . Here was faith as it should be. Would any Catholic think like this? No, he thought regretfully. Christ Himself was in the blessed sacrament of the altar for them, but their faith was so limited that it could not reach over the boundary to Him . . . so there were few miracles. They prayed to God to come to them, instead of boldly going to Him.

'Can I help in any way?' he asked. 'Is there anything I can do?'

Peter turned to the priest again: 'You can, if you will. John wouldn't suspect you. You could get more tablets and see that he takes them. If the men don't get the other . . . this done tonight, there may not be another chance for days. And then it may be too late.'

Father Bailey looked steadily at Peter Bracken: 'Why are you taking all this trouble over someone who has done you such a terrible injury?'

Peter's eyes closed, and his face set in lines of pain. He had lost the mainspring of his life and hopes, for Christine would have carried on his ideas. She had been brave; more so than him in some ways, for he was vulnerable to jibes – how many deaths had he died these past three days because of the attitude that had been taken towards Christine. It was as if his girl did not count . . . as if she too had not died the same death as the child, even the blame for the tragedy, in some subtle way, had been laid on her, while the perpetrator of it had even come in for a modicum of sympathy from a section of the people, and he himself was more hated and feared than before . . . and his heart was sore within him.

But he answered the priest calmly: 'Because I believe in the Great Plan of Life. I believe all that has happened had to happen. What I am doing I must do, for I feel also that it isn't in the Plan for John to commit a crime and suffer for it. There are other things for him, he has begun to think, and nothing can stop him evolving.'

As if expecting some deprecating remark, Peter's eyes held those of the priest for a moment before he went on: 'I believe he will eventually do something for the betterment of his people . . . I know he will, for Christine has told me; and she knows, for, you see, she loved him.'

Father Bailey's gaze was almost tender as he looked at this old man, who, strangely enough, held views which were in exact keeping with some of his own; did he himself not always say that the path was all mapped out for each one of us from the day he was born, that the great Creator knew the shape of every pebble to be trodden by our feet. This man was a thinker, and was possessed of a spirit that wasn't un-Christlike. He preached that he was part of Christ in his understanding and in his power, and although the doctrine he taught was divided by insurmountable barriers from his own, nevertheless the essence was very much the same. And he must talk to him; for whether he knew it or not, at this moment his need was great. Father Bailey knew that to extend to Peter Bracken the hand of friendship would be a Herculean task; the main stumbling block would be, not so much the difference of their religions or opinions, but the priest now lying on the mat between them; and not him alone, but others of his breed, who with a little learning packing the narrow channels of their minds, set up theories bred of their own enlarged egos and used them under the stamp of the Church . . . Well, this was one time he was going to make a stand. If this man and he could never see eye to eye, they would have gone far if each could respect the other's point of view . . . A flash of enlightening candour through the priest's mind told him that the trying would be his work alone, for this man in his humility was advanced far beyond him.

He put out his hand and touched Peter Bracken's sleeve: 'I'll fix up that lad next door: then perhaps we can have a talk.'

After Father Bailey had gone, Peter, his eyes bright and head raised, stood by the side of the sleeping priest. He spoke as if to someone near: 'You were right, my dear; your going had a purpose. Never could this have come about otherwise. Will you ask all the guides of tolerance to help this man here? I, too, will work on him, that he may become more like him just gone.'

While Peter Bracken was sitting at the head of Father O'Malley the priest jerked violently – it was as if his spirit was up in arms at this outrage. From time to time his lips and cheeks would puff out and emit sounds like 'Pooh! Poo-pooh!'

Peter did not smile – it needed Father Bailey to appreciate the humour of the situation.

The tin alarm clock on the mantelpiece showed twelve-thirty. Father Bailey sat looking at it, and from time to time he wondered whether it had stopped. But as he stared, the hand would give a slight movement, and once again he would tell himself that these were the longest three hours he had spent in his life . . . and the oddest. Was there ever such a situation! Here he was, sitting in this kitchen, after midnight, with this toil-worn woman opposite, so still she might be dead; and three cups on the table, the largest holding the white powder already mixed with the milk. And there on the hob was the teapot, stewing its inside out. They would likely all die from tannin poisoning if they were to drink the stuff. Well, pray God there would be no need. Less than half an hour now, and the men would be here and gone, and John could remain asleep or wake up just as he pleased, and no harm done . . . And for himself, he would go next door, where at least there was a comfortable chair to recline in while waiting for the grand awakening, as he termed it, of his superior . . . Was there ever such a situation! There next door was lying the man who was the sworn enemy of all spiritualists, and of Peter Bracken in particular and being tended gently by the man himself.

Father Bailey felt his eyes closing and he was thinking sleepily that it was many years since he enjoyed a conversation like the one this evening . . . a very enlightened man that. Of course, God help him, he was entirely wrong in many of his opinions, but there were some which tied up amazingly with those of the Church. Peter Bracken's idea, for instance, that the spirits, termed guides, and through whom the healing was done, were the good people who had gone on, whom he and all Catholics termed saints. Now that was an interesting point . . . He was awakened, startlingly, by a gasp from Mary Ellen.

They exchanged glances and looked towards the bedroom door; the bed was creaking heavily. There was a shuffling, a short silence, and John appeared at the open door.

It was only two days since Father Bailey last saw John, yet the change in him hurt the priest; he looked gaunt and twice his age.

But now was not the time, Father Bailey told himself, to waste on useless pity. Of all the times John could have chosen to wake up this was the worst; even if he drank the stuff this minute, as strong as it was, it was doubtful whether it would take effect before the arrival of the men.

John shook his head and ran his hand over his forehead. Then he looked dully but enquiringly at the priest.

And Father Bailey said promptly, 'Your father's not too good, John. Your mother called me in.'

John accepted this, and looked at his mother; then from her to the clock . . . twenty minutes to one! The pain of his existence flooded back to him . . . he had slept for hours! They would have got him away then. Well he had to sleep some time. But, oh God, why couldn't he have got him first, then this agony would have been appeased. Now it would go on for ever.

'Have this cup of tea, lad.' Mary Ellen was pouring the black tea into the cup with shaking hands.

John ran his hand round his face and shook his head: 'I'll have a wash first.'

'I could do with another, myself, Mrs O'Brien. Have a cup with me, John, it'll pull you together.'

The priest took the cup from Mary Ellen's hand and stirring it vigorously, passed it to John.

Without demur, John took it and drank a mouthful of the hot tea. He pursed his lips before replacing the cup on the table. Huh! the taste . . . his mouth was dry and thick!

Going to the hearth, he picked up the kettle. It was empty; and the occurrence was so unusual that he shook the kettle, then glanced at his mother. It seemed a symbol of the new life . . . nothing would ever be the same again.

Mary Ellen took the kettle from John's hand, whilst he went to the table and finished his tea. The priest sighed and sat down heavily, saying to John, 'Sit down, lad.'

Docilely, John sat down, as if his being knew nothing of hatred and the craving impulse to destroy.

Mary Ellen passed between him and the priest and placed the kettle on the fire. Then she too sat down, and the silence became heavy; until Father Bailey exclaimed, 'Well, Mrs O'Brien, I must soon be making my way home.' But he didn't move; and into the renewed silence came a soft padding. It bore no relation to footsteps. Mary Ellen and the priest exchanged quick glances, but John went on looking at the kettle, which had begun to hiss softly.

The padding which came from the wall at John's back now passed on to the ceiling. The priest turned his gaze from Mary Ellen and stared into the fire . . . Well, if they made no more noise than that, it would be all right – the old stockings round their boots were quite effective. Another two or three minutes, and it would be over.

The minutes passed, and John stood up and lifted the kettle from the fire, forcing back into himself the urge to be going. What was he idling here for, anyway? In another few minutes he'd be asleep again. And there was still the chance he might find him; for how did they know how long he would sleep. They might have been afraid to risk getting him away. This time he would stay at the bottom end of the streets; it was ten to one he was there, for his cronies were in that quarter.

'That water isn't hot,' Mary Ellen broke in, getting to her feet – in the scullery he would be standing under the staircase and the padding had started again.

'It'll do.'

As he made to pass her, he was brought to a halt by the sound of something falling on to the floor above. It could have been a chair or a box, or any piece of Peggy Flaherty's ménage. Perhaps John would have let it pass as just that had he not looked at his mother and from her to the priest. The apprehension in their exchanging glances was like a revelation to him . . . 'The bitch!' The words were forced out through his clenched teeth – at this moment he wasn't thinking of Dominic so much as Peggy Flaherty. It was as clear as daylight . . . In the street, he ran as he had never run before, round the bottom corner and up the back lane. But when he reached the backyard he found only Mary Ellen and Peggy there. They were standing by the kitchen door, an epitome of the conspiracy against him and of its successful close.

In the moment of his pausing he was made aware of the effects of the drug, for he had the desire to push past them into the kitchen and to sit down. But the desire was swept away and he turned and ran again, for the main road now. However they tried to evade him, eventually they must make for the main road.

A cold drizzle was falling, and already his shirt was wet; but this would keep him awake. There was no-one in sight, as far as he could see, and he stood in the shadow of the wall, scanning the openings to the streets. There was a lamp at each corner, but so far did the streets seem to stretch away into the darkness that he realised he must keep on the move if he hoped to discern any movement from the lower streets.

His lids felt heavy and drooped slowly over his eyes. He stretched them and swore grimly to himself. They had only to play a waiting game . . . they were in there somewhere still, he was sure. How much longer could he fight against this increasing drowsiness?

He had to lean against the wall. Gradually his anger died in him, and all he wanted to do was to lie down . . . Blast them!

He started to walk, briskly as he thought, but soon stopped again and leaned against a lamp post. His head was throbbing to the rhythm of approaching horses' hooves. Soon the black shape of a cab rocketed towards him, and ahead of it, on the pavement, he made out the scurrying figure of Father Bailey.

Panting, the priest came alongside John and laid a hand on his arm. He murmured something, but John did nor hear what it was. He was looking at the cab, which was now abreast of him . . . and there was Dominic's face! His eyes were turned towards the window. They were sockets of darkness in a white blur. Time seemed to stand suspended, giving the brothers the opportunity to exchange their last looks of hatred. Then something sprang from John and leaped upon the sneering face of his brother. But whatever it was it had no effect . . . the cab rolled on, the bandaged face disappeared. And John, like a child, allowed himself to be led gently away by the priest; he was thinking dimly that all his life there would be a want in him . . . something uncompleted.

Chapter Thirteen

Renunciation

THE UNDER-MANAGER of the sawmill watched John jump the wall; he was waiting for him on the pavement of the main road.

'You know, that's a punishable offence,' he said evenly.

John straightened his cap. 'I suppose so.'

'Well, I don't want to seem stiff,' – the man was almost apologetic – 'but it's got to stop. I shouldn't mind if it was just one doing it, but it only needs a start you know, and we'll have everybody living in Jarrow coming out this way, and I leave you to guess what'll happen to the timber . . . It's got to stop you see.'

John merely nodded before moving off; and the man, looking after him, thought 'poor devil'. It was right what they said, he had gone a bit queer. What other reason could there be for him not using the dock gates – for though the sawmill yard might be a short cut to Jarrow, it was difficult of access. Perhaps the lad thought he was still chasing his brother. Well, whatever he thought he was doing now, he'd have to find some other way of doing it but by this wall . . .

John realised this as he strode homewards. But there was no other way to avoid meeting Mary; if he used the main gate sooner or later they would be bound to meet. For four weeks now he had come out by the wall; it cut off the arches and the length of road past the Simonside bank. It did not cut off the gut – no deviation could cut off the gut. At first, he was determined to avoid Mary only until he should feel strong enough to face her; but with each passing day he became weaker, and told himself that in the silence between them the madness would fade and he would not have to see her. Then her letters started to come. Every day for the past three weeks there had been a letter. They were all neatly stacked in his box under the bed . . . and all unopened. With the coming of the first one he knew he must not open it, for the words it held would break down his reserve.

In the long stretches of the night he would think of the letters and what they held, and it would seem as if their substance created Mary herself, bringing her into the room to him . . . at times, even into the bed. He would feel her there, even smell the faint perfume that was hers, and his arms would go out to her, and in pulling her to him he would come to himself and, getting up, would stand on the cold floor, staring out of the window into the black square of the backyard, or up at the piece of sky visible between the houses, and know that Mary and the magic world that she alone could make was not for him – this wherein he stood was his world, this his night view for all time . . . this was his far horizon; this was the limit to all his wild hopes; here in this house he would have to work out his salvation. Sometimes he would lean his head against the window frame and murmur, 'Katie, Katie,' as if asking her forgiveness . . . If only he had never had the idea of making her a teacher! It was his fault, for she was a child and would have forgotten about it. Then he would never have got dressed up to go and see . . . her. And not seeing her, he would have come to love Christine; and the issue between him and Dominic would have been finished earlier, and his Katie and Christine would have been alive today . . . Again, had the Brackens not come next door, and, like a disciple, he had not sat at Peter's feet, lapping up all his mad ideas about the power of thought, this would never have happened.

Well, he was finished with thinking . . . his mother was right – it got you nowhere. There would be no more wild imagining for him. The road he was on held no space for flights of fancy. He had been mad in a number of ways. Between her and Peter he had gone crazy for a time. She even made him believe that the quaint thoughts which came into his head were unpolished gems, holding poetic qualities . . . and Peter, that life held something gigantic for him, that one day he would lead men, not into battle, but out of it . . . Out of the battle with squalor into brighter and better conditions. Peter even egged him to take on the job of being a delegate to the Labourers' and General Workers' Union . . . God! How far above the earth he had walked; until that business of Nancy Kelly's! Even then he saw his Mecca in America. But now it was all over. He knew where his Mecca lay . . . in this house, in the fifteen streets and in the docks, working to feed his mother and father and Molly and that other growing Dominic.

Yet as he walked up the road, he knew that it wasn't all over; the hardest part for him was yet to come. He would have to see her and finish it. Far better to make a clean cut than try to keep dodging her. Once it was done, he would feel better; he could not feel worse.

Saturdays were like the opening afresh of a wound; the weekends altogether were a torture. And now another was upon him. Since jumping the sawmill wall, he knew how he must spend this one . . . he must read the letters! . . .

When he entered the kitchen, his eyes, in spite of himself, were forced to the mantelpiece. There was yet another letter against the clock. He thrust it into his pocket, then washed himself before sitting down to dinner. Shane was already at the table, and John, out of the pity growing in him for his father, answered his questions patiently . . . Yes, the first boat of the year was in from Sweden with Lulea ore, and it seemed heavier than ever . . . yes, there was one due in on Monday from Bilbao.

'That'll mean piecework,' his father said . . . 'five shillings a shift.' He shook his head and looked down at his trembling hands. 'Perhaps if I made a start I would steady up . . . eh, lad?'

'Give yourself time,' said John, knowing that all the time in the world wouldn't put his father back in the docks.

'Yes. Another week then,' said Shane, with pitiable relief.

Silently, Mary Ellen moved between the oven and the table. Into the love she held for this son of hers was creeping a feeling of awe. The letters were creating it. The lass was writing to him every day, yet he was standing out against her. If ever a lad was in love, he was. But he was renouncing her . . . and for them. Where did he get his strength? She recognised him as a man with a man's needs, and her humility ignored the origin of his strength in herself. If only in some way he could have the lass . . . But it was impossible, the house depended on him; they could only live by him.

Here was another Saturday. How she dreaded and hated Saturdays! She seemed to spend her weeks gathering strength to face the Saturdays. Yet life went on. Round the doors, it was back to normal. Already the incident was being referred to as something long past, in remarks, such as, 'That was a Saturday, wasn't it?' or, 'That day the two bairns went down.' The only ones outside the house who still felt the weight of that day were Peggy Flaherty and the Kellys . . . Peggy, because John, as she said, wouldn't look the side she was on. He wouldn't forgive her for duping him, and her fat was visibly disappearing through the worry of it. Her simple soul felt that until she was on speaking terms with John again nothing would be right. The Kellys were affected because now there could be no redress for Nancy. They would be saddled with her child and their scraping to live would become more difficult, while the possibility of yet another Nancy would be growing under their eyes. Mary Ellen, too, often thought of this. In a short while now, the child would be born, and she would be a grandmother. And always there would be Dominic across the street from her . . . from behind the curtains, she would look for the traits to show. She could see herself doing just that all down the years, for there was no possibility of her ever leaving the fifteen streets. Nor did she want to now; all desire for a change had long since left her, and she knew she must see life out to its close here. This did not worry her, but what did was that her lad would have to do the same. She hadn't wanted him to go to America, but that wasn't saying she wanted him to be stuck in the fifteen streets all his life . . . Dear God, no . . .

The meal was over, and while Molly cleared away Mary Ellen, taking Mick's shirt from the top of the pile of mending, cut off the tail and pinned it across the shoulders, before sitting down opposite Shane and beginning to sew.

John came from the bedroom, and looking hard at Molly, asked, 'Did someone call here a while ago? You know who I mean.'

Molly, after staring back at him for a second, hung her head and answered, 'Yes.'

'Why didn't you say?'

Molly turned her head a little and stared down to her mother's lap . . . How could she say to him, 'You were all mad when she came'? She recalled going to the door on the Sunday afternoon and seeing Miss Llewellyn standing there. She had asked to see her mother or father, and Molly had said she couldn't, they were both bad. It felt nice, at the time, to deny something to her one-time teacher, a teacher who had never taken any notice of her; and when she was able to deny her John, saying that he was out and she didn't know where he was, she experienced a definite pleasure. There was no room in her to feel sorry for Miss Llewellyn, who looked pale and bad. She didn't want her here, anyway. She guessed that Miss Llewellyn had clicked with their John, and she was puzzled, yet made bold, by sensing the comedown it was for anyone so swanky to click with their John. And so, after Miss Llewellyn had gone, she forgot about her. And now here was John blaming her, and she didn't want him to be vexed, for the daily aim of her life was that he and her ma would come to like her as they had liked Katie.

When she gave him no reply, John went back to the bedroom. He picked up the letter he had been reading . . . 'Dearest, I felt I must come and see you. Judged by my own sorrow, yours and your people's must be unbearable . . . ' She had come here, to this house. Through the open door she must have glimpsed the conditions from the bareness of the front room, yet it had not put her off; nor the fifteen streets themselves. Nothing would put her off. She would go on believing that when he had accepted his sorrow he would come again to her.

He picked up another letter . . . 'Beloved, I understand. I will wait patiently. Each night I go to the lane, and I know that if you are not there there is always the following night, or the one after, or yet the one after that . . . ' He ground his fist into the palm of his hand, and getting up, began to pace the floor in his stockinged feet . . . How much could a man endure! Of all the millions of women in the world, this one, who stood out above them, had to offer him a love such as this, a love men dreamed of, and died with it still but a dream. And it was his, it was being offered to him, John O'Brien, of 10 Fadden Street, of the fifteen streets. Yet he must renounce it, and do so now, this day. He must tell her in words that the mad dream was over. He must do it quickly and cleanly; the cut must be made without sentiment; there must be no tender goodbyes, and no holding out hopes for the future. He knew what the future held for him . . . he was a gaffer, and he'd remain a gaffer; and there was not even the remotest chance of her even becoming a gaffer's wife.

John caught sight of Mary before she saw him. She wasn't in the lane but on the main road, walking slowly with her back towards him, and the setting sun cast an aura of white light about her as she moved. He paused and drew in to the side of the road. The sight of her back had taken all the strength and determination out of him – what hope had he then to stand firm when he faced her. It was easy to be brave in a room talking to oneself. There you asked the questions and fired the answers; there were no eyes to bore into your heart and no touch to set the blood racing. In the bedroom he had been brave enough to don his old style of dress; with a grim defiance he had knotted the muffler ends around his braces, put on his old trousers and heavy boots, and lastly his mackintosh and cap. This, he told himself, was getting back to what he really was, and it would make things easier for her; she would have less regret at what she imagined she was losing. But now he wasn't so sure. His decent clothes would at least have left him free of thinking of himself. Fingering his muffler he could only think of her reaction when she saw him like this – well, wasn't that what he wanted? He continued to watch her for some minutes, and his heart defying his head, cried out, 'Mary – oh! Mary!'

As if the voice of his longing had become audible, she turned, and John, knowing that the time had come, stepped into the centre of the path and walked slowly towards her.

Mary remained still, gazing over the distance towards him. She did not see his clothes, only his face. Even from a distance it sent out its lostness to her, and she murmured aloud, 'My dear! My dear!' and with a little cry she picked up her skirts and ran to him. John halted before she reached him, and the resistance needed to stop the automatic gesture of holding out his arms became a pain.

'Oh John! My dear!' Her hands were on his chest.

He swallowed as if ridding himself of a piece of granite, and said, 'Hallo, Mary.'

'Hallo, my dear,' she smiled at him gently; 'how are you?'

'All right.' He could not take his eyes from her face. She was pale, but she was more beautiful than he had ever seen her, and the tenderness in her eyes caused him to groan inwardly.

'How is your mother?' she asked softly.

'All right.'

'And is your father better?'

'Yes.'

Her eyes fell from his to her hand. Her fingers were softly stroking his muffler. 'I've missed you, dear.'

It was unbearable. No flesh and blood could stand it. He moved brusquely away from her and began to walk; and in a second she was by his side with her hand in his arm. 'What is it, John?'

He did not reply, and she went on, 'Shall we go up the lane?'

He turned into the lane without speaking, his arm hanging straight and stiff under her touch. The action was boorish, but he knew that if he allowed himself one tender move he would be finished. They stopped by the field gate, where they had been wont to lean and watch the moon and make love. Beyond, the afterglow was tinting the field of young wheat with sweeping strokes of pastel colour. John did not lean against the gate but stood staring into the field.

'Talk about it, my dear. Katie would want it so. It will make you feel better.' Mary had withdrawn her hand from his arm, and now she stood by the side of him, waiting.

'No talking would make any difference to that,' he replied tersely; 'but there's something else I've got to talk about.'

She remained silent, and he went on, swiftly now, 'I am not going to America – that's finished. This business has put paid to my father. He'll never work again. And Molly and Mick are still at school. There's no money coming in, only mine.' He turned now and looked at her; the afterglow which was mellowing the world around had no softening effect upon his face. 'Nothing can come of it now – it's no good going on. You understand?'

'No,' she said, 'I don't.'

He moved his head impatiently: 'How can I? What will there be to live on?'

'We could wait . . . you asked me to wait while you were in America.'

'That was different. What could there be to wait for now?'

'Molly leaves school this summer, and your brother will soon be fourteen.'

'And what about my mother and father?'

'There are ways and means. You could always manage to keep them.'

'Out of what?' he almost shouted. It was as if he were fighting her now, and some part of him was shocked; but he went on, 'Where would we live, and on what? Just tell me that.'

She made no answer. And his head dropped, and he murmured, 'I'm sorry.'

'There's no need to be sorry.' She took a step nearer to him, but did not touch him. 'John, look at me.' She waited until he raised his head before going on: 'We love each other. There won't be anyone else for either of us – we know that – so don't let this happen. There is a way out, there must be – there is a way out of everything.'

Peter's words – 'There is a way out of everything. Use your mind and it will give you the solution.' Peter's reasoning, added to the appeal of her voice and the entreaty of her eyes, broke the tension of his body for the moment, and he allowed his mind to clutch at a fleeting hope – could there be some way out? Could the madness be resurrected? Oh the joyful bewilderment of touching her again! Her face blurred before his eyes, and her voice became blended with the evensong of the birds.

'If you'll only listen to me, darling – I don't mind where I live or how I live, as long as I'm with you. We could be married and I'd go on working. John – I'll come to the fifteen streets . . . '

The blur cleared. The mention of the fifteen streets held the power to betray dreams for what they were. No longer did he see the pleading in her eyes. He saw only her well-cut costume, the gold wristwatch, the ring on her finger with the large amber stone in the centre, the patent leather of her narrow shoes, and the glimpse of grey stockings, which were of silk; and covering all, the perfume which emanated from her was in his nostrils, the perfume whose ingredients lay not in any bottle but in a sequence starting from a scented bath to fresh linen – and she said she would come to the fifteen streets! He laughed inwardly, harsh, bitter laughter, and said sharply, 'Be quiet! You don't know what you're talking about. Have you ever been inside a house in the fifteen streets?'

'No.'

'It's a pity you haven't.'

'There's no disgrace in being poor.'

'No? I used to think that at one time, but I don't any longer – it's a crying disgrace, but one that I can't alter. But I can do this – I can save you from yourself. You shall never come to the fifteen streets through me.'

'John, darling, listen.'

'I can't listen, I've got to go.' He stepped back from her outstretched hand.

'John, please . . . Oh, don't go like this – John, I love you . . . Don't you see, I can't go on without you?'

The stillness of the field settled on them. Outwardly they appeared lifeless things, fixed in their staring. Then, in spite of himself, he spoke her name, 'Mary.' And like a caress it touched her. But the caress was short-lived, for he went on, 'This has got to be – it's got to finish right now. It's no use going on – no – no!' – he silenced her quietly and with upraised hand. 'All the talking in the world won't make it any different. You'll forget – time will help.'

'It won't – I know that deep within my soul you'll remain with me for ever; I won't be able to forget you – John, oh, John –

please! Please let us try to find a way out.' She held out her arms to him, and the humility in their appeal probed a fresh depth of pain in him. But he did not touch them, and Mary made a desperate final effort: 'Katie would have wanted it – she loved to think that we . . . '

'Don't! . . . Goodbye, Mary.' For a second longer he allowed his gaze to linger on her. A lark in the field beyond suddenly rose, singing, from the grass and soared into the dusk of the closing evening. When he saw the mist of tears blinding her eyes, he turned from her and went down the lane.

It was done!

CHAPTER FOURTEEN

WHITHER THOU GOEST

MARY ELLEN WAS puzzled by her own emotions. The sorrow of Katie's loss had not died or faded – it was as poignant as the hour when it happened – but she could bear it now with equanimity because of use. What puzzled her was that it seemed to have moved aside to make room for the sorrow she was feeling for John. Daily she watched him closing up – life seemed to be dying in him. He was becoming the kind of dock man he had never been, even before he had taken to wearing collars and ties. He had not yet taken to drink or lounging at the corners, but he never seemed to get out of his working clothes, and he never moved from the house once he came home from work. Nor did he sit in the kitchen, but spent hours in the bedroom – wrestling, Mary Ellen thought, with himself.

It was a fortnight since the letters ceased, and in some strange way their cessation had brought an added emptiness to her days. With their daily arrival, there remained the hope, however faint, that things would come right for her lad. Now hope was dead, and with it the part of him that had survived Katie's loss was dying too.

What was there to live for now? Mary Ellen asked herself, as she banged the poss-stick up and down in the tub full of clothes.

With no possibility of happiness for her lad and nothing she could do about it, her usual incentive to 'cope' was gone – if only an act of God would finish them all off and leave John free! But God never did things like that – nothing with any sense or reason in it . . . There she was, going again. Her bouts of defiance against God brought her hours of fear and remorse in the night, yet mixed with her fear was a tinge of admiration at her daytime audacity at facing up to Him, and strange, too, was the contradictory feeling of late that she wanted to go to church – not to Mass, so escaping Father O'Malley's censure, but just to sit quietly in church, with no-one there, and perhaps come to terms with God. She did not actually think of it like this – she had not advanced so far in her bravery to do so – but the feeling in her urged that should she go to church and sit quiet she would feel better. The feeling was strong in her now, and she stopped possing and whispered aloud, 'I'll go – I'll go now!' She rubbed her wet arm across her forehead and shook her head, and muttered, 'For God's sake, what's come over you? Have you gone completely up the pole? There's another two hours washing in front of you yet!' She stooped, and lifting the clothes from the tub, began running them into the mangle. There was a series of groans, squeaks and loud jolts, as garment followed garment.

The tub empty of clothes, she dragged it into the yard and poured the water down the sink, and she made no effort to move as the dirty foam swirled about her feet. Rolling the tub back into the wash-house again, she happened to glance up, and met Shane's eyes on her. He was standing at the kitchen window and his face bore the look of despair that covered them all. Although he had made no mention of it for weeks now, she knew that he, too, was continually crying out inside himself for Katie, and also that he was suffering because of the knowledge that through his dependence things were not right with John. She stood leaning over the empty tub for a moment, her eyes gazing down at the water-worn wood. Then, as if she had found a command written there, she hurriedly left the wash-house.

In the kitchen, she dried her arms and combed the top of her hair. Shane watched her silently. Even when she put her coat on he did not question her. With her face turned from him, she said, 'I won't be long.' Then, as if compelled to expose her madness to him, she added, 'I'm going to the church.'

That any woman could leave her washing at two o'clock in the afternoon to go to church must prove, she thought, to a man like Shane that she was mad; but he made no comment on her extraordinary behaviour. Not until she was going through the front room did he speak.

'Mary Ellen.'

She turned: 'Yes?'

He was groping in his trouser pocket. 'Will you light me a candle?' He handed her a penny and their eyes met over it; and perhaps for the first time in their married lives they felt joined in thought and purpose.

As Mary Ellen opened the front door a pantechnicon passed and stopped at Peter Bracken's, and she saw Peter himself standing on his doorstep. For a space they looked at each other, and she knew that she should go to this man and say some word, for her son had been the means of killing his lass; yet through his lass she had lost Katie. With his very coming here, tragedy had entered her life. Peter's eyes were asking her to speak, but she found it impossible. It was strange that only once had this man and she exchanged words – that day in the kitchen, the day the bairn was born. Before she turned away she tried to send him some kindly message; but whether she succeeded or not she couldn't tell. She hurried away down the street, knowing that she had looked her last on Peter Bracken – he was leaving the fifteen streets and never again would they meet. Why had he come here in the first place? To relieve poverty and ignorance, he said. Oh, God, how happy she would have been in her poverty and ignorance had she still Katie. Yet she could feel no virile bitterness against him, which was strange. Instead, she felt they were sharing the same sorrow, and she wasn't troubled at her manner towards him, knowing intuitively that he understood . . .

The day was dull and the sky low. Inside the church the light was as dim as if it were evening, and the air, as usual, was different from that outside – thick and heavy with the weight of stale incense. At the top of the centre aisle, Mary Ellen, her head bowed, made a deep genuflection. She did not look towards the altar, where always and forever reposed Jesus in the Blessed Sacrament; somehow she wanted no 'truck' with Him; it was His mother she needed. She went down the side aisle walking softly, as if trying to escape the notice of the Holy Ones standing in their niches with flowers at their feet.

There were no candles burning on the half-moon stand to the side of Our Lady, and she stood in shadow until Mary Ellen lit her candles, one for Shane, one for John and one for herself. Then the Virgin was illuminated, smiling down on Mary Ellen, half holding the Child out to her.

Mary Ellen knew she should kneel and say a prayer, and ask the Virgin about Katie and tell her about John, but she felt very tired and all she wanted to do was to sit. She sat in the end of the front pew, as near as she could get to the Virgin, and gazed at her, preparatory to speaking about her lad. But as she sat on, her feet resting on the long wooden kneeler and her hands joined in her lap, she found she couldn't think of John. It was as if he and his troubles had shrunk, her mind groping for them in vain. As the flame of the candles lengthened, the smile of the Virgin deepened, and it seemed to Mary Ellen that she moved and hitched the Infant higher up on to her arm as she herself used to do with Katie. The light of the candles grew brighter and brighter as she stared at them, and the church outside the ring of light became darker. A great peace swept over Mary Ellen.

It started in her feet with a tingling warmth and coursed through her body, flooding her being with a happiness she could never remember experiencing before, or ever imagined possible. So great was her happiness that it left no room for fear when she saw the Virgin move and gently push someone towards her.

When Katie stood at the end of the pew and, smiling shyly, said, 'Oh, Ma!' Mary Ellen felt no surprise. She leaned forward and gripped Katie's hands. 'Why, hinny, I thought you were – gone.' She wouldn't say 'dead'. And when Katie answered her, saying, 'It was only for a few minutes, Ma. Things went black and then it was over,' Mary Ellen took it as a natural answer, and went on, 'You're not out there then, hinny? – Not out in the sea?'

Katie's laugh tinkled through the church, and she glanced back at the Virgin, and the Virgin's smile broadened. 'We never went out there, did we, Christine?'

Katie turned her head and spoke into the shadows, and Mary Ellen asked, 'The lass, is she with you?'

'Why, of course! We're waiting together – it's nice waiting.'

'Waiting?' repeated Mary Ellen. 'For what, hinny?'

'For the time to come when we should have died, and then we'll go on – we went too soon, Ma.'

'Yes, hinny, you did.'

Now death had been mentioned, a sweet contentment was added to Mary Ellen's happiness – she felt she was with death, and it was a pleasant thing, not only pleasant, but strangely exciting. Her bairn was in it, and was happy. 'How long must you wait, hinny?'

'We don't know; but once it's over we'll start growing again – a different growing, getting ready to come back – won't we, Christine?'

Mary Ellen peered into the shadows but could see nothing, and Katie went on, 'Before we go, I'll come and see you again – and Ma . . . '

'Yes, hinny?'

'Don't worry about John; he's going to be happy, so very happy.'

'How can you tell, hinny?'

'We know about those we love. Go home now, Ma.'

Katie's lips rested on Mary Ellen's and the sweetness of them pressed down into her being . . . the sweetness like a gentle perfume was in her nostrils when she opened her eyes.

'Katie, hinny—' She put out her hand, gropingly. She could not see Katie, but something stronger than reason told her she was there. She whispered again, 'Katie, hinny,' then looked towards the Virgin. She was as she had first seen her, yet different, for her face seemed to hold the knowledge of all eternity.

Katie and Christine were all right . . . they were with her. It did not enter Mary Ellen's head to question how Christine – the spook's daughter – could be with the Virgin, who, above all others, was a Catholic first and the Mother of God after.

Smiling gently to herself, Mary Ellen left the church. Katie was happy, oh indeed she was happy – and everything was going to be all right for her lad. Katie had said so.

The ghoulish picture of Katie floating in deep water that had filled her mind for weeks had gone – Katie wasn't there – she knew where Katie was . . .

Going homewards Mary Ellen walked with a lighter tread; there was an urgency in her to reach the house and tell Shane, although how she was going to tell Shane about Katie without him thinking her completely mad she didn't know. But Shane needed comfort, and if she could tell him in a sensible way that she had seen Katie she had no doubt that he would feel as she did now. She hurried up the backyard, ignoring the dead fire under the wash-house pot and the mounds of unfinished washing, and entered the kitchen. Shane was there, sitting in his armchair beside the fireplace, while opposite him sat the lass. Mary Ellen had never met Mary Llewellyn, but there was no need for anyone to tell her who this was.

Bright spots of red burned in the dull colour of Shane's cheeks: 'I told the lass to stay – you wouldn't be long.'

Mary rose to her feet and watched the little woman unpin her hat and hang her coat carefully behind the kitchen door. She had not spoken, and Mary began, 'I hope you don't mind, Mrs O'Brien . . . I wanted to talk to you.'

'Sit down, miss,' said Mary Ellen with strange gentleness, 'you're quite welcome. Can I offer you a cup of tea?'

'Please; I should like one.'

Mary Ellen pressed the kettle, which was standing on the hob, further into the fire. At the same time Shane rose, saying, 'I'll be lying down for a while.' He left the kitchen without glancing at Mary – it was as if she had been there always and was likely to remain. The room door closed behind Shane and the two women were left alone.

Mary Ellen, filled with a growing awe and wonder, silently placed the teapot to warm, and unhooked the cups from the back of the cupboard and put them on the table. Oh, Katie, Katie. Can this mean what you said about John's life? She dare not look at the lass in case she should disappear as Katie had done.

'How is John, Mrs O'Brien?'

Mary Ellen was forced to stop in her trotting to and fro and look at this woman, whom her lad loved. She said simply, 'He's not too grand, miss.'

Mary turned her gaze towards the fire, and after a moment asked, 'Do you agree with his decision?' Then before Mary Ellen could make a reply, she turned to her again and went on rapidly, 'Please believe me . . . I understand . . . I know that you have only him now to look after you, and I want him to do that always. But that is no reason why we should be separated – is it, Mrs O'Brien? We care for each other – very deeply, and there is a way out if only he would listen to reason.'

'You can't marry without money, lass.'

'Did you wait until you had money?'

Mary Ellen shook her head. 'This is different . . . you're different. He'd want money to give you a home.'

'I don't want that kind of a home, Mrs O'Brien,' – Mary leaned forward and took hold of Mary Ellen's hands – 'the solution is for me to come and live here. I must show him that I can do it. There are always empty houses going, and I could continue my work. Even if I didn't, I have a little money, enough to keep us a couple of years, living simply . . . How much is the rent of these houses?'

'Four and tuppence.' Mary Ellen, her hands locked in the soft firmness of Mary's, was trying to measure the cost it had been to her lad to give up this lass, whose charm was already telling on her . . . Aye, but it wouldn't work out. She would never be able to stick it here; it would strip her of everything but the capacity to regret . . . Yet why should she stick here? Wouldn't John fight with every fibre of his being to take her out of this? That is, if she persisted in coming here and persuaded him to marry . . . Peter Bracken's gone, the house next door is empty . . . It was almost as if Katie was at her elbow – the voice in her head was Katie's. She remained still, listening to both Katie and the lass.

'Will you help me, Mrs O'Brien? I can assure you that you'll not suffer for it. Please, Mrs O'Brien, do help me. I want to come and live here, somewhere near. He will know nothing about it until it's done. I must show him that I can live here successfully . . . will you?'

'There's a house empty right next door, lass.' It was as if Katie had nudged her. 'It was the Brackens' you know . . . the lass . . . '

'Yes, yes, I know . . . Oh, Mrs O'Brien, tell me what to do. Who do I see about it?' In her excitement Mary stood up, and Mary Ellen, her mind suddenly filled with doubt, turned away and mashed the tea. Would John want to live in a house where the lass Christine had lived? . . . She seemed to hear Katie's laugh tinkling again as it had done in the church. Now it was deriding her superstitions, and Mary Ellen set down the teapot, and turning back to Mary, said resolutely, 'I'll do anything to see my lad happy; although I'd better tell you, lass, it'll be hard for you . . . at the very best it'll be hard going.'

'You doubt that I'll be able to stand it?'

'No, somehow I don't. If you care for him enough it'll keep the iron out of your soul.'

With a sigh that swept the tenseness from her body, Mary sat down again. As she took the cup of tea from Mary Ellen, they smiled at each other and a quietness settled on the kitchen as they sat drinking and thinking, their thoughts in different channels but flowing the one way.

The flat cart was at the door – a clean, respectable flat cart, but the sight of it and its import had prostrated Beatrice Llewellyn. She lay on her bed, faint with rage and self-pity. There was rage, too, in James Llewellyn's voice as he talked to Mary from the doorway of her room, moving from time to time to allow the removal man to pass. He only spoke in the man's absence, talking rapidly to get in all he had to say.

'You'll regret this to your dying day . . . do you hear me?'

'I hear you.' Mary, with her back to him, went on lifting books from the shelves and packing them into a tea chest.

'You don't know what you're doing – you can't! Why, woman, the scum of the earth live in the fifteen streets – he's not a man! No man who could lay any claim to the name would ask anyone like you to go there.'

'He hasn't asked me, he has refused even to see me.'

'And you have so little pride you are going to live there and push yourself on him?'

'Yes, I have so little pride I am going to do just that.'

The man came in and as he lifted the tea chest asked, 'Is this the lot, miss?'

'Yes . . . except the two trunks and the cases in the hall.'

James Llewellyn threw a murderous glance at the unfortunate man as he lumbered past him with the box. 'Have you got the place furnished?' He barked the question at her.

'No.'

'No? You mean to say you are going to live there with those few odds and ends?' He nodded towards the hall.

'I have bought a bed and a table . . . just the necessary things.' Mary kept her face turned from her father. She thought of the problem the buying of the bed had caused – whether to be modest and buy a single bed, or to be true to herself and buy what she hoped would be necessary. She had not asked Mary Ellen's advice about this. It was something she had to decide for herself . . . And was she brave enough to face the comments of her future neighbours? For she did not delude herself into thinking it would escape their notice; and she could practically hear their comments on a single lass buying a new double bed. She knew already that the hardest thing to bear in the fifteen streets would be her lack of privacy.

She had ordered a double bed and by now it would have been delivered. She glanced for the last time round the room, her eyes avoiding her father's. He was standing, black and massive, filling the doorway. She did not mind her mother's censure, but his cut deep into her. She would have gone happily to the fifteen streets had he given her some kind word.

'You'll be the talk of the town – a laughing stock!' He barred her way, and she waited, eyes cast down, until he would move aside.

'I'll not be the first, or the last.'

'Your mother's ill.'

'My mother isn't ill . . . she's merely angry, and you know it.' She lifted her eyes to his. His face was mottled with his emotions, and she could not bear to witness it any longer.

'I must go . . . ' She stepped towards the door, but her father did not move. He stood staring at her, his face working, fighting against the softening emotion that was breaking him down – his lass going to live in the fifteen streets! His Mary, who loved colour, and light and laughter, who was so close to him, closer than his wife, who could reason like him and laugh at the same things. She was going to live in one of those wrecks of houses, just to be near that big docker . . . God Almighty! It was unbelievable . . . Yet he had given her credit for being able to reason like himself. Then could she be so far wrong? . . . Was there something worthwhile in the fellow? Worthwhile or not, she had no right to be doing this. She was mad.

'Mary, lass, don't go . . . I'll try to fix something . . . a job or something, for him.' His face fell into pitying lines of entreaty.

She shook her head slowly and put out her hand to him, speaking with difficulty.

'It wouldn't work . . . he'd refuse. This is the only way, to take whatever he has to offer, however small, and make it do . . . Perhaps later –'

'Oh, lass,' – he pulled her into his arms – 'oh, Mary, lass!'

They held each other for a moment, tight and hard. Then, thrusting her from him he went hurriedly down the passage, and Mary, trying to stem the flood of tears, listened in amazement to him barking down the drive at the carrier.

'Come in here, and give a hand with these things.' He came back, followed by the man, whom he bewildered with his torrent of orders.

'Get that china cabinet out, and that bookcase. And the couch and chair. Then up with this carpet.'

'Father – no, don't. Listen to me,' she protested, 'I don't want them . . . I must go as I am. It will only make it more difficult. He wouldn't want . . . ' She stopped. Her father wasn't listening; he was in a frenzy of action. He passed her, carrying one end of the heavy bookcase, almost pushing the man off his feet, both with his confused orders and force, and she knew she must let him do this for her. However more difficult it would make the work ahead, she must accept these things.

When the room was at last bare, she walked down to the gate, her father at her side. In deep embarrassment they stood facing each other.

'Well, good luck, lass. I dare say I'll find my way to see you . . . what's the number?'

'Twelve Fadden Street.'

'You can always come back, you know.'

'Thanks, my dear. '

'Goodbye, lass.'

'Goodbye.' It was impossible to say more. Blindly she went down the road. The cart on ahead was a blur, and it remained so until she came within sight of the fifteen streets.

All afternoon they worked. They cut the carpet, and it covered the floor of the front room and bedroom. The kitchen boards were bare except for two rugs, which to Mary Ellen's mind were far too bright and grand for such a room. The things the lass had brought were lovely! She was glad the lass's father had made her take them, for now one of the main problems to the marriage, as she saw it, was removed . . . they were set up. But her happiness in this new turn of events was marred, and it was the statue that was responsible . . . that great white, bare woman, as naked as the day she was born, and standing on a box where anyone at the front door would get an eyeful of her. The lass was respectable, she knew that, and apparently to her mind this naked woman meant nothing except what she was, a statue. But let them about the doors get a glimpse of it, and Mary Ellen knew the result as if it had already taken place. The women would dub the lass 'a loose piece', and from the start her life in the fifteen streets would be suspect. They would conjure up the men she'd had, and her lad would become an object of pity for having been caught, and never would the lass be able to pass the corners of the streets without hungry eyes and low laughter following her. If only she could explain to her . . . but it was a hard thing to explain. Mary Ellen knew she wasn't at her best with words, but actions now . . . yes. If she were to knock the thing flying accidentally . . . She stood looking at it. There wasn't much time left, for John was due any minute now. Molly was on the watch for him at the corner, and the lass was in the kitchen getting her first meal ready. Well, it was now or never. She lifted her hand and swiped the naked woman to the floor. As it crashed, she heard a gasp, and there, standing in the doorway, her face white and shocked, was Mary.

Across the debris they stared at each other. Mary Ellen, her face working, tried to explain. 'I had to do it, lass . . . they would think . . . the women would say . . . They wouldn't understand around these doors . . . I want you to have a good start.'

Mary gazed down on the fragments of her expression. The statue had been a symbol of truth to her; a figure indeed of her emancipation from cant and hypocrisy; a symbol of her growing freedom. But now it was gone. Never until this moment had she fully realised what coming to the fifteen streets would mean. She imagined at worst it meant living meagrely. Now she saw that was but a small part of it. To live happily, her life would not only have to be altered from the outside, but from within. Not only her actions, but her thoughts, must be restricted. This little woman had not broken the statue from malice; but from a desire to help her. Some deep knowledge of her own people had urged her to its destruction, and it might be only one of the many things which must be destroyed if she were to suffer this life. Could she suffer it?

'Lass, I didn't mean to hurt you.' Mary Ellen's face was pitiable, and her fingers, as always when she was in distress, picked nervously at the button of her blouse. Had she, with her mad action, destroyed what she wanted most? Happiness for her lad. The lass looked hurt and bewildered. She wanted her off to a good start, but she had achieved just the opposite. She bent her head in an effort to hide the raining tears . . . was nothing ever to go right?

When she felt the lass's arms go about her, she leant against her, faint with relief, and felt herself almost a child again as Mary patted her back, saying, 'There, there! It's all right. I understand. I should have had more sense than to bring it. Please don't cry! Just think,' – she gave a little laugh – 'if Father O'Malley had seen it!' They both began to shake, small, rippling tremors, which mounted into laughter; quiet, relaxing laughter such as Mary Ellen never thought to laugh again. Oh, the lass would get by. She knew what to laugh at.

They both stopped abruptly when a knock came on the front door, and Mary Ellen opened it to Molly.

'He's coming up the road, Ma.'

'All right,' said Mary Ellen, 'you know what to do. Tell him I want him to come in the front way.'

Without looking again at Mary, she said, 'Well, lass, I'll get myself away in,' and she went through the kitchen and out of the back door.

In her own backyard she paused a moment. Within the next few minutes she would have lost her lad, for she had no doubt that once he stepped inside that door he would be gone from her and another woman would have him. She wanted his happiness didn't she? Yes, above all things she wanted his happiness. But with it she hadn't thought to feel this added sense of loneliness. Well, she'd have to turn her mind to the others. Shane, for instance, who needed her as never before. And Molly, who seemed to have been born when Katie died. And Mick, who'd need two steady hands on him to keep him from Dominic's path. Yes, she still had a lot to cope with. And her lad would be next door for some time yet – Rome wasn't built in a day.

Left alone, Mary felt unable to move. There were a dozen and one things she wanted to accomplish before seeing him; among them to change her apron and do her hair. But now she could only stand rooted. A few minutes ago she had asked herself if she could suffer this life. What a ridiculous question to ask, when her whole being told her she could suffer no life that did not hold him.

The heavy tread of his steps reached her, and she lifted her head to the sound. All the colour of life, all the essence of the music she had heard, all the beauty she had seen and felt with her soul's capacity, rose in her, and she moved towards the door. Not until she heard the sound of the knocker on his own door did she lift the latch.

It was some time before he turned his head towards her, and then he did it slowly as if afraid of what he would see. She held out her hand, and he moved towards her but did not touch her. It was she who took his arm and drew him over the threshold and closed the door behind them. Walking ahead of her into the room he looked about him, and his face was drained of its colour. He brought his gaze from the fragments of the broken statue lying by the fireside to her face, and he said grimly, 'No, Mary. You can't do it . . . that's how you'll end, like that – broken.'

'Some things are better broken.'

'I'll not let you do it.'

'You can't stop me, dear . . . it's done. Here I am, and here I stay until you have me . . . and after.'

His eyes travelled again around the room, and she smiled gently at him. 'Do you like it?' He made no reply, and she said, 'Come and see the kitchen.'

In the kitchen he stared at a table set in shining whiteness for two. The kettle, startlingly new, was singing on the hob. It caused something to break in him. He closed his eyes, striving to fight the weakness. 'You don't know what you're doing . . . you'll regret it . . . your father should –'

He could say no more. She was leaning against him, her arms about his neck. The oval of her face was lost in light. 'Hold me, John.'

His arms, telling his hunger, crushed her to him. The faint perfume of her body mingled with the acrid smell of iron ore, and in the ever increasing murmur of his endearments and the searching of his lips her words were lost:

> Whither thou goest, I will go: and where thou lodgest, I will lodge: thy people shall be my people, and thy God: Where thou diest, will I die, and there will I be buried: the Lord do so to me, and more also, if ought but death part thee and me.

The End